COOKIE'S CASE

A NOVEL

ANDY SIEGEL

ROCKWELL PRESS | NEW YORK

Rockwell Press
New York, NY
info@rockwellpress.com

Interior design by Renata Di Biase
Cover design by Faceout Studio, Charles Brock, www.faceoutstudio.com
Tug Wyler Mystery Series logo by Andy Siegel and Rebecca Cantrell
Author photographs by Michael Paras

ISBN 1981553266
ISBN-13 9781981553266

*"I'm only left with shreds of sensation
as to what my life once was."*
—A young client who was run over by a bus

I dedicate this book to those inflicted with personal injury from an unexpected instance of negligent conduct. I've seen how after this traumatic event there is often no return to the normal existence once taken for granted. The courageous way these survivors have coped with their life situations has inspired this work.

Although The Tug Wyler Mystery Series is meant to be entertaining, I am well aware there is nothing humorous about being the victim of personal injury or medical malpractice.

There are always people who will take advantage of others. Unfortunately, their victims are usually predisposed to becoming . . . well, victims.

In my line of work, the story invariably opens with an unfortunate event. And often ends with the injured party receiving monetary compensation for pain and suffering. There can, however, be other sorts of outcomes. This is one of those.

COOKIE'S CASE

THE UNFORTUNATE EVENT

Scalpel."

"Scalpel," repeats the nurse. She delivers the instrument with just the right authority.

The neurosurgeon slits his patient's throat in one fluid motion. The incision is quick, decisive, and skillful. A seeping red river fills the canal.

"Give me some suction here."

"Suction," repeats the nurse. She vacuums the blood. Unexpectedly, Dr. McElroy breaks into song. "Stairway to Heaven."

The nurse looks at him, taken aback. His a cappella is as good as his surgical technique, but she disapproves of the buds in his ears.

"Doctor," she asks, "do you really think you should be listening to Led Zeppelin while performing surgery between the jugular and the base of this young woman's brain?"

Ignoring her, the surgeon proceeds to carry out the necessary dissection through the various layers of soft tissue that will take him where he needs to be. He uses his arrival at a deep ligament as a natural breaking point where he can respond.

"Nurse, tell me your name again."

"Molina."

"Nurse Molina," he says, as blood collects, "a study almost published in the *New England Journal of Medicine* presented correlations indicating that certain harmonies in this song were shown to elevate serotonin levels. Serotonin plays an important role as a neurotransmitter for the regulation of mood—and it relaxes me. Of course, skeptical peer reviewers claimed the study was based on unreplicable methodology. There's always a divide among the members of the medical community, isn't there?" Then he adds, "You were off on your landmarks, by the way. I'm nowhere near the base of this girl's brain, anatomically speaking, that is. Now give me more suction."

"Suction," she repeats, clearly annoyed.

McElroy resumes the song but is finished with the scalpel. With a long reach in front of Molina, he returns the blood-tinged instrument to the surgical tray. It would be possible to perceive this bypassing of Molina, the surgical nurse, as a snub. He breaks off his singing.

"Retractors here . . . here . . . here . . . and here." He points to four spots along the edges of the incision.

"Retractors," repeats Nurse Molina, applying them, two on each side. She's unhappy about their exchange—and about the snub—but understands a good working relationship in the OR takes time to develop. Nonetheless, she regards this young doctor as a cowboy, given his decision to perform spine surgery through the front of the neck.

"Give me a little more exposure with those retractors, Nurse." Pause. "That's better. Now more suction."

"Suction."

"Give me a fifteen blade."

"Fifteen blade," she repeats. She hands it to him.

McElroy inserts the blade, crooning, "Oooooh . . ." transitioning from the song's mellow front end into its up-tempo crescendo in perfect pitch.

"Pay attention!" bursts out Nurse Molina. She can't help herself. "To what you're doing," she finishes, in a more collected tone. "I think you nicked her."

"Thank you, Nurse."

"No, I mean I think you accidentally cut through the lining of her spinal cord, the dura into the arachnoid."

"Thank you for defining the medical terms, Nurse."

Frustrated, she tries again. "Doctor, I mean lower on her neck. Near the fourth cervical vertebrae, away from where you're operating up at C2." Molina points to the lower aspect of the exposed surgical field. "Over here."

"Thank you, Nurse," McElroy responds in a firm tone. He is dismissing her.

Molina takes two determined steps, nudging Reggie, the physician's assistant, who is keeping mum, out of the way. She moves closer to McElroy, invading his space. This is a clear violation of the unwritten rules and regulations of operating room decorum. He stops and withdraws. She looks deep into the neck cavern where glistening white vertebral bones are visible. Molina points and counts, "C2, C3," as she moves down the stack. "Right here, Doctor, at C4, there's a fluid leak. That shouldn't be."

She points to a clear liquid slowly leaking out of a thin layer of tissue, one microdrop at a time. Drip . . . drip . . . drip.

"See it?" She gestures emphatically. "You somehow punctured those layers, into the subarachnoid space, and now she has a cerebral spinal fluid leak. You better take care of that right now." Her tone is insistent.

"How about I'll be the doctor and you be the nurse?"

"Dr. McElroy," she says, angered, "if you don't stop that leak this very instant, she'll lose too much fluid, and then we'll have a real problem on our hands."

Staying focused, he responds, "Nurse, I may be new to this hospital, but I've had enough of you. Leave the OR this minute. You're distracting me."

At this, she turns adamant. "I won't leave until I know that hole is sealed, the fluid bathing her brain has stopped leaking, and she's out of harm's way." The OR team—Reggie, the two circulating nurses, the anesthesiologist, and the anesthesiology resident—all freeze, waiting for his response.

Dr. McElroy raises his head, and now he and his antagonist share their first sustained eye contact since the initial incision. Reciprocal glares result.

"Leave this instant!" he commands. "I said you're distracting me!" Molina, still angrily staring at him, pulls off her rubber gloves, which creates violent snapping sounds.

"I'll leave all right," she retorts. "I don't want to be a part of this. Your patient can sustain irreversible brain damage or die on the table if she loses too much fluid. I've been the senior neurosurgical scrub nurse here for eleven years, and I know such leaks can be disastrous if not addressed promptly. And there're post-operative complications associated with continued spinal fluid leakage, as well. You're setting her up for a spinal tap if that fluid collects and compresses her nerve structures."

"Thank you, Nurse. Good-bye. Reggie, step in here."

He watches as she stomps out, slamming through the OR doors, which fly back, though designed not to. He reorients himself to his patient. "Now where was I? Oh, yes." He delivers the song's famous last line—a touch out of tune.

Drip . . . drip . . . drip.

Self-Limiting

Two well-manicured but sausage-fingered hands are holding a piece of paper. It is a surgical report.

REPORT OF OPERATION
PATIENT NAME: CLAUDETTE KRUMKE
MEDICAL RECORD NUMBER: 06041933
DATE OF OPERATION:
SURGEON: DR. JAMES McELROY
ASSISTANT SURGEON: REGGIE HARRIS, PA

PREOPERATIVE DIAGNOSIS: NERVE COMPRESSION IN
THE NECK AT C2 SECONDARY TO TRAUMA
POSTOPERATIVE DIAGNOSIS: SAME
ANESTHESIA: GENERAL
OPERATION PERFORMED: ANTERIOR CERVICAL
DISCECTOMY AND FUSION
COMPLICATIONS: NONE
INDICATIONS: This is a 25-year-old female with no prior
surgical history who has developed progressive, severe,
intractable neck pain with radiation and associated
symptoms of numbness and weakness to her hands from a
job-related injury. After thorough discussion with the
patient about her condition—findings; indications;
benefits, risks, and alternatives to surgery—she requested
to proceed. Complications include, but are not limited to,
loss of voice, swallowing difficulties, quadriplegia, and
death. No complications occurred during surgery.

The hospital risk manager looks up from his reading of McElroy's operative report and rests it on his desk. He skims through page two, which contains the significant body of the report. Dr. McElroy and Nurse Molina are sitting next to each other across from him. Up to this point, neither has acknowledged the other. The body language of each clearly indicates mutual contempt.

"I've read enough," says the risk manager. "Nurse Molina, it makes no mention of a complication of a tear or laceration or hole into the subarachnoid space at the C4 level with a resultant cerebral spinal fluid leak."

"Well, I was there, and I know what I saw. You should make him," she nods in McElroy's direction, "redictate that report. Or include an addendum. If this patient develops future complications, no one would ever know to consider that leak if not given reason to. That's one of the principle purposes of an operative report." Her tone is determined. "To state what went on during surgery, allowing a subsequent treating doctor to act accordingly in the event something comes of it. It's part of the written rules and regulations of this institution, and is in the best interests of the patient."

"I have to agree with you there, Nurse," replies the risk manager. "Well, what do you have to say about this, Dr. McElroy?"

"There was a small leak at the C4 level," he responds calmly. "I'm not really sure how it occurred. I could've stitched it closed or sealed it with heat or applied some bonding agent to it. But I felt, given such an insignificant hole, I'd be making things worse by intervening, so I monitored it during the entire operation. As I proceeded, the leaking slowed and, within an hour, it stopped. It was self-limiting, as I expected. No harm, no foul, end of story. Had Nurse Molina been able to conduct herself appropriately, she would've witnessed the reparation marvels of the human body. It's been two days and Miss Krumke, my patient, has not had one post-op complication or complaint. When I discharge her later today, it will be a thing of the past. Why dwell on it?"

Their listener looks at the two of them. "As risk manager here," he says judiciously, "I find your explanation is reasonable. Although I ask that you amend your operative report, Dr. McElroy, so that it reflects the date of the procedure in the heading. I see it's dated underneath your signature, but it's hospital policy to have the date of surgery in the heading. Is that satisfactory to you, Nurse Molina?"

Her face is red with fury. "That's ridiculous. We haven't heard the last from this patient. At the very least, a post-op MRI should be performed." She stands up. "*Pendejos*," she mutters under her breath, then turns before leaving to make a final statement. "That's not managing risk, that's creating it."

1.

Major watches Cookie prepare. She's getting out her bag, the one in which she packs her special outfits before heading to the club. Tonight, she's planning to appear onstage garbed as a saucy police officer. It's intended as a tribute to the men in blue.

The whip she'll be cracking is her extra touch. It goes in first.

To every costume she wears, Cookie adds an offbeat accessory—for the surprise value. It's her trademark. Machine gun–toting nurse, ax-wielding librarian, banana-eating buccaneer; she likes to keep her fans guessing.

However, she's retired the banana, ever since what became known as "The Fall." Just about all the guys who frequent Manhattan's gentlemen's clubs know and love Cookie. They're aware of what went down one night as she was exiting the stage. What went down was Cookie.

Now checking that her Sergeant Sexy name tag is securely attached to her dark blue shirt, Cookie smooths out a wrinkle with her hand, then neatly folds and tucks the authentic NYPD uniform into her bag. She'd received it, tag included, as a gift from a loyal customer, a veteran cop. She'd had it altered to suit her professional needs so she could tear it off mid-dance without missing a step.

"Watch out!" Major yells from the living room. Cookie has been kneeling and now starts to rise. *Bang!* Too late. Her head contraption has struck the side of the closet's door frame, rendering her a tad unsteady.

"Whoops!" she says, laughing it off as she extends her arms with the grace of a ballerina to recapture her balance. Taking two shaky steps forward, she puts her bag down at the front door. Then, gingerly, she turns and walks back toward the living room, one careful step at a time.

Major takes note of her gait pattern.

Entering, she carefully maneuvers herself down onto the couch. He watches as she takes a few deep breaths to collect herself.

"Whew," she says and smiles at him. What he's doing is studying her. Suddenly her smile begins to fade. Major can tell it's time. She's displaying her distinctive grimace, the one she tries to suppress as long as possible. It's not just *any* frown but rather a look that sends a critical message.

For his part, he'd never ask. This Major has his own MO. His way is to play things out until the last moment. Nonetheless, thoughts of his reward start infiltrating his mind—and his loins. Although he won't initiate what's about to happen, dropping a subtle hint is completely acceptable when it comes to Major's little game of needing her to need him. He's become expert at finding clever ways to spark the cycle of mutual reciprocation.

Cookie, on the other hand, has issues asking any person to do anything. Girls from Sheepshead Bay are raised to be self-reliant. It's a Brooklyn thing. The fact that she actively resists dependence makes their relationship all the more difficult for outsiders to understand. And that's over and above the age difference of forty-two years and their unmatched levels of attractiveness.

Major is a gray-haired, well-groomed, retired doctor. He's the type who belongs in Boca, practicing putting. You might trust him instinctively, but you'd never look at him twice. He could easily be mistaken for her father or grandfather. Cookie, on the other hand, is a tall, slender, extremely pretty exotic dancer. A hot cookie indeed, she's also as sincere and genuine as they come, entirely confounding the stereotype of her chosen profession.

"Are you sure you should be dancing tonight?" he worries aloud. "You know what your doctor said."

"What does she know?" Cookie snaps back in a rare moment of exasperation. "I wouldn't be wearing this thing around my head if these doctors really knew anything. What am I going to do? Hurt myself?" She giggles, then gives him one of her rare, utterly serious looks. He understands she's only venting. He's aware few others could handle such a situation with so much courage, grace, and reserve. It's been three long, hard years of pain and suffering since the surgery that changed her life.

"I've had three neck procedures," she points out, although it's hardly news to him. "So what's a little dancing going to do to me? Besides, it's been seven weeks since the last one, and I'm just itching to get back in there. I can't sit around here anymore." It was as close to a complaint as she'd ever express. "You know I don't like to disappoint my regulars. My dancing's like going to therapy for them, and they depend on my advice. I've saved twenty-three marriages," she proudly states. "And counting. Besides, I don't want Ruby trying to snap up my guys for the wrong reason, making them feel special just to pinch their hard-earned cash."

"I'm simply questioning whether it's a good idea, Cookie. You know you have a tendency to overdo it. And it's not as if you need the money." Instantly, he realized his mistake. But it was too late.

"I appreciate all the wonderful things you've surrounded me with for the last three years." Cookie's tone manages to be both earnest and severe. "But I told you before I moved in with you that I'm always going to want to feel independent and productive. Dancing for my clients satisfies my needs, and theirs."

Her sincerity is evident, and so is her resolve. Then a cloud passes over her face.

Continuing to watch her closely, he understands that the

pressure is building. He knows the signs. Her composure, there-fore, is remarkable.

"I'm sorry," he says. "You know I'm supportive of everything you do. It's only that I don't want to see you compromise your recovery by going back to work too soon. It's unfortunate but true that too much activity can cause headaches in your condition."

There it is. The hint has been dropped—at just the perfect moment. Major waits. Then Cookie crumbles. She looks at him in a summoning way, a needing way. It's the most she'll allow her-self when it comes to requesting anything from anyone else. Major responds now, in accordance with their routine.

"Come on, Cookie, it's time for tap."

"Yes . . . I think it is."

She shimmies her bottom to the edge of the couch and gets up slowly. As she walks into the kitchen, she pretends she's on a bal-ance beam, placing one foot in front of the other, heel to toe, with arms spread wide. Going over to her junk drawer, she takes out a pair of Ray-Bans—the classic gold-tone aviators. She holds them up to the light for inspection. Bright light magnifies the intensity of the pounding in her head. The medical term for this sensitivity is photophobia.

She buffs the lenses, then slides on the sunglasses. Although they hide her dark chocolate eyes, the shades bring her other fea-tures into relief. The high cheekbones with dimples underneath, the regal nose and pointed chin, the latter with a cleft so deep you could do a shot of vodka out of it.

But, in fact, she's wearing the Ray-Bans for Major's benefit. Cookie knows he loves the way she looks in them—topless, that is. He'd told her this once on a trip to Santorini, before her condition made travel ill-advised.

Now she's heading toward the dining room, falling off her pretend beam three times as she does so. The medical term is disequilibrium. Once she's reached the heavy wooden table, she readies herself for the procedure. As she begins to unbutton her shirt, she's a little clumsy. The pressure inside her head is compromising her fine motor skills, and she knows it.

Her breasts, once she's removed the shirt, jut out from the openings in the custom-fitted plastic medical vest she has to wear. It serves as an anchor for the contraption affixed to her head. She stops for a moment, then pulls out one of the hand-carved high-backed chairs and turns it around. Sitting down backward on the red velvet cushion, she straddles it with her long, shapely legs. Then she leans forward and hugs the back of the chair.

"All set!" she calls out. At this point, anguish can be heard in her voice. Her statement of readiness more resembles a plea for help. She's in pain, real pain. Once the pressure inside her skull begins, it will soon turn overwhelming. Without immediate medical attention, inevitably it will result in a seizure that will send her into a coma. Within a matter of minutes, she'll die from brain stem compression, brain herniation, or both.

Major has played the role of spectator up to this point, watching from his Eames lounge chair like a pervert at a peep show of the surgically disabled. And who could blame him? She's beautiful, even in all her pain. He stands and, in his movements, reveals himself as old.

Once upright, though, his pace quickens. He's heading for the surgical pouch kept on the kitchen's center island. As he reaches it, Cookie says, "Oh, I forgot."

Major looks over.

She sits up and takes a red hair scrunchie off of her wrist. She reaches behind her head and, despite the obstacle presented by the bars of the obtrusive metal device, executes a ponytail. Then she reassumes the position, with her lower back angled at forty-five degrees so Major won't have to bend too much.

He walks over carrying the already prepared pouch and places it on the table. Once it's opened, he returns to the kitchen where, at the sink, he carefully performs a hand scrub. After rinsing, he uses the inside of his left elbow to push the hot water control into the off position, all the while keeping his hands face up to ensure their continued sterility. He'd changed the faucet himself, for just this purpose. Major does all the maintenance in his luxury apartment, with its spectacular East River views, himself. He's very private.

Peering inside the pouch, he looks up and says, "More gauze is needed." Cookie winces. She knows the journey to get it from the other room will take approximately thirty seconds for the round trip.

"Um, just use a paper towel if you need to. The pressure is getting bad. Hurry, please." Her resistance to making any complaints is breaking down.

"Will do," he responds. He moves behind her using the upper aspect of her sacrum as his anatomical landmark. Counting the notches between her individual vertebrae he makes his way up. "L5, L4, L3 . . . perfect. Right here."

"Hurry. Please," she says again.

"Soon, my dear, soon." Major hadn't needed to identify his entry point, knowing it to be the intervertebral space just above a birthmark shaped like the isle of Ios. But he counts each time anyway, as a matter of medical procedure and precaution.

Now wearing disposable latex gloves, he first wipes her back with an antiseptic pad, then puts iodine onto the last piece of gauze, making sure not to spill any on the antique Persian rug.

"Hurry!" she reiterates.

From the pouch, he now removes a small plastic syringe. It's for the local anesthetic. He addresses her lower back at the predetermined mark. "A little sting," he says, just as he always does.

"Sting, sting . . . sting, sting," she responds. His jabs are fast and skillful, but it helps Cookie to comment like this. It is, after all, happening to her.

Next he prepares a different sort of syringe—a bigger, metal one. It has a built-in spinal-fluid pressure gauge and a glass collection tube running through its center. A large spinal needle is attached to one end, with three circular finger rings on the other.

Clearly, it's designed for the withdrawal of fluid. He sterilizes the needle, at last ready to get down to business.

"Just a pinch," he tells her. "That's all." Nonetheless, Cookie squeezes the back of the chair. She's well aware what's next.

Major inserts the hollowed needle point into her spine, where it meets with resistance. "Slow, slow, slow," Cookie says as he pushes forward steadily.

"Easy, Cookie. Easy, girl," he soothes her. He applies a little more force. Suddenly, the resistance lets up.

"We're in." Cookie sighs with relief. Major looks at the gauge. "Hmm, I've never seen your fluid pressure so high. And you weren't due for a tap today—that's why you chose tonight to go to the club in the first place. You just can't accurately predict this, as we've learned."

He now inserts his three middle fingers through the rings, curling them, then slowly pulls on the plunger, filling the barrel of the collecting tube with Cookie's cerebral spinal fluid.

"Yeah, that's it, baby," she says, exhaling. "I can feel the relief already. Keep going. *That's it.* That's how I like it."

Major smiles. He relishes the foreplay surrounding the tap, even as he's aware of its peculiarity. "We're done. And your fluid's nice and clear. Hold still now." He withdraws the spinal needle and immediately applies direct pressure over the access site with the iodine-soaked gauze.

After a minute more of compression, he inspects the area. "You're good to go."

"Hey, I feel great! Ready to dance, dance, dance. Gee, I hope this thing on my head doesn't get in the way too much." She rolls her eyes drolly at the thought. "I need a tall glass of cranberry and Red Bull. The usual." He follows her into their kitchen, where he puts away his medical supplies. Peeling off the gloves, he discards them along with the rest of the medical refuse into a special container. Major then puts away his treasured spinal syringe, knowing it'll be needed again.

"Go sit in your chair," she instructs him. "I'll tend to you in a minute."

Obeying her command, he stares at Cookie, thinking how sexy she looks. He whispers under his breath, "She's mine, all mine."

Then he waits.

Cookie finishes her drink and heads over. Major feels his excitement build as she approaches. Stopping in front of him, she places the tip of her finger on her bottom lip, then slowly inserts it into her mouth, giving it a sensual suck.

He sighs in pleasure.

"You like that, you dirty old man?" she teases. Then she asks, "Are you a good doctor or an evil doctor?" Her naughty-girl voice is adorable.

"I'm a good doctor *and* an evil doctor."

Cookie laughs. "You don't have an evil bone in your body. Even the one growing between your legs has good intentions."

Kneeling now, she gently maneuvers down his pants, sliding one leg out, exactly as she has done so many times before. "You just sit back and relax. I'm not a doctor, and I don't have a fancy medical pouch," she says with a giggle, "but I have just the right treatment plan to release *your* mounting pressure."

He smiles. Cookie is beautiful, funny, smart, caring, and attentive. What she's doing is no easy job given the device she's wearing. But she's determined. Several minutes of hard work produce a few satisfying grunts.

Major says, "That was nice. Thank you, dear."

"No. Thank you for being there for me every time. For giving me the help that only you can give." The truth in her statement gratifies him. "Now, though, I need a few moments to myself," she adds.

She gets up and walks to her room, closing the door. Major had insisted on separate quarters when he convinced her to move in. "It will help you maintain your independence," he'd explained.

As she passes the exotic plants he bought for her, she takes in the scent of a rare desert flower and admires the antique iron plant stand—another gift from him—on which they're displayed. She fingers the dusty soil of a few, checking their moisture level. She takes great care maintaining them, the same way she intuitively takes care of those around her.

Entering her bathroom, Cookie studies her reflection. She rests her hands flush on the black marble to give support to her upper body. Having to wear the device takes its toll, interfering, as it does, with her sleep, and more.

She continues to stare at herself for the next several minutes, deep in thought. Suddenly, tears erupt uncontrollably. Their ritual has been unchanging for the last two and a half years. The only difference now is the addition of her headgear.

Cookie looks intently, thinking about her loss of freedom and her relationship with Major. Before this happened, life was limitless. Now she's condemned to an existence of bondage and quiet suffering, despite his good nature and her gratitude to him.

She takes a deep breath and lets it out. She doesn't want to worry him. "A banana peel," she says aloud. "Who would've thought?" She takes a second deep breath. On the exhale, she whispers to her reflection.

"Mirror, mirror on the wall, why did I have to slip and fall?"

2.

'm meeting Dr. Mickey Mack at his place, which happens to be a strip club. As I cruise down Broadway through the theatre district, I take in the city through the cab windows. It's alive with flickering lights and trendy scenesters on the go. And taxi drivers on the hustle just like mine is. After he slams to a halt at a light, I automatically straighten my tie, the way one does after being tossed a bit.

Then, as if summoned, I jerk my head to the right. Booyah! What a babe! She's standing at the curb, innocently still as everyone swirls around her. I lower my window a tad more and offer a flirty smile.

So now the jury's out, as they say in my profession. I'm either a creepy older dude in a suit, clinging to his forties, in end-stage pattern baldness, taking a long shot by hitting on her or I'm a distinguished-looking man of interest who fashionably buzz-cuts what's left of his thinning hair and is now making a reasonable play for a young woman not averse to greater exposure to education and culture.

Here comes the verdict.

She smiles. Then gives me the finger. A high, hard one. Man, I love this city. Why would anyone want to live anywhere else? The light turns green, I give her a nod good-bye, and she yells, "Loser!" Onward we go. I think I have a crush on her.

When we pull up in front of my destination, I hand over a stack of singles. After getting a shine in Grand Central this morning, I took back a wad of twenty-five ones from a fifty. The shine-guy got a healthy tip and nine of the local homeless found themselves a dollar richer before I left the terminal. A buck dispensed here and there on the streets of New York is a gesture I learned from my mother. But since I had to be able to fold my wallet to get it in my pocket comfortably, this time my handouts were more about necessity than generosity.

At least I admit it.

I'm pretty sure a fat wallet won't be my problem by the time I head home later. Coming up with a good explanation for my wife as to why I was spending time at Jingles will be my quandary. I shall admit and qualify. That's what I do most of the day, anyway. That is, when I can't throw out an honest, sweet-tasting denial.

As I exit the cab, my phone vibrates. It's not the first time. I pull it out. It says *Private Caller*. I hit the ignore button, then scroll down my call log and count. Eleven incoming attempts to reach me by this "Private Caller" since I left my office twenty-three minutes ago. Whoever it is wants to speak to me badly. Wouldn't you think, wanting to chat so persistently, he'd leave a message?

I don't pick up private callers anymore. If you want to speak to me, identify yourself. That's how it works. Let *me* decide. Answering a phone while wondering who's on the other end is a thing of the past. Then again, it depends on my mood.

On the sidewalk outside Jingles, I see a trio of women holding *The Watchtower*. "Good evening," I say as I pass them.

"The end is near," the middle one says. I stop, push my cuff up, and look at my watch.

"You wouldn't happen to know how near? Like an hour? Two hours? I have to meet a couple of friends inside." I nod toward the door. "Then I gotta travel back to Westchester. Am I good?"

"We're living in the final days," she tells me.

"Oh, *days*. Thanks, I appreciate the info. I just wanted to make sure I had enough time to see my family again before this all went down. I wouldn't mind shoveling in one last plate of pastrami and eggs up in the Bronx either. I reserve that treat for when I do good for a client, but I think living in the final days would also qualify. You agree?"

I could have sworn she gave me a judgmental look. But I know better. Having selected juries in Brooklyn, where many of these people live, I know they're not supposed to sit in judgment.

And anyway, if she were passing judgment, she'd be wrong. I don't, in fact, make a habit of going to gentlemen's clubs. The thing is, I've been dodging Mick for a while now, so I need to make up for it. However, just because I don't make a habit of it, doesn't mean I don't enjoy a well-choreographed dance. Yes, the choreography, that's what I'm here for. "Honey," I'll reason, "it was the choreography, I tell you. I was looking for a talented danseuse to choreograph Penelope's next solo." (Penelope is my dancing seven-year-old daughter. My life project: keeping her off the pole. Not that there's anything wrong with it.)

I approach one of the giants manning Jingles' door. He's a large black dude whose black turtleneck is tucked in at his forty-six-inch waist, over which he's sporting a full-length black leather duster. It's seventy-five degrees out.

His function is to screen patrons. Keeping the riffraff outside keeps the peace inside. Your basic doorman tenet. The fellows to his left and right are the interventional muscle, while the one behind them opens and closes the door for those passing muster. He also provides backup support as needed.

Doormen in New York make up a distinct subculture, one that's in continuous touch with the beating heart of the city and its inhabitants. Whenever you want to know the truth about something or someone, ask a doorman. They're also a great source of cases for me, seeing as I'm an injury lawyer.

"I'm Mick's friend," I say, looking up at Mr. Duster.

"You Benson?"

"No. I'm the other guy. Wyler. Tug Wyler."

"Go on in. He's at six o'clock."

"Thanks." I start through the door, then pause and turn back to him. "I worked my way through law school as a bouncer."

"That ain't funny, man."

"No, really." He gives me an unflattering up-and-down. I turn to the side so he can see where I got part of my ear shot off. I puff out my chest, standing six-foot-one, mid-two-thirties. The problem is that I definitely present that nebbish attorney look, more paper pusher than badass. The fact that I'm in a suit with a briefcase in my hand may also have something to do with it.

"You know karate or something?"

"Second-degree black belt. 'Hava Nagila'–style. My sensei was Ari Goldberg, Temple Beth El, third grade."

He rolls his eyes. I don't blame him. "Mick's at six o'clock. Like I said."

Ten feet in, I'm standing in front of what looks like a ticket window at the train station. "I'm Mick's friend," I say to the gorgeous girl behind the glass.

"Oh, okay. That'll be forty dollars, please."

"Um, I was supposed to be comped."

"Let me look at the list. What's your name?"

"Tug Wyler."

She extracts a compact from a small leopard print hand pouch and flips open the mirror. She looks at herself, then takes out lipstick. Making a pucker in the mirror, she freshens her color and then deigns to remember I'm there waiting.

"Nope, sorry, you're not on the list. Forty, please."

"But you didn't look at—"

"We don't have a list. Forty."

After paying, I enter the main area.

There's an eight-foot-wide catwalk jutting way out from the main stage extending into a large circular dance floor. Sitting front and center is my friend Mick, just where Mr. Duster told me.

He's dressed as he always is: in ripped jeans, basic white T, black belt, and biker boots. Mick's my age—midforties—and, despite being the best neurologist I've ever met, he was forced into retirement by his peers on a medical ethics board with whom he didn't see eye to eye. His involuntary surrendering of his license didn't affect him financially though, because he was already rolling in dough. He'd invented and patented an ouch-less tape that was sold to a major medical manufacturer and used in hospitals around the world.

He stands and gives me a big hug. "Man, this is way overdue. Like you asked, I left the name of your friend Benson at the door."

"Yeah, I'm surprised he didn't beat me here."

Just then a familiar voice addresses us. "Gentlemen. Good evening." It's Benson.

I turn around. "Good to see you, Henry. This is Dr. Mickey Mack, the guy I told you has been helping out on some of your cases."

"Glad to finally meet you. I expected someone a little older, don't ask me why. But thanks for your input. It's been invaluable. When Tug told me he was seeing you here tonight, I insisted on coming to personally thank you."

Henry smiles at me. What he came for was the hot ass. And, for the record—lawyers love that phrase to highlight a point of distinction—*hot ass* is his descriptive term, not mine.

"No problem," returns Mick. Before he sits down, Henry swivels his head, radar-style, scoping out the place.

"Well, I'm pretty sure I'm the only one in here mixing Viagra with cardiac meds," he quips. We chuckle like fourth graders. The majority of adult males in New York City are simply mature-appearing fourth graders. This is a fact not open for debate.

Henry's in his late sixties, just shy of six feet, and likes to wear Italian designer pinstripe suits with cowboy boots. Henry commands attention, but I'll explain more about him later since the house lights are dimming now.

Not an Angel's Halo

"Good evening and welcome to Jingles Dance Bonanza." The crowd goes quiet at the sound of the anonymous male voice coming over the speaker system. "We're proud to present for your viewing pleasure one of your all-time favorites." He pauses. "That's right, gentlemen," he continues, "I know many of you have missed her, but tonight she's back and better than ever."

Clapping and cheers erupt. But before the announcer can complete his intro, a happy chant—"Cook-ie! Cook-ie! Cook-ie!"—begins to sweep the room.

I lean into Mick. "So what's with this Cookie?"

"I'm not a real regular," he explains. "But her situation—her reputation—is unusual. It's like she's more than a dancer. She's a friend to a lot of these guys, an actual friend. Not just looking for the quick lap-dance cash-out. She actually cares about her customers and what they have to say. I only met her once, a while ago, but I gotta tell you, she left me feeling good, too. She has a gift that way. And it's sincere."

"Yeah, Mick, I'm certain she cares about you."

He gives me a look. "You'll see," he says.

The announcer continues. "So, without any further ado, Jingles Dance Bonanza proudly presents Cooooookieeeeeee!"

The lights start flickering and, up high, a vintage disco ball starts spinning. The pulsating reflections remind me of my bar mitzvah and the Bee Gees. It's virtually a given that "I Will Survive" will begin playing as the black velvet curtain splits open. And it does. Yep. However, what I see on the stage causes me to give my eyes a rub and do a double take. And it's not just me. The entire room seems to be in shock, too.

This Cookie *did* survive, by the looks of things. Just not unscathed.

She's tall, dark-haired, and wearing a police uniform, posing aggressively with her hands on her hips. In her right hand, she's holding a big black whip that's curling down to the floor. But that's not why the crowd's wide-eyed. What's shocking them is the thing on her head. She's got a halo. Not an angel's halo but rather a medical one, a brace of the sort worn by broken-neck survivors.

Henry pokes me. "What's that around her head?"

I turn to Mick. He actually looks taken aback himself. "You do the honors."

He nods and asks Henry, "You want the simple explanation or the detailed one?"

"I'm a man who prefers detail but, given the circumstances, how about splitting the difference?"

"You got it. That's a halo brace. It's generally used in the treatment of neck fractures located at the second cervical vertebrae, referred to by doctors as C2, just below the base of the skull. That black metal ring running around her forehead—why it's called a halo brace—is secured by screws drilled directly into her skull. They penetrate the bone approximately one-eighth of an inch and, once tightened, exert about six pounds of pressure per pin site. So the ring is held in position by the pressure of the pins, rather than their depth.

"Enough tension, meanwhile, is created to stabilize her head and neck. Underneath her shirt, she's wearing a plastic, padded stabilizing vest, attached to which are the four metal rods you see coming up from her shoulders—two in front, two in back. These are securely attached to the halo to arrest neck movement, since the medical recommendation for halo-wearing patients is little or no activity. Pressure on the device can disrupt the anatomical alignment of the surgically set vertebral bone fractures. The danger lies in too much movement causing a fracture fragment to migrate and sever the spinal cord, resulting in instant paraplegia. And possibly death. That's about it."

"Thanks," Henry responds. "I'll remember to ask for the simple version next time." He looks at us with a serious expression. "Gentlemen, we can only salute this girl's uncommon dedication to her art form. I think it's safe to say that never before could exotic dancing have carried the risk of such serious consequences."

I quickly turn my attention back to the stage. I don't want to miss a thing.

Strutting down the catwalk, Cookie does seem a little nervous. Suddenly, one guy initiates a loud slow clap, breaking the hush. He stands, soon joined by more and more of the audience. When the entire room is on their feet, cheering starts up. They've gotten over the initial shock of seeing the head contraption she's wearing, with its daunting black rods jutting up past the top of her head.

Cookie herself is teary-eyed and wearing a big smile. It's plain to see how happy she is. She waves to several obvious regulars, who're excited to be acknowledged.

Now she picks up her pace, increasing the suggestiveness of her body language. Yet something's not right; she begins pitching forward with her right hand outstretched.

"Oh, shit!" Mick yells. "She's going down!"

"Head first!" Henry adds.

The whole place falls silent again. I realize I haven't been breathing.

Then, to my amazement, Cookie's audience erupts into cheers. She's not going down. What appeared to be a halo-busting, spinal cord–piercing forward plunge has evolved into a neatly executed front one-handed cartwheel. I can hardly believe my eyes a second time.

She completes the maneuver with the precision of a gymnast. But my breath stopped again as I watched the rod tips barely clear the floor.

Her fans are loving it. "More!" one patron pleads as she cartwheels again, landing in a front split a few feet from my astonished gaze. Though the crowd is roaring, those in the know—Dr. Mickey Mack and I—are caught between the world of entertainment and the world of deep concern for her.

Cookie is looking around, turning at the waist from the spread eagle position with her head fixed. You feel as if she's touching each individual there with her careful regard. Her arms are wide-open with palms up, as if assuring us all, "I'm here for you." Yanking off her breakaway top, she reveals an extraordinary pair of breasts. They are popping out from the openings in the device's anchoring vest. When she tears away her pants, the room roars in honor and admiration as she twirls them lasso-style.

Suddenly, the fabric catches on the right front prong of her halo, and her pants wind up hanging over her face. We're close enough to hear her. "Oops!" she says. Laughing at herself, she tosses them aside turning an awkward moment into sublime entertainment.

Gracefully, she rises and continues to dance seductively up and down the catwalk with her head fixed in position the entire time. The visual is totally unnatural but, at the same time, sexy as hell. Now, in addition to the bumps and grinds, with every wisecrack she makes, the house goes nuts.

A guy across from us takes out a cigarette, which Cookie instantly whip-snaps out of his mouth. "There's no smoking in here, buddy," she reminds him. He grins, and the crowd erupts further. She totally owns them and they're adoring every minute of it.

"Mendel, what did I tell you?" she reprimands a scrawny accountant type with his mouth hanging open. "Didn't I say you look better without that hedgehog on your keppie?" With a gentle flick of the whip, she relieves him of his hairpiece.

All this, and she speaks Yiddish, too.

The song plays out just as Cookie returns to her starting pose. As she takes a stiff bow, the applause is explosive.

"It's good to be back, y'all. I love you guys." She throws kisses, and once more tears fill her eyes. It's an emotional homecoming, and she deserves every bit of the homage she's receiving. Waving good-bye, she disappears backstage.

I turn to Mick, shaking my head in wonder. "What the hell was that all about?"

"Like I said, she's got a big following."

"Yeah, she *is* amazing, and so are her fans."

"When she did that move," Henry says, incredulously—which isn't his usual mode, "I thought she was going to kill herself."

"I gotta tell ya," Mick answers, "like I said, just about any form of activity is contraindicated in her situation. But Cookie, she's definitely one of a kind."

Just as things settle down, we're distracted by a fresh round of applause. We turn and see her. She's making her rounds on the floor, offering careful hugs and cheek kisses. I also notice Cookie's refusal to take any of the money being pressed upon her. She's one of a kind, all right.

When she gets to the fellow with the toupee, they embrace extra warmly, as if too much time's gone by.

"Ruth sends her love," I'm close enough to hear him say. "She wants to know if you and Major are ever going to come over for a nice home-cooked dinner."

"You tell her it'll be one night soon. I got a few screws stuck in my head right about now. Did she like my turkey meatloaf recipe?"

"We both did." She gently caresses his face as she moves past him. I wonder how my wife would react if I brought home Cookie and this Major guy. Okay, she likes learning new recipes. But still, I'm not sure it would be enough.

Cookie makes her way to us, as Henry stands up to offer a personal round of applause. Some people merely clap, but Henry has such a commanding presence that when he puts his hands together, he does it with the kind of confidence that lends it a greater importance.

"Young lady," he says, "that was quite an astounding performance." He puts out his hand for a shake, then slides a folded bill into her unsuspecting palm. She looks. It's a hundred.

"That's extremely generous of you, but completely unnecessary." She hands him back the bill.

"Are you sure?" he asks. "That was a death-defying act."

"I'm positive. Please, I don't want it. Besides, I don't even know you, sir."

"Please, call me Henry. 'Sir' makes me feel like an old man."

She smiles. "Well, Major's older than you, I bet. But you're both handsome and distinguished, and I'm not just saying that."

Unless I'm mistaken, Henry blushes. In my book, it's a first.

As the two of them are talking, I take the opportunity to inspect the halo. Being a personal injury attorney, I can't help myself. I've had a number of cases involving broken necks, with about a dozen halo wearers. Of course, the million-dollar question, and I mean it literally, is: Does she have an injury claim? I have every confidence that, at just the right moment, I'll find the opening to head us down that road.

That is, if Henry doesn't beat me to it. He's one of my referring attorneys. Meaning, he sends me injury cases, and it works out for both of us. That is, I do the work and he gets half the legal fee. But here, I have a chance to make the first move.

This Is Madness

Sensing she's ready to continue her rounds, Henry, with his usual perfect timing, says, "Well, Cookie, I enjoyed meeting you. I can see why you have so many loyal fans around here, and it's clear many of them are still waiting to greet you." She rewards him with a radiant smile.

Wait a minute here. Isn't Henry going to say something? Could he really be dropping the ball? If so, Cookie really casts some spell. Mick, a casual observer up to this point, now steps in.

"Say, Cookie, how'd you end up in a halo, anyway?"

Thanks, Mick. I look at Henry, who's realized a second too late that the opening's mine.

She pauses and takes a deep breath, like the last thing she wants is to tell the story again. By the look on her face, I know it's a tale of trauma. How could it not be?

"Well," she begins, "hard as it may be to believe, it all started when I slipped on a banana peel. At the end of a dance number. It was entirely my fault. I never should've used it as a prop, but the guys love it when I do. At first I thought it was no big deal, but I wound up having an operation. Now, I'm three surgeries in. Two of them to fix what the first guy did—and that's about it."

"That's horrible." Mick shakes his head. "But I gotta tell you, I used to be a neurologist, and something doesn't sound right." He looks at me. "You should have this guy check it all out for you. Tug's the best damn malpractice lawyer in the state. He's even got trophies."

"You have trophies?" she repeats in an awed tone.

"Please, Mick," I correct him, "I don't have trophies."

"Well, you have plaques."

"Yes, I have some plaques, but no trophies. Besides, I'm sure Cookie isn't interested in a malpractice case." She shoots me a look that implies I'm wrong. Dead wrong. Wow. What's going on here?

"Actually, I already have a lawyer. The case has been going on for almost three years now." Suddenly, her expression is hard to read.

"Well, who is he?" Mick wants to know. "Tug can tell you if you're in the right pair of legal hands. He knows everybody. Malpractice cases are challenging, and most attorneys aren't experienced enough to handle them properly. But my man Tug over here," Mick says, putting his hand on my shoulder meaningfully, "is the top guy."

Cookie shrugs. Maybe she doesn't realize the importance of a seasoned courtroom attorney to the prosecution of a malpractice case.

She turns to me. "My lawyer's Chris Charles. Do you know him?"

"I can't say that I do. What firm is he with?"

"Um, he doesn't have a firm. He works out of his basement. In Brooklyn."

Huh? That doesn't sound good. But I don't want to worry her.

"Well," I say in a comforting tone, "that's okay. As long as he's experienced, it doesn't really matter where he works from." I kind of believe my last statement. But not really.

"Oh, he's experienced. I made sure of that. I'm his fifth case."

"Fifth neck case?" I ask, concerned with the answer I think I'm about to hear.

"I don't know. He just said I was his fifth case. Five is pretty good."

"I see." I'm trying to stay neutral here, but it's hard. There's nothing worse for an injury victim than an inexperienced malpractice lawyer. Frankly, they should be outlawed, especially the ones working from basements. At the same time, I don't approve of snaking clients from colleagues. The only time I'll take such a case is when there's a high probability the injured party's rights will be compromised by the attorney representing him. I can't allow that to happen. We have a bad enough name already.

"I'm curious," I say. "Who referred you to this attorney?"

"The same person who referred me to the doctor I sued. My boyfriend, Major."

That doesn't sound right either. I look over at Henry. He shakes his head. Although naive, she's smart enough to pick up on our unspoken doubts, and so she rushes on, trying to make it better. It doesn't work.

"Well, he wasn't my boyfriend at the time he referred me to Dr. McElroy, or when he suggested I retain Chris Charles. But he's my boyfriend now. Anyhow, it doesn't really matter. Chris said they've offered me two hundred fifty thousand dollars to settle the case. He says it's a good number. So he's sending me the papers to sign, and then I can get my lawsuit money."

"Did I hear you correctly, Cookie?" Henry interjects. "Are you saying your boyfriend referred you to the doctor whom you're suing for malpractice, and also to your lawyer?"

"That's right." A look of confusion brought on by Henry's tone crosses her face.

"By any chance," Henry asks, "this Dr. McElroy and this Chris Charles—did they happen to know each other before the lawsuit?"

"Why, yes. They did. How'd you know?"

"Just an assumption. Based on your boyfriend, this Major, sending you to both these individuals. He was acquainted with each, so a reasonable inference is that they also knew each other."

"Oh, you mean like that Kevin Bacon thing, how everybody knows somebody who knows him, kinda."

"Yes, like that, I imagine. Nonetheless, what you're saying is that after three surgeries, while still in that halo, and uncertain as to the permanency of your medical condition, you're being offered two hundred fifty thousand dollars to settle the case?" His tone drips horrified disapproval.

Cookie now looks bewildered. Worry that hadn't been there before crosses her face.

Just then, a man taps Cookie on the shoulder. His presence is dignified, his manner refined. She slowly turns, from the hips. The halo on her head gives her no choice.

"Major!" The embrace she gives him is warm in a different way from the others she's been offering. "I wanted you here for my comeback show. I looked for you." She's pouting.

"I caught the tail end of it, my dear. I'm sorry. I'd fallen asleep in my chair." She nods understandingly, unsurprised. His next utterance startles me. "Please tell me you didn't open with the cartwheels. You promised." She smiles at his concern.

"No worries. I'm doing just fine." She turns back to us. "Major, these are my new friends. This is Mick, this is Henry, and this is Tug."

Henry, one of New York's most famous and talented criminal attorneys, is about to erupt. I can see it. Cross-examining a witness is one of his specialties. In a stern and commanding voice, he now begins his inquisition.

"You are the boyfriend who referred Cookie to the surgeon, McElroy, I understand."

"Why, yes, that's correct."

"And that would also make you the same boyfriend who sent her to the lawyer in her malpractice action."

"That's right."

"And this lawyer—this Chris Charles—knew Dr. McElroy before he sued him for malpractice?"

"Why, yes."

Henry pauses. It's a staged hesitation and a highly effective one. He continues the cross. "Would you consider them friends?"

"Well, yes, in some regard."

"And how do you know this surgeon?"

"Well, he rotated through my department when I was teaching medicine."

"You're a doctor? I assumed you were in the army."

"No, I'm a doctor. Don't let my name throw you off." Henry gives him a look, and the guy has no idea why. I sense it coming.

"This is madness," Henry says to himself but loudly enough to be heard.

"What's madness?" Major asks, appearing merely curious.

"I'll do the questioning here, my friend. Got that?"

Major glances quickly at Cookie.

Catching the look, Henry asks, "Do you care about this young lady?"

"Yes, of course I care about her. I love her."

"We'll just see about that." In an instant he's now completely in command. This Major guy came over to say hello to his gal and has found himself on the hot seat. Yet he seems clueless.

His ignorance is more than troubling; it makes no sense.

"If you care about Cookie," Henry now tells him, "then I'll see you in my office tomorrow at ten o'clock." Henry turns to me. "Is ten good for you?"

"You may recall, Henry, I have a court appearance in the morning, the Josefina Ruiz matter. Could we do noon?"

"Oh yes, Ruiz." He turns to Cookie. "That time good for you?"

"Um, uh . . ." she looks to Major for consent. He nods.

"Can I assume by your nod that the time works for you, Major?"

"Yes, it's fine."

"Then it's confirmed. Tug, you're going to run along home to get a good night's sleep. We don't want our clients thinking that their new lawyer makes a habit of late hours in clubs before he goes to court." He smiles at Cookie. "Not that there's anything wrong with the environment, of course."

I give Henry a look. One that says: Hey, I don't get out to these environments too often and I haven't yet had a drink or taken in the sights. He reads me loud and clear.

"You're on your way home, Tug. Give the gentleman one of your cards." I comply. Major looks at it, then puts it in his wallet.

"Come on now," Henry coaxes, nudging me toward the door as I resist. "I'll take care of getting them to my office. You just show up at noon. Let's go."

He shoves me again. "I'll walk you out." To Cookie and the Major he says, "Be right back."

I give in, and we head for the door. As if I have a choice. "Bye, Mick, sorry."

He nods, understanding.

Ten steps into the march of disappointment, I turn to Henry. "Is this really necessary? I don't get out like this very often."

"Appearances, my boy, appearances."

"But how could she hold this against me? She's a dancer. It's her club."

"It's not her I'm worried about. It's that Major guy. He obviously pulls all the strings. I'm not going to lose this case because of him. If you stay, he'll spend the rest of the evening gathering up information based on your conduct here to throw at her when they get home later."

"Information? What information?"

"Any and all information. Any and all, my boy. A guy like that has to be insecure having a girl like Cookie. Look at the two of them together." I turn back. He's right.

"This needs to be a Tug-free zone. When you interact with either of them from now on, it's got to be in a professional setting. Do you get me?" I could argue, but we're already almost to the door. "See you later, litigator," Henry says genially. "We'll talk tomorrow."

You'd think he'd wish me good luck on Ruiz.

Outside, I pass the doorman in the black leather duster. He's curious, and I don't blame him. "Why you out so soon?"

"I just came to say hello to a friend, that's all."

"Nah, man. That ain't right. You go tell that shit to somebody else." He turns away like I've insulted him. I remind myself he's a doorman and more instinctive than most people. Still on the sidewalk are my new friends with *The Watchtower*.

"The dawn of a new age is upon you," the talker says. She, at least, is happy to see me leaving.

"Yeah, well it wasn't voluntary," I assure her. "It's more like I got a new case and then was forced to leave by my referring attorney. But I'll go with the 'dawn of a new age' if my choreography explanation fails with the wife."

Confused would best describe her expression after hearing this.

I pull out my phone, which has been vibrating against my chest since I walked into the place. Private Caller has made nine more attempts. Who is this person and why is he so persistent? It's getting under my skin. Whoever it is needs a talking-to.

I pocket my phone and head to Grand Central, making it back to the burbs earlier than expected.

There, at home in Westchester, I find myself in bed next to my wife, Tyler—yes, that's right, her name is Tyler Wyler—by ten fifteen. Her pillow tower is already in place, the better to muffle my anticipated snoring. I'm just happy she's asleep. If I'm lucky, I'll be out of the house in the morning before she wakes, avoiding her kitchen disposition. Then, by the time I see her tomorrow night, she'll be more likely to ask if I have any spare cash, having forgotten to inquire about my evening with Henry and Mick.

Nice.

Just as I complete that thought, she pulls the pillows off her head. Instantly, I'm on the wrong foot. But that's because I'm dealing with an expert.

"You smell like alcohol, smoke, and cheap perfume. Where were you?"

The thing is, Jingles is smoke-free, I didn't drink, and Cookie wasn't wearing any fragrance. Did I mention Tyler is an attorney, too? Only now she confines her practice to tennis. Hmm. I need to think fast. Better skip the choreography thing. Best to go for vague and simple.

"I met Mick and Henry. It was fun. I picked up a case. I'm meeting the client tomorrow. The dawn of a new age is upon us. Love you, honey. I've got to crash. Big day in court *mañana*."

"Don't snore," she commands.

"I'll try not to, honey," I answer, knowing this response will spark a heated exchange. A trade-off I'm willing to accept for heading off the interrogation of my evening's activity.

"Better try hard."

"I will."

"Real hard."

"Okay, honey."

"You better not snore tonight. I had to play two tie-breakers today."

"I understand."

"Well, you better do more than just understand. You better not snore."

"I won't." That is the answer she was looking for. Now I can rest—or so I think. She's not done.

"It's the couch for you if you snore. I mean it."

"But I need a good night's sleep. Like I said, I have a big day in court tomorrow."

"Don't snore or breathe heavy, and you'll get a good night's sleep. Now stop talking already."

"Okay."

"Shush!"

"Sorry."

"I hear you breathing. Quiet."

"I have to breathe."

"No, you don't."

3.

wake up early—in the den. Funny thing is, I don't remember either my eviction or the journey downstairs. But I imagine I continued breathing, which is how I found myself here.

I stand and tiptoe upstairs, making sure not to disturb Tyler. I'm now thinking about her kitchen disposition. When I'm dressed and heading back downstairs again, the dogs are watching. Where they're waiting marks the border of our in-home dog containment system. They dare not move closer or it's zap time. I step through their invisible barrier, give my big guy, Otis, his morning head pat, and they lead me through our kitchen, which has the biggest center island in town. (When we built the house, I asked my wife why we needed such a big island. It's six feet wide by twelve feet long. She didn't hesitate. "Because we do.")

As I make my way past the island, the dogs are keeping an eye on me in anticipation of their freedom. After letting them out, all I can think about is that dancer, Cookie. She slips on a banana, becomes a victim of malpractice, gets two corrective procedures, moves in with an elderly boyfriend who gets her mixed up with a crappy doctor and a basement lawyer, and she ends up in a halo. Yet, she's out there doing cartwheels. I'm also thinking, in the most respectful of ways, about her great legs, her fine ass, and, of course, her perfect breasts popping gloriously through that halo vest. I propose the aforementioned counts as normal male reflection.

At least I admit it.

As I let in the dogs, I see Penelope coming down the kitchen stairs. She looks pissed. You'd think a seven-year-old wouldn't wake up ticked off. Actually, most of the time she's the most adorable, intelligent, intuitive, and hilarious little girl I've ever met. She's also a talented dancer, which makes me connect her to Cookie. No way, Little Munch, no pole for you. Not while I'm alive. And I say this while acknowledging the important civic service that pole dancing provides.

She stops five steps up from the bottom landing and sits down with authority, putting her elbows on her knees and resting her chin in her hands. She means business.

"What's up, Little Munch?"

"The boys, Dad, the boys. I can't stand them."

"You mean Brooks and Connor, your brothers?"

"What other boys would I be talking about? I'm too young to date, right?"

"Uh, right, Munch. So what's the problem?"

"Control issues, Dad, control issues."

"How old are you again?"

"Dad," she responds, "c'mon, I'm serious."

"I'm listening." I can't wait to hear what she believes is a control issue. But there's no doubt, she'll be on the money.

"They think they own the TVs in this house. Brooks is addicted to those old stupid baseball games and hogs the one in the family room, and Connor hogs the one in the den, watching Classic NBA. I just don't get it. But it's not fair. So what are you going to do about this?"

This kid wants results. She's her mother's daughter.

"You're right. They shouldn't be allowed to control both televisions. I'll do something about it. Still, we must respect that your brothers are students of the games."

"Whatever, Dad. Just fix it. I want to watch *my* shows, too."

"I will, I will. I agree it's not fair. Just because they're older doesn't mean they get to control the TVs."

"Older? What are you talking about? They don't control them because they're older."

"Oh, really," I say. "So tell me then, why do they control the televisions?"

"Please, Dad," she says. Like, how could I not know the answer? "They control them because they're men." I refrain from chuckling. This is serious to her.

"First of all, they're not men. Brooks is ten and Connor is nine. They're boys."

She nods.

"And second of all, they have no gender-based right to control the televisions. Do you understand me?"

"Whatever. But you'll take care of it?"

"Listen carefully. As a girl in this world, you need to stand up for yourself and never let a guy think he has more rights than you, your brothers included. Understood?"

"Yes." She stands and turns back toward the stairs.

I say in a serious tone, "Penelope." She looks at me like she knows she's in for a lesson, and she's right.

"Sit back down."

She complies, reluctantly.

"Now, what are men?"

"Dirty dogs."

"Right. I've taught you well." To her, it's like our pups needing a trip to the groomer. But it still serves the purpose. For the time being. After all, what are dads for?

"Can I go now?"

"Last thing. No one has the right to control anyone else."

She nods.

"And you always have to be independent and do what makes you happy. Got that, Little Munch?"

"Got it."

Ooh-Dat! Ooh-Dat! Ooh-Dat!

As I walk out my front door, my phone goes wild. It doesn't always get reception inside, so what was sent during the evening is now making a mass run at the thing. I don't want to miss my train, so I'll browse the incomings during my commute.

I get a choice seat on the train and begin to scroll away. There it is again. Six private calls leaving not one message. Next time, when whoever it is tries to call, we're definitely going to chat. The device suddenly vibrates in my hand. I look, and there he is now. It's time to confront.

"Hello. Are you the guy who's been calling me incessantly?"

"I don't know," he says, a little unsure of himself. "What does incess . . . incess . . . incess—"

"*Incessantly*," I say, helping him out.

"Yeah, what does that mean?" His voice reveals, right off the bat, that he's a little slow. Having fought to bring justice for many children who were victims of traumatic brain injury, I'm ultrasensitive to this.

I'd better take it easy with him.

"*Incessantly* means all the time. Has that been you calling me all the time, young man?"

"Yes. That's me."

"Well, what do you want?" My tone is gentle.

"Tell . . . name . . . first," he says, haltingly, sounding like a second grader attempting to read from a note card.

"Excuse me," I say.

"Oh, sorry, mister. I'm reading off my sheet that tells me how to do this. The one they gave me. I can read, you know."

"I'm proud of you, that you can read. Why don't you tell me your name?"

"My name is Robert Killroy. But I didn't kill no Roy, and I didn't kill nobody. That's just my name."

"I understand, Robert. Why don't you tell me how you got my cell number before we go any further."

"I did my investigation."

"I see. Well, you're a pretty decent investigator, given that this isn't a number you can find that easily. Good job, Robert."

"Thank you, mister. Investigating things is part of my job. I'm an investigator. Granny says I gots to be financially independent before she dies."

"Your granny is a smart lady," I say. "But, tell me, what kind of investigator are you, Robert?"

"I investigates why peoples don't pay their bills."

"Well, are you an investigator or a bill collector?"

"Well, they told me I was a bill collector. But my granny don't like them bill collectors, so they said I could be an investigator instead, since I investigates things."

"I understand. Like your grandmother, I don't like bill collectors, either. But I like investigators. In fact, I work with one myself. Her name is Pusska."

"I done never heard that kind of name before, mister."

"Yes, well, she's from Eastern Europe."

"Is that near Eastern Parkway?

"No, Robert, it's a whole other country."

"Well if it got eastern in it and it ain't in Brooklyn near Granny and me, then it got to be in Queens. Right?"

"Well, it's close, Robert."

"I just knowed that. Didn't think it was all the way in Staten Island."

"You're absolutely right. Now that we have that settled, how can I help you today, Robert Killroy?"

"Okay," he says, "this part is easy. I'm calling to collect a debt. You owe Wang's Dry Cleaning fourteen dollars and seventy-nine cents. Did I read that right, mister?"

"Yes, Robert, I think you read that right. You tell Mr. Wang I'm not paying him that money, and he can keep the suit of mine he ruined, okay?"

"Yes, mister." But his voice is uncertain.

"Thank you, Robert. Could you also tell him to just forget about this, and I won't sue him for the seven hundred fifty dollars he cost me by ruining my new suit?" There's semisilence on the other end. I say *semi* because I can hear Robert's heavy breathing. He's likely a large young man from the sound of things.

"Hello, Robert, I know you're there. I hear you breathing."

"Mister, you paid seven hundred fifty dollars for a suit?"

"Yes, I did."

"Just one?"

"Yes, just one."

"Well, you must be rich, mister. So why don't you pay Mr. Wang his fourteen dollars and seventy-nine cents that you owe him? He's a really nice man."

"Robert, I'm not going to pay Mr. Wang because this is a matter of principle, not money. Do you know what I mean?"

"No, mister. You see, I'm a little bit retarded." This statement shocks me.

"Robert, did you just say you were a little bit retarded?"

"Yes, mister."

"Well, you don't sound it to me."

"It's okay, mister. It don't bother me none. Granny says we gots to embrace who we are or we be living a lie." The guy sitting across from me just flashed me a dirty look. Who could blame him? I hate when people talk on the train, too.

"Listen, Robert, I have to go now. Don't forget to tell Mr. Wang what we discussed. And your granny sounds like a wise woman. Have a nice day now, okay?"

"Ooh-dat! Ooh-dat! Ooh-dat!" he howls. Not just any wail but an uncontrolled shriek of pain.

"Robert! Robert!" I call out, disturbing the guy across from me again. "Are you all right? Are you all right?" I'm definitely concerned on his behalf, and I don't even know him.

"Yes, mister. I just gots the pains."

"The pains?" I ask. "What are the pains?"

"In my ankle. From that van. The one that runned me over. I'll tell Mr. Wang what you said. I gots to go, mister. I needs to chop them out. Ooh-dat!" *Click.*

Damn. I think I just missed a case. A very natural thought for a personal injury attorney.

At least I admit it.

From Grand Central, I take the 4 train down to the Brooklyn Bridge stop. The ads plastered all over the subway car feature one of my competitors. I like his approach. It's original. In giant letters it wants to know: *HAVE YOU BEEN INJURED IN AN ACCIDENT?*

Back on the street, I walk a few blocks and then pause, looking up at the massive Corinthian columns of the New York Supreme Court. Above them the words of George Washington are engraved: *The true administration of justice is the firmest pillar of good government.* The funny thing is, it's been said that the word *true* was actually penned by Washington as *due*. Interesting. The building where lawyers gather to make oral arguments has a misquote inscribed on its facade. Who'd have thought? What's more, the word they got wrong is *true*, as in truth. What I've learned over the years is that any single event is riddled with several versions of truth. It all depends on whom you ask.

Just as I'm mounting the familiar steps, I feel my phone start vibrating in my inside lapel pocket. Crap. I'm certain it's not Robert Killroy, whose call I'd take. The problem is, I really don't like taking any calls at all before appearing in court. The wrong one can be too much of a distraction when it comes to the task at hand. I pull it out.

The screen reads *Home*. This can't be good.

"Hi, honey."

"Don't 'hi honey' me," my wife says. "Why is Penelope insisting her name is Summer? What did you do?"

"I didn't *do* anything. I mean, we had a little philosophical talk this morning about being an independent person, but nothing about—"

"You're an idiot." *Click*. At least she didn't call me a stupid idiot.

A few steps up, I sense the vibration again. Crap. I take it out. Home again. It's unlikely to be Tyler since she already had the last word. I hit *answer*. Before I even get a chance to say anything, Penelope speaks.

"Dad, it's me, Summer. Will you tell Mom to stop calling me Penelope? That's not my name anymore."

"Hold on there, Little Munch. What're you talking about?"

"Well, I love the name Summer, and after we had our father-daughter talk this morning, I decided to change my name. As a show of independence. You can do that, you know. Change your name, that is."

"That wasn't the point of our conversation. Your name's Penelope, and that's final!"

"It's Summer!" *Click*.

I keep my phone in my hand. This ain't over. Five steps farther, and the phone does its thing again. It's not going to be Summer—I mean, Penelope—for the same reason it wasn't her mother. I pick up.

"Dad, it's me, Dirk."

"Dirk?" I question. "Connor, is that you?"

"Dad, I used to be Connor. Now I'm Dirk. I like that name better. It's tougher-sounding. What time are you coming home tonight? I want to pitch to you."

"Connor," I say sternly, "forget about what time I'm coming home tonight and forget about changing your name to Dirk. Tell everybody to stop calling me. I have to make my argument in court this morning. Got it?"

"Okay, Dad, but I'm still changing my name to Dirk. Summer told me I have to be independent. She said you lectured her on that this morning."

"That's not what I meant, and you're not changing your name!"

"Am too. Penelope changed hers, so I'm changing mine. Bye!" *Click*.

Damn that last word. The phone remains in my hand. Two steps later, it vibrates. "Yeah," I say. You could call my tone surly.

"When you get home, you better fix this," Tyler snaps.

"Honey, I just—"

"I just . . . I just," she mocks, cutting me off. "Listen to me, you stupid idiot. You want to 'just' something, I'll tell you what you can 'just' do. You can just fix this. And need I remind you that today is Tuesday?" *Click.*

That went well. Now *idiot* had been ratcheted up to *stupid idiot*, and she'd dropped in the Tuesday reminder. Crap.

"Hello!" My phone has rung again.

"Hi, Dad. It's me, Brooks. You sound mad."

"Hi, Brooks. I'm just irritated, not mad. What's up? Let me guess: you changed your name."

"No, Dad, I like my name."

"Good. So, make it quick. I'm at the courthouse."

"Can you tell Dirk and Summer to stop hiding the television remote from each other. I can't find it and—"

"Brooks," I cut in, "do me a favor. Call them by their right names so they don't take this thing any further, okay?"

"Okay, Dad."

"Now, what are you kids doing home from school today, anyway?"

"There're parent-teacher conferences. Hold on, Dad, Dirk wants to talk to you."

"Brooks, I said call them by their—"

"Hi, Dad."

"Connor, tell everybody to stop calling me! Give Brooks the remote! Or, better yet, give it to Penelope. And nobody's changing his or her name! Bye!" *Click.*

That felt good. But I knew it was only a time-out.

$4.$

t's a big day in court. There's my lawyer. That's right. I'm going to court this morning, not as the attorney but, instead, as the client.

"Roscoe!" I call out. "Jenkins!" He turns around and smiles. Jauntily, with a pop in his step, he walks toward me.

Roscoe Jenkins is a young, good-looking black man. He's about ten years into his legal career, and attorneys in the city who find themselves with a Disciplinary Committee problem often consider retaining him. The Disciplinary Committee oversees attorney conduct and has the authority to suspend your license, permanently. Roscoe has a certain approach to things—looking out for your best interests, in his own special way. Some may suggest his way is unethical, but I never said that. He has a certain swagger and is very, very likable. He's wearing his trademark hand-knotted burgundy bow tie and three-piece custom-tailored suit. His glasses are wire-rimmed and round.

"S'up, my man?"

"S'up, Roscoe, is that I hate this crap."

"All part of the game, my man. All part of the game."

So here's what he's talking about. I've gotten my client a million-dollar offer of settlement as compensation for the amputation of three of her toes. The ones you hardly even use. This sum represents the entirety of the insurance coverage, with the defendant bankrupt. This makes it impossible ever to get a penny more. Nonetheless, my client, who was likely to lose those toes in the near future thanks to her uncontrolled diabetes, has gone and fired me. She did so because she wants 1.1 million, not the million on the table, despite my explaining to her in simple English that the coverage is one million, the company is defunct, and a penny over one mil will never, ever happen.

I'm not done.

Her first new "incoming attorney" visited my office, read her file, then looked up at me and said, "Great job. I'm not taking this case." I mean, why would he? I got the insurance company to tender their entire policy, so there's nothing this lawyer could do to get even one penny more. Smart guy.

The next one came and did the same thing. "Excellent job," he said, after two hours with his head in the file. "I want no part of it," he told me and walked out of my office. But before he did, he retained me as trial counsel on a case *he* has coming up.

Of course, both of these guys knew that I, as "outgoing counsel," am entitled to a fee for my work. That fee, given that I've gotten the defense counsel to offer all the money that will ever result from this case, will amount to nearly all the attorney percentage of the recovery. No lawyer ever wants to substitute out another attorney and litigate a case with no upside. At least, no lawyer with half a brain.

But there's a reason I'm here in court today on this matter. It's the third attorney she hired. He doesn't have a brain. Not half, not a quarter—*none!*

This guy—I think of him as Wilbur, in tribute to the rather dim owner of Mr. Ed, the talking horse—called me up and advised me he was Josefina's new attorney. I said, "Great, want to come look at the file before you take it?" presuming that he, like his two predecessors, would likely turn it down once he got the facts.

"Nope," he replied.

"Okay," I said, curious as to why he wouldn't want to review it. It's standard operating procedure to look at a file before you snatch it from another lawyer, just to make sure it's worth the steal. "I'll need you to sign an acknowledgment of my attorney fee and lien on the file before I turn the case over to you," I continued.

"I'm not signing shit."

"Then you're not getting the file."

"We'll see."

"Yeah, we'll see. If you think I'm going to roll over and play dead with the hefty fee I earned at risk, you've got another think coming."

"You're the one who's got something coming, amigo. You're the one." He hangs up on me.

Well, he was right. I had something coming. Something I could never have seen even if it was a foot in front of my face.

Wilbur claimed, in open court, in response to my motion to establish my fee *prior* to turning over my file, that I had suborned perjury at my client's oral examination before trial, commonly referred to as an EBT. That I knowingly advised her to testify falsely and that she did so testify. If this allegation were believed, this conduct unbecoming a lawyer would extinguish my right to a fee, but that's the least of it. I'd also face criminal prosecution and lose my license because, as everyone knows, suborning perjury is a serious crime.

Just so we are clear here, alleging that a lawyer suborned perjury—meaning, told his client to lie under oath—is like calling a kindergarten teacher a pedophile.

It's *that* bad.

And if I'm found guilty by the Honorable Brown, who sits on the bench as both judge and jury, she's next required to notify the Disciplinary Committee and the District Attorney's office. It's all downhill from there. Therefore, the fact that today is Tuesday will be of no consequence when I go to bed tonight, for clearly, my mind will be elsewhere.

"If some client of mine falsely accused me of that crime," Roscoe says, "I'd get one of the boys to deal with it in the appropriate manner. But I never said that." Ah. It's this singular phrase that embodies his special way of giving legal advice.

I look at him. He smiles.

"Roscoe," I say, "I know Josefina well. She doesn't have the mental capacity to have come up with this plan. It's her new lawyer who's the architect of this scheme. She's his puppet. Besides, you're an ethics lawyer. Not only is it your specialty, but you teach ethics courses at two law schools. How could you say you'd go for the unwritten approach to justice?"

"Didn't I just tell you 'I never said that'?"

"Yes. You never said that, despite saying it—giving me advice on the sly—in my best interest. I get it. But only, you did say it."

"Look," he begins, "they don't teach shit like this in law school. This is street law. We're dealing with a street guy who just happened to get himself a law degree. This thug sees a big, cool fee flashing before his eyes, one he could never achieve on his own. Well, he's got no problem with ruining your reputation or putting you behind bars to get at it. It's about cool, quick cash, bro, just that. So, yeah, if this shit happened to me, I'd have the Fidge bring down some curbside justice on this scoundrel. But I never said that."

The Fidge is a guy Roscoe and I know who takes care of things that need taking care of, and his reach is long. "You wouldn't really get the Fidge involved in a civil matter like this, would you?"

"I never said that, did I?" We look at each other.

"Come on, we've got to go inside," he reminds me. "I'm going to cross-examine the shit out of your former client for you." He turns to go up the courthouse steps.

"Yo, Roscoe, I got this one."

"What?" he yells, stopping abruptly.

"I said, I got this one."

"I'm your lawyer, Tug. That's what you hired me for."

"Yeah, I know, but my license is on the line here. It's more than just money involved. I know you'd do a great job in there, but I've been handling her underlying case for three years. I know her better than anyone else. Not just stuff in the file you read, but stuff only in my head, and I know how she thinks, too. It's only right that I do her cross." It's a winning argument. Roscoe sighs. He knows me, but still, he wasn't expecting this.

"Okay, you do it," he says.

We walk in together.

Let the Games Begin

Yesterday was Josefina's direct exam, when she testified against me with Wilbur feeding her the questions. He was practically moving her mouth with his hand up her ass. It sucked, hearing my client, whom I busted my butt for, claim I did something that I did not do.

Now, in the courtroom, I look over at Josefina. Even from this distance, I can see her eyes are bloodshot. I'd like to think it was from sleeping badly, owing to a guilty conscience for what she's attempting to do at the direction of her new lawyer. But I know it's not. More likely she's strung out on whatever painkiller cocktail or street drug she's currently taking.

As I'm walking toward the trial table, my phone vibrates in my pocket. Shit. I forgot to shut it off when I entered the building. I take it out. It's a message from Tyler, my wife, who loves me in her special way. It reads: *Connor and Penelope are telling all their friends about their new names. You better fix this when you get home. And by the way, you just might as well forget it's Tuesday.*

Bye, bye, Tuesday Night Hand Job (TNHJ). But that's the least of my worries at this moment.

"Phone off and away, Mr. Wyler," instructs Judge Brown, "or it will be confiscated by my court officer."

"Sorry, Your Honor. It was a message of support from my wife. She knows, understands, and appreciates how important this proceeding is."

"Take your seats, Counsel," Judge Brown says. "Take your seats," she repeats. This is a nonjury matter, so our little group consists of Wilbur, the court staff, Roscoe, and me. Plus, of course, my former client Josefina Ruiz, who's sitting in the chair up on the witness stand, minus three toes. It's also a closed hearing. Meaning that no one else is allowed in, and no one will be able to view the trial transcript. Thank God for that, given the horrible allegation against me.

In a hearing like this, where the claim is that you told your client to testify to something other than the truth under oath—which you are categorically denying—the credibility of both parties is directly at issue. It's a "he said, she said," situation. Literally. So my entire goal is to establish that Josefina is unworthy of belief.

Once the preliminaries are out of the way, Judge Brown gets down to business.

"Let the record reflect that the witness, Josefina Ruiz, is sitting in the witness chair." Josefina looks up and smiles upon hearing her name. "She's your witness, Mr. Jenkins, you may cross-examine her."

"Well, uh, you see . . ." I rise from my seat. "Your Honor, I'll be cross-examining the witness, not Mr. Jenkins."

"You?" she asks, surprised.

"Yes, me."

"The party-litigant crossing their adverse party. I've never had this in my thirty years on the bench. It's highly unusual."

"As is the bogus claim against me, Your Honor."

"Objection!" Wilbur barks.

I turn to him. "Pipe down, Wilbur, there's no jury here to grandstand for."

"You talking to me?"

"You're the only Wilbur in here."

He grits his teeth. "My name's not Wilbur! And you damn well know that."

"Enough, gentlemen. Mr. Wyler, she's your witness."

"Thank you, Your Honor. Mr. Jenkins will be making legal argument on my behalf, in response to Wilbur's objections, should the need arise during my cross of this witness."

"Duly noted, Counselor. You may inquire." I slowly walk over and place myself right in front of the witness box. Most times when I do this, it's in a more threatening manner. But not now. In this instance, I'm placing myself here in such a way so as to make Josefina feel comfortable, which is why I walked over so deliberately and why I offered my former client a kindly smile when I stopped in front of her.

There are two basic ways to take down a witness. You can go directly for their jugular, an aggressive, attacking, quick-kill approach that they can see coming. Which was the original plan. Or, you can make nice as you slowly drain blood from the witness's smaller collateral vessels without them knowing it. By the time they become aware of what's seeping away—their credibility—it's too late. I'm now opting for the latter exsanguination. It's taken only a glance at Josefina to realize I need to make a change on the fly. She looks pathetic. If I play the cutthroat lawyer taking advantage of her less-than-perfect intelligence, I become the bad guy. For real. Not going to happen. Let the games begin. My laptop is plugged into the court reporter's steno machine, and this is how the testimony reads in real time:

> Q: Josefina, yesterday you testified that one year ago, in my office conference room, I told you to lie under oath during our predeposition prep session. Correct?
>
> A: *Sí.*
>
> Q: And you and I were alone in this room when you say I told you to lie. Correct?

A: *Sí, abogado.*

Q: And when we finished talking and were ready to begin your deposition, I pushed a button on the phone and told Lily, my paralegal, to send everybody in. Correct?

A: Correct.

Q: And the court reporter walked into my conference room first. Correct?

A: Yes.

Q: And she began setting up her machine. Correct?

A: Correct.

Q: And in response to your attorney's questioning here in court yesterday, you testified what happened next is that the truck driver who ran over your foot and his lawyer walked into the room. Correct?

A: *Sí.*

Q: And you saw this truck driver on that day with your own two eyes. Correct?

A: *Sí.*

Q: He was a tall white man. Correct?

A: Yes. *Sí.*

Q: No issue—meaning you are certain— that when he walked into the room, you looked at him and saw him standing there before you. Correct?

A: Yes, I see him.

Q: Not only did you see him, but he felt so bad about the accident that the first thing he said when he came into the room was, "I'm so sorry for running over your foot." True?

A: Yes, that is true. He say he sorry.

Q: So, not only did you see him, but you heard him also. Correct?

A: Yes, *abogado*. I hear him. *Sí*.

Q: And he felt so bad about running over your foot that when he came into the room, he took your hand in his and gave it an apologetic rub as he said sorry to you. Correct?

A: *Sí*, that is true.

Q: So you not only saw him, but you heard him and also felt his hand as he held yours. True?

A: Yes, that is true. *Sí*.

Q: No issue for Judge Brown here. You saw, heard, and felt the hand of the truck driver on that day. Correct?

A: Correct.

Q: It is as clear in your mind as I am clearly standing before you at this very instant. Correct?

A: Yes.

Q: As clear today, as it was one year ago, when you gave your testimony, the testimony you claim I told you to lie about. Correct?

A: Yes, very clear.

I look up to Judge Brown. She doesn't know where I'm going with this, but she will soon. "Your Honor, may I approach the bench, please?"

"What for, Counselor?"

"I want to hand the court a copy of the deposition transcript of Josefina for the day she gave her EBT testimony, as I intend to make reference to it."

"Hand it to the court officer, and the court officer will give it to me."

I comply. "May I continue with my questioning, Your Honor?"

"You may continue, Mr. Wyler."

I return my focus to Josefina. As much as I hate her for doing this to me, I know it's her new attorney who's been orchestrating it. I slowly walk over and stand behind the court reporter.

> Q: You see this court reporter here today moving her fingers over the keys of her machine, don't you?
>
> A: Yes, I see her.
>
> Q: You know she's taking down everything being said in this courtroom. Correct?
>
> A: Yes, I know that.
>
> Q: And do you remember, just a few minutes ago, during the preliminaries, when Judge Brown instructed us to note our appearances for the record?
>
> A: Sí, I remember that.
>
> Q: And when everybody said their names, the court reporter moved her fingers over the keys of her machine and pressed them down. You saw that? Correct?
>
> A: Yes, I see that.
>
> Q: Do you know why she did that?

A: To put in that machine everybody's
name.

Q: Correct, Josefina. To take down
everybody's name. And do you know why she
takes down everybody's name?

A: No, I no know.

Q: The reason she takes down
everybody's name is so the world will
know who was there in the courtroom when
a witness gave testimony. That's why. Do
you understand this now?

A: Yes, I understand now. So
everybody know.

Q: And, not only do court reporters
take down who was present in a courtroom,
but they also take down who was present
at a pretrial deposition, an EBT, like
the one you are claiming I told you to
lie at. Did you know that?

A: No, I no know that.

Judge Brown at this moment understands. I see her open Josefina's pretrial transcript, which I had handed her, and flip through the first couple of pages. A grin slides onto her face. If she was suspicious that Wilbur was attempting to steal my fee before, she's goddamned certain of it now.

Time for me to ask her to take judicial notice.

Judicial notice is a court rule that allows a fact to be introduced into evidence that is so authoritatively attested that it cannot reasonably be doubted. Facts admitted under judicial notice are accepted without being formally introduced by a witness or other rule of evidence. The easiest example would be what day of the week a particular date was two years ago. You go to an old calendar, and the judge can take judicial notice that the 17th of May was a Friday.

"At this time, Your Honor, I would like the court to take judicial notice of who was in the deposition room on the date Josefina gave testimony in the underlying matter—the matter where she claims I suborned perjury—as taken down under the heading of 'Appearances' in Josefina's EBT transcript."

"Yes, Mr. Wyler, I deem that to be appropriate at this time. Let the record reflect that I have in my hand the pretrial transcript of Josefina Ruiz, taken before a notary public of the state of New York, and the appearances as noted in this transcript are Mr. Tug Wyler for Josefina Ruiz and Ralph Hope, attorney for the defendant."

"Your Honor, so the record is clear, was there any appearance on that day for the truck driver himself?"

"No, Mr. Wyler. There was no truck driver in that room, not according to the appearance sheet."

"And, Your Honor, I hate to belabor the point, but my license is on the line here. Could you just read into the record what it says in that transcript relative to his appearance?" She nods.

"Let the record reflect that on page three of the transcript, under the heading of 'Appearances,' it reads: defendant, John Livingston, no appearance." I look over to Wilbur. He's got sweat on his brow.

I think you should have come and looked at the file, douche-bag, before making such an accusation against me in open court in order to steal my hard-earned money and ruin my life.

"May I continue cross-examining the witness, Your Honor?"

"You may," she says. Meanwhile, she continues flipping methodically through the transcript, one page at a time, like a speed-reader. I look at Josefina. It's clear she doesn't understand what just happened.

> Q: Josefina, we have now established
> that the truck driver was not in the room
> on that day. Yet you just testified that

```
you saw him, you heard him, and you felt
him by the touch of his hand.

    A:  Yes, I see him.

    Q:  Well, Josefina, he wasn't there to
see. Or to hear or feel, for that matter.

    A:  [No response]
```

She looks confused. "Let the record reflect that the witness has a look of confusion on her face."

"Objection!" Wilbur yells. "I move to strike Mr. Wyler's interpretation of the witness's facial expression."

"So stricken, Counsel. But let the record reflect that based on my observation, it did appear that she had a confused look on her face." Judge Brown leans toward the witness box. "Miss Ruiz, are you confused?"

"Yes, I confused."

The judge nods. "You may continue with your questioning, Mr. Wyler."

Time to play multiple choice. At this stage, if you do that, you're at least giving the witness a chance. The thing is, I don't want sympathy developing for her as a result of any of my actions.

```
    Q:  Josefina, let me give you some
options. Choose a letter. (A) The truck
driver was not there, and your memory
of the events of that day is faulty.
(B) Your new lawyer told you to say
that the truck driver was present for
your deposition. (C) That day, you
were experiencing auditory and visual
hallucinations, which you had been
diagnosed as suffering with, according to
your medical records. Or (D) all of the
above. Which is it?
```

> A: I'm sorry, *abogado*. I no
> understand.
>
> Q: Which one explains why you say you
> saw the truck driver that day, yet he was
> not there—(A) your faulty memory, (B)
> your new lawyer told you to lie, (C)
> hallucinations, or (D) all of the above?

She looks up at the ceiling as if the answer is written on the dirty gray acoustic tile, then brings her head back down as if she found it. Wilbur looks super nervous, for good cause, I'm sure.

"E," says Josefina.

Bang! Bang! Bang! goes the gavel. Brown gets our attention but quick. "Ramona," she says to the female court officer, "help Ms. Ruiz off the stand and sit her in the back." She looks to us. A judicial order is forthcoming. "All counsel in chambers, now!" As she's leaving the bench, she turns and reaches for the EBT transcript.

I look to Roscoe, lifting an eyebrow. Wilbur looks even more nervous. No surprise.

"After you, Wilburrrrr," I say.

"My name is not Wilbur, it's Wilberto, and if you call me Wilbur again, I'm gonna punch you in the nose."

We proceed into Judge Brown's chambers. I've got two tight fists, just in case.

She's out of her robe. There are four chairs in front of her desk, each pair on either side of a small table dividing the good guys from the bad. As we seat ourselves, she gives a stern look to Wilbur.

"Mr. Hernandez, do you know why I brought you back here?"

"Uh, no, Your Honor."

"I brought you back here because you have made a very serious allegation in open court. You stated, on the record, that Mr. Wyler suborned perjury by having his client testify that the front wheel of the truck ran over his client's foot, and not the rear wheel, as she believed to be the truth. Am I correct on that?"

"Um, yes, Your Honor."

"Can you tell me on what page and line number it is in her transcript where she testified falsely that the front wheel of the truck ran over her foot?"

"No, I cannot, Your Honor."

"And why not, Mr. Hernandez?"

"Because I don't possess a copy of her transcript."

"You mean to tell me you made an allegation of suborning perjury in open court against another attorney without first having in your hands the subject transcript to verify the claim and back up your assertion?"

"Yes, Your Honor. But my client was sure."

"Well, certainly you must have gone to Mr. Wyler's office and at least reviewed the transcript before making this allegation in open court."

"No, Your Honor."

Quickly, things become hostile. She shakes her head in disapproval.

"*Tsk, tsk, tsk,* Counselor. Well, I just read every word of this transcript, and nowhere here does she testify that it was the front wheel of the truck that ran over her foot, the proposed statement of suborned perjury. In fact, it states the exact opposite. She testified that the rear wheel of the truck ran over her foot, which is what she testified to be the truth of the matter here in court yesterday. So, by definition, there can be no perjury or the suborning thereof, because she testified both at her EBT and again here in court to what she believed to be the truth of the matter. Would you like to read this deposition to confirm what I am saying?" She extends the transcript to him across the desk.

"No, Your Honor. I'll take your word for it. Her memory, it seems, may be faulty."

"Mr. Hernandez, when we go back on the record, I am going to dismiss the allegations against Mr. Wyler in their entirety and issue an order entitling him to ninety-five percent of the attorney fee. You will, however, have to earn your five percent by taking this matter to trial—since your client won't consent to a settlement—and end up with the same amount after a verdict, assuming you win. And I say 'assuming you win' because you do not have an ideal witness in Ms. Ruiz. Do I make myself clear, Mr. Hernandez?"

"Yes, Your Honor."

"Good. But I'm not done with you." She pauses, then begins again, her tone grave.

"Mr. Hernandez, my obligation is to report your reckless conduct to the Disciplinary Committee, where you could easily have your license suspended for this egregious behavior. But I will leave that decision up to Mr. Wyler." She turns to me. In my head, I hear his threat to punch me in the nose again.

"Well, Mr. Wyler, what do you want me to do?" I hesitate. Telling her that I'd like him to lick my ass in Macy's window will not reflect well upon me.

"Your Honor, I don't believe it will be necessary for you to make a report to the Disciplinary Committee. I think your ruling on this matter achieves justice, and as long as counsel stipulates not to appeal your decision, that would be enough." She looks to Wilbur.

"Well, sir?"

"Yes, Your Honor, I'll so stipulate, on the record."

"And one other thing, Your Honor."

"I'm listening, Mr. Wyler."

"I think that Wilbur should apologize to me for what he attempted to do here."

"Yes, Mr. Wyler, I do think an apology is in order." Judge Brown turns to him. He nods.

"I'm sorry," he says, in a low voice. Judge Brown intervenes. Again.

"Mr. Hernandez, that really didn't sound very sincere. If an apology is not sincere, then it's not an apology at all. Do you agree with me on that, Mr. Wyler?"

I love her sense of justice. "You know, I was just thinking the same thing, Your Honor."

She gives me a smirk, and we turn back to Wilbur. This guy is on the ropes.

"I'm sorry," he repeats, sounding a little more genuine. But not that much.

"For what, Mr. Hernandez? For what are you sorry? Look Mr. Wyler in the eye and tell him."

He understands what he needs to do but is struggling. "I'm sorry for falsely claiming in open court that you suborned perjury."

"And . . ." this very forthright judge prompts.

"And for attempting to steal your fee."

Justice comes in all forms, I think to myself. Sometimes even a simple apology does the trick. Everyone deserves a second chance. That's what makes this country great.

A little later, after we go through the formality of placing the resolution on the record, Roscoe walks out of the building with me. We stop at the bottom of the courthouse steps. I sigh. But it's a happy one. The thing is, even though I've just saved my ass, I can't even stop to congratulate myself. Roscoe gives me the nod.

"So, where you off to?"

I point across the street.

"Benson?"

His guess is on the money.

"Good luck," he says. "But just remember what I've told you time and again: some day one of his referrals is going to be the end of you. It easily could've happened this morning with this . . . What do you call Henry's referrals again?"

"HICs."

"Right, this HIC."

"Got ya," I reply. And sigh again. This time, a heavy one.

But this is what I do. And this is who I am.

5.

As I walk across the street through Foley Square to Henry Benson's office, I'm thinking about our relationship.

The reason Henry, a celebrated criminal defense attorney, no longer handles injury matters is because he managed to commit legal malpractice on the last civil case he presented to a jury. Now he can no longer obtain professional insurance that will cover injury matters. Thus, I became the lucky recipient of Henry's injured criminals—or HICs—as my paralegal, Lily, and I have nicknamed them.

Henry, by his own admission, chose me—a complete stranger—mostly so he could say fuck you to his 'best friend,' Dominic Keller, the self-proclaimed king of all injury cases. Though, to be fair to myself, I know he'd been impressed by what he'd heard about my expertise in courtroom medicine. Dominic, in fact, had been the guy who'd once mentioned my skills to Henry, making the fuck you extra sweet.

So far, every HIC case has been accompanied by some form of wrinkle. One way or another, they don't ever fit the description "straightforward." It's also fallen to me to figure out which HIC cases are legitimate injury claims and which might be trying to bilk the legal system. Since getting involved with Henry, I've learned—after the fact—that, occasionally, I guess wrong.

At least I admit it.

But what you need to know is that my first commitment is to my client. It's an ethical violation to tell the opposing attorney that a case may be tenuous at best or even lack merit should it become evident after being retained.

So this is how I went from having a quiet but steadily growing practice, at which I made a decent living, to being a guy up close and personal with not just the unexpected but the truly scary. I've been beaten up, drugged, kidnapped, run off the highway, and knocked into a coma. I've also committed forgery in the interests of justice, found myself in alliance with murderers and their co-conspirators, and faced the Disciplinary Committee an embarrassing number of times. I imagine you get the picture.

Plus, I look like Mike Tyson bit a piece of my ear off. But that's the good news. It's the permanent reminder of a gunshot to the head, which I survived while pursuing justice in the case of one very special brain-damaged girl, little Suzy Williams. Which is a whole other story.

Still, as Henry promised, my bank account has definitely benefited. At the same time, believe me, I'm just a guy who wants to do the right thing.

As far as Cookie is concerned, she's technically not an HIC. But Henry's involved himself, and so there's just no telling. Case in point: my morning events. Josefina Ruiz, although referred by Henry, was not an HIC—because she had no criminal past. The part Henry left out was her drug addiction, an unfortunate omission since addicts will say or do anything to support their habits.

When I enter Henry's office, he's seated in one of the client chairs flicking playing cards into a specially placed wastebasket.

"Bored, Henry?"

"Did you preserve our fee on Ruiz?" That's his way of showing concern.

"Fee preservation achieved."

"Good. And no, not really," he says. *Flick, flick.*

"No, not really, what?" I ask.

"I'm not bored." *Flick, flick.* "You're early," he adds, still concentrating on what he's doing, which doesn't involve looking at me.

"I know I'm early. Do you want me to leave and come back?"

"No, stay. This Cookie matter looks to be a big case." *Flick, flick.* "Three neck surgeries—you and I know two hundred and fifty thousand's ridiculous. But you tell me. You're the pro." *Flick, flick.*

"Without seeing her records, my take is that it could either definitely be big—or no case at all. We'll just have to wait and see. But the fact that she's doing cartwheels in headgear is strong evidence that she's on the road to recovery. Anyway, that was an artful cross you did of Major. Now he has no choice but to come here."

Henry flicks two more cards, then stops. He likes to flick in pairs. He glances up for the first time.

"Let's stop bullshitting each other. Since we both met her at the same time, I won't consider her a direct referral. Instead of giving me fifty percent of the fee, I'll just take twenty-five since you're going to have to work out a fee arrangement with this Chris Charles, the outgoing attorney. Sound fair?"

"Yup. Sounds fair." He's always been fair with me, so no need to point out it was my buddy, Mick, who made the score.

There's a buzz. "Mr. Benson," his receptionist says, "Ms. Cookie Krumke and Dr. Major Dodd are here to see you. I'm sending them back per your instruction."

I almost forgot he's a doctor. It's part of the weirdness here.

Just Agree

At this cue, Henry gets up and, with the toe of his ridiculously pointy cowboy boot, kicks two cards that fell short under his desk. Next, putting on his jacket and tightening his tie, he moves behind his desk, taking the trash can with him.

"Let me do the talking," he instructs. "You stand there." He points to his right. "Just agree. You got that?" I nod. Generally, I don't like to play third wheel, but he's got the home-field advantage.

Cookie and Major appear at the door. "Come in," Henry invites them. "Please sit down." She proceeds gingerly, possibly paying the price for last night's cartwheels today.

Henry picks up on it. "You seem stiff today, Cookie. Is everything all right?"

"Well, I guess I overdid it. My neck's killing me, but I should be fine in a couple of days."

Henry nods in sympathy, then turns his focus to Major, staring at him just long enough to make him uncomfortable. Then he shifts his attention back to Cookie.

"First things first," Henry begins reasonably enough. "Cookie, two hundred fifty thousand dollars does not, we believe, constitute fair and reasonable compensation for what you've been through. Agreed, Tug?" He looks over to me.

"Agreed," I respond. The first of many to come.

"Without even seeing your medicals or even knowing what the totality of the claim is, I feel justified in deeming two hundred fifty thousand an insult. Agreed, Tug?"

"Agreed." Damn, Henry, I just told you there might not even be a case.

"I don't know what the basis for the offer of settlement is, but I do believe that for this Chris Charles to recommend it, he must lack the fundamental skill set it takes to handle a complex medical malpractice case properly. Agreed, Tug?"

"Agreed."

"Under no circumstances, then, are you to accept that offer of settlement before we have an opportunity to look into things. Agreed, Tug?"

"Agreed."

Cookie, though, has something to say. It's as clear as the dimple in her chin.

"But that's a lot of money, Mr. Benson," she interjects.

"I understand that it may sound like a lot of money to you, young lady, but it doesn't mean it's fair under the circumstances.

And it's these circumstances that I've brought you here to discuss today. If that money is on the table, it will always be on the table. Don't worry about that."

"Um, I'm not sure that's exactly true, Mr. Benson," Major says. He's biting his lip but appears composed.

"Oh, really?" Henry replies, confident he knows otherwise. "Why's that?"

"Chris Charles explained that they were willing to pay this money if we accepted it within the next seven days, before they incur any more expense in defending the case. Otherwise, they're going to take it off the table. It's their position—McElroy's lawyers, that is—that the only thing he may have done wrong was put a screw in improperly, which was corrected by the first remedial surgery. It's also their position that the next procedure came about because Cookie was having difficulties with bone healing. Which was unfortunate—yet we all know, I think, that it can happen in the best of surgical hands. Therefore, they're offering the two fifty for one otherwise unnecessary surgery, taking the position that the last operation was a result of healing insufficiencies rather than malpractice."

"You seem to be well informed."

"I'm just trying to help Cookie make the right decisions."

"You helped enough already, don't you think?"

Ouch. Yet Major doesn't react. He genuinely seems concerned—for Cookie, not himself.

"Besides," Henry continues, "even if the last procedure was the result of delayed bone union—that's what you're saying, right?"

"Yes, sir. Well, actually nonunion of bone at the fusion site."

"Well, even so, that doesn't relieve Dr. McElroy of responsibility under the law. Those surgeries are items of damage imputed to him. The legal doctrine is called 'the eggshell plaintiff.' Meaning, if Cookie sustained a greater injury than someone else would have who didn't have a healing insufficiency, McElroy is nonetheless responsible because you take the plaintiff as you find her. Agreed, Tug?"

"Agreed." I'm keeping to my side of the bargain. But we need to connect the nonunion to McElroy's malpractice to collect for it.

"Thus, this case is worth more than two fifty based on the two subsequent surgeries alone. Agreed, Tug?"

"Agreed." Like I said.

"As far as their taking the money off the table, that's just a negotiation ploy. It never happens. Once the money is there, it's always there. Agreed, Tug?"

"Agreed," I say. The truth is, though, I'm way less confident with this one. I've been in situations, rare as they may be, where it happened. Now you see it, now you don't.

"What we must do at this juncture is discuss the circumstances that brought you two here," Henry says, turning purposefully to Major. "It was quite a fortuitous chance we met, I believe. Since then, you've had time to reflect on what we talked about—and I'd like to pick it up from there. I made reference to an important aspect of this being 'madness.' Do you recall? And do you understand what my meaning was, why I used that word?"

"Well, it obviously has something to do with the relationships between Chris Charles, Dr. McElroy, and me—which is to say, our various connections," Major replies with surprising forthrightness.

"You hit the nail on the head. Now I'd like to hear the specifics."

"That part I'm really not too sure about."

Henry gives him a look. There's a long pause before he says, "What the devil is the matter with you? I'm talking about the inherent conflicts of interest among the defendant, the surgeon; his friend, the lawyer; you, the boyfriend; and Cookie, the injured malpractice victim. Don't you see it, man?"

"Well, not exactly."

"Then I'll make it clear. Cookie deserves legal representation that's not influenced or compromised by personal relationships. She needs an attorney who'll represent her zealously, not some novice working out of his basement suing his friend, whom he may not want to hurt financially or professionally." He stops to let this sink in, although any of it should have been obvious in this situation from the word *go*.

"Is this lawyer," he continues, "going to go after his doctor pal's credibility and expose all the wrongful things he's done? I think not, because that would end their friendship. Now, Cookie's damages are certainly worth more than two hundred fifty thousand, but the question here is, what if they're worth more than the doctor's insurance coverage? Is this lawyer going to go after his buddy personally in an effort to get Cookie fairly compensated? Or will he be more concerned with the financial harm it might bring to his friend?"

Henry slams his hands down on his desk. Okay, it's overdramatic, but he knows what he's doing. "And that's only the beginning! Truly, it couldn't be more fundamental!" Henry and Major lock eyes. Henry's the alpha dog, so he keeps on going. Cookie is watching anxiously, protectively. She's concerned for her man, yet a door has been opened.

"Many of the conflicts with which this situation is plagued should give you pause, Major," Henry continues. "What if you and Cookie split up for some reason? It's obvious you two share a close bond, but for discussion's sake, let's say a bad breakup occurs. She'll be on the outside of your cozy threesome. What then?" He can see he's broken through to Major finally, and so can I. It was the possibility of breaking up, however hypothetical, that did it.

"So I'd suggest the current situation is not entirely in Cookie's best interests, yet her best interests are what you want for her, correct?" With this last thrust, Henry's got Major wearing the look he should be wearing.

"Yes, yes, of course I want what's in Cookie's best interests. I just never realized the potential here for conflict. I'd felt terrible about referring her to Dr. McElroy, who did what he did. Even felt responsible for what happened to her. I was trying to make things better by getting her to a lawyer. But I understand what you're talking about now. The circle is too small." Major looks at Cookie. "I'm sorry, my dear. I just didn't realize. But I should have."

"I know you were doing what you believed was best."

As they share this loving moment, I have to question how these two ever became a couple in the first place.

Henry points to me. Cookie and I lock eyes, and she smiles at me. She's really something. I smile back, not a flirty smile, but one that acknowledges her in a respectful way.

"Now, I've had a long-standing relationship with Mr. Wyler here," Henry says, "and I know he's the right man for the job. Still, I intend to personally oversee your case, and that way you get double expertise, experience, and insight. How does that sound to you, Cookie?"

"Can I really do that? I mean, can I really change attorneys?"

"Of course you can. People do it every day for one reason or another. You just sign a piece of paper and poof, you have a new lawyer, just like that."

"But what about Chris?" she says with concern. "I mean, I don't want to hurt his feelings or get him mad at me. I called him early this morning to let him know I was coming here. I didn't want to do it behind his back. And it seemed he was pretty upset. This is the biggest case he ever had. I feel really uncomfortable firing him. I mean, I never fired anyone before. It just doesn't feel right, especially since he got me so much money."

I want to ask Henry if he'd mind if I said something. But I know he's just about to close the deal so I don't. One of the most difficult things for a lawyer ever to do is to keep his mouth shut. I'm no exception.

At least I admit it.

"Well, I'll talk to Chris and explain to him how his lack of experience made him unable to identify the conflict." Henry's irony is lost on everyone but me. "Technically, he should be disqualified by a judge and this matter brought to the attention of the Office of Professional Conduct. But we don't want to see him in any trouble now, do we?" He looks at Cookie.

"Oh, gosh, no," she says, in a tone that makes clear the fact she's never brought harm to anybody or anything.

"So don't worry then; he won't be. I'll effectuate the change of attorney and have your file in my hands in less than a week. Sound good to you?"

She looks to Major. He gives her the nod. The same nod of approval he gave her at Jingles. Her best interests are clearly what matters to him.

"Gee, thanks, Mr. Benson."

"Now, you just call me Henry, young lady." He gives her a benevolent smile, then turns back to Major. The smile vanishes. "Are we all on the same page here?"

"Yes, we are. I really appreciate your firmness and candor. Cookie and I have little experience with lawsuits and lawyers. I think I speak for the both of us when I say we feel more comfortable already."

Henry, hearing this, picks up the Consent to Change Attorney form he just happens to have on his desk and places it in front of Cookie. Reaching into his leather desk tray, he takes out a black-and-gold Mont Blanc and twists the top. He gets up, leans forward, and hands it to Cookie.

"This first document is the Consent to Change Attorney, substituting us in as your new counsel, with Charles out. This other document is a letter we drafted on your behalf directing him not to contact you regarding this matter. Now, this is serious business, so he should not be getting in touch with you, and you should not be contacting him. Do you think you can comply with this rule despite any gratitude you may feel?"

"Yes, Mr. Benson."

"Call me Henry. Good. Now, should Charles contact you in violation of this directive, it then becomes your obligation to tell either Tug or me so we can deal with that in the appropriate manner. Will you do this?"

"Yes," she answers. But she's not extremely happy with the idea, I can see.

"Good," he says again. "Now, sign here," he directs, pointing to the appropriate places.

At first, she begins to try to scan the official-looking documents, filled with their legal mumbo jumbo. Then she hesitates, as if she has a question.

"Um, are you sure they can't take the money off the table, Mr. Benson? I mean, Henry. Two hundred and fifty thousand dollars is a lot of money. And I've been out of work so much since this all happened that I don't want to risk losing that kind of money. It's a lot of lap dances." She giggles. "And, like I said, I want to pay everybody back who's helped me through this, everyone who insisted I take money even when I told them I wanted to do it on my own."

"Cookie," Henry says in a stern tone, "once the insurance carrier gets notice that Tug is involved, that number is only going to go up. That two fifty won't be taken off the table, I assure you. Agreed?" he says, looking over at me.

I have no choice.

"Yes, Henry, agreed." I really wish he wouldn't do this. It's improper, from an ethical point of view, to make assurances about money offers. Ones that can, at any time, be withdrawn.

Cookie attempts a shrug, but it's not easy with her halo. She hesitates, thinking hard, then looks up. Major has remained silent. "Okay then, I trust you guys," she says. And she signs on the dotted line.

Claudette Krumke.

6.

As I head out of Henry's building, I realize my contribution amounted to eight *agreeds* and a reciprocating smile to Cookie. I wish all my retentions were that easy. I also wish all my referrals from Henry were like Cookie, kind, and thoughtful, appreciative, felony-free hottie nuggets.

So I'm feeling good about my new case. But I'm also aware that what's in the file will determine just how big a payday lies ahead. It's three years old with two fifty on the table after all, and that means the malpractice carrier views it in just the way Major stated, as an otherwise unnecessary surgery case. Still, they're offering top dollar for one of those, so they're obviously factoring in all the surgeries, despite their stated position.

One thing to consider is the uncertainty regarding the permanency of her condition. It's clear to me that Chris Charles is jumping the gun by recommending acceptance of an offer while she's still in the recovery phase.

In my view, the case is worth seven hundred fifty thousand at a minimum, based on the three surgeries alone.

Two things continue to bother me, however. One is how could an intelligent, medically trained guy like Major be so ignorant about the obvious conflicts? And two is his unlikely relationship with Cookie. Opposites attract, sure, and women look for father figures. But I don't know . . . It's still just pretty weird. Also, I really wish Henry hadn't said the current offer would never be pulled off the table.

Oops, as Cookie would say, that makes three.

Once I turn on my phone, which I'd switched off for the meeting, there's a blast of messages. *Bzzzz*. It's my favorite "Private Caller." I'm enjoying this new unseen pal, plus I'd like to find out about the van that caused his painful ooh-dats. I hit the *answer* button.

"Hello, Robert."

"My name is Robert Killroy, but I didn't kill no Roy, and I didn't kill nobody."

"How have you been? Long time, no speak."

"I'm sorry," he says, sounding confused. "I musta dialed the wrong number."

"No, wait, Robert, you've got the right number. Why are you saying that?"

"'Cause the person I be looking for spoke to me this morning. Nice man but owes Mr. Wang some money."

"That's me, Robert."

"Oh, so you *do* owe Mr. Wang the money. That's good 'cause that's what he says too."

"No, Robert. I *don't* owe him the money. But I *am* the guy you spoke to this morning. What's up?"

"I thought that was you, mister. Then you told me 'long time, no speak,' and I just knowed we spoke this morning. That threw me off directly."

"It's only a figure of speech, Robert, so don't worry. What's going on?"

"Okay, now according to these rules, I got to tell you I'm calling to collect a debt."

"I understand."

"Okay now," he continues, "I called up Mr. Wang, and he says that you are dead wrong. He didn't ruin your suit, and it was all messed up when you brought it in. So can you pay him the four-teen dollars and seventy-nine cents you owe him and pick up your seven-hundred-fifty-dollar suit? That's a lot of money for a suit, mister."

"Robert, no, I can't pay him that money. Like I said, it's a matter of principle."

"I don't think Mr. Wang is no principal. I think Mr. Wang cleans clothes for people. He don't work at no school, that's what I think."

"I agree, Robert. Mr. Wang is not a school principal. But I don't owe him that money."

"Ooh-dat! Ooh-dat! Ooh-dat! Oh, da pains, they be bad," he yelps suddenly. What's that new sound? Like slapping, or punching.

"Are you okay, Robert?"

"That be the pains, mister. Down in my ankle."

"Robert, why don't you tell me what happened to you."

"Got runned over by a van. Ruint my ankle. Granny says I drag it along when I walk, but I can ride like the wind. That's what Granny says."

I need to ask. It's what I do. "Robert, do you have a lawyer?"

"Not no more. Granny fired the one I got. Said he wasn't bony fried."

"Well, do you have a new lawyer handling your case?"

"No, mister. Granny says lawyers ain't no good. She's taking care of it herself."

"Is Granny a lawyer?"

He laughs. "Naw, Granny ain't no lawyer. She takes care of me."

"I see, Robert. Tell me, not that it matters, but which ankle did you injure?"

"Hold on fer a sec," he responds. "Hey Granny! Hey Granny!" he yells. "Which one of my ankles gots hurt? My right or my left?"

"Your right one, boy," I hear a sharp old voice respond. "How many times I got to tell you that?"

Now Robert's breathing heavily, like the reprimand elevated his respirations. "My right, mister. Now what about that fourteen dollars and seventy-nine cents?"

"Robert, do me a favor and put Granny on the phone."

"Can't do that," he quickly responds.

"Why not?"

"'Cause I'm opposed to be collecting money now. I got to have what Granny calls my financial independence. I got to get this job right." The distinct implication is that he may have failed in previous ones. But I'd be surprised at that, with his perseverance.

"Just tell her to pick up for a second, Robert." Before he gets a chance to respond, I hear Granny again in the background.

"Who you speaking to, Robert? You supposed to be collecting a debt, practicing that job, not talking about your ankle, boy."

"Granny, I knowed what I'm opposed to be doing, and I am collecting a debt. But my pains came along and . . ." I hear the classic sound of one person wrestling a phone out of another's hand.

"Who's this on the phone?" Granny asks, all soured up. "You the man that owes Mr. Wang the money?"

"You got the right guy, but I don't owe Wang any money."

"I see. Well, he ain't allowed to use the phone but for business. Why you taking him away from what he needs to be keeping on at?"

"Granny," I say, "Robert was in pain. So I asked him why. That's all. He didn't do anything wrong, I assure you."

"Okay then, I'll put him back on the line."

"Wait!" I say with urgency. "Maybe I can help you out on Robert's case." I sense quiet caution on the other end of the line.

"You a lawyer?"

"Yes, I am."

"I don't trust no lawyers."

"Me, neither."

"That's a good snap back."

"It was a truthful one."

"How come you don't trust no lawyers, seeing you're one of them?"

"The list is too long," I tell her.

"Ha, I got me a list, too. Hmm," she says, contemplating, "let me ask you this—do you believe what your clients tell ya?"

"Depends on the client. If it were Robert," I add, "the answer would be yes." And I mean it.

"That's straight on. Want to know why?"

"Sure do."

"You see, Robert here, he's a boy who ain't told a lie since the day he was born. No threat of ass-whop or nothing."

"That's right, Granny," I hear him say in the background. "I don't tell no lies."

"Hush, boy," she says to him. "You see me jawing on the phone. And his own lawyer," she says to me, "the one I fired—he didn't believe Robert. Thought he was lying. Decided the boy caused his own accident 'cause that's what the police report says. Ain't no sense having a lawyer if he don't believe ya."

"I have to agree with you on that."

"One thing is for certain," she states with conviction. "Robert didn't cause no accident."

"That's right, Granny," I hear him agree. "I didn't cause no accident."

"Well, I can tell you this," I respond, "I'm certain too that Robert didn't cause the accident. There's no doubt in my mind."

Now there's quiet on the other end. The wheels are spinning inside her head. I can tell Granny's not just smart but cagey.

"What's your name, lawyer?"

"Tug Wyler."

"You bona fide?"

"Do you mean am I admitted to the bar? Then the answer's yes, I'm bona fide."

"Still," she continues, "I don't trust no lawyers. So I'll be handling the case myself."

"May I ask your name, please?"

"Just did." I hear her snicker at the fun she poked at me. "Just playing. The name's Ethel."

"Ethel, do you really think that's a good idea? Handling Robert's case yourself?"

She waits a beat or two before answering. "Probably not, but like I'm saying for the third time, I don't trust no lawyers."

"Give me the top reason on your list why not."

"They're after the quick money, for one thing. Robert's lawyer was trying to have him take forty-seven thousand five hundred dollars for his case. Said it's good money since Robert caused his own injury—"

"Which he didn't," I interject.

"Now you're catching on, Mr. Lawyer. But that ain't hardly enough for what this boy's been through. So I fired him. He was trying to take advantage, and for certain he was not no bona fide lawyer. We Killroys may not have a lot of dollars, but we chock full of common cents."

She's listening, I can tell, to see if I get her little joke. I chuckle appreciatively.

"That was a smart move, Ethel. But why not make another good move now? Let me take a look at Robert's file."

"No."

"I'm concerned with your grandson's best interests here, I assure you. He sounds to me like he's in real pain. He's probably got a neuroma or reflex sympathetic dystrophy in that ankle."

"Hmmph. That's exactly what he got. Just the problem is, I don't want to be scammed by no lawyer."

"How about if I work for free?"

"For free?"

"Yes, for free."

"Why would you go and do that? For a stranger who's trying his best to make sure you pay your bills."

"A few reasons."

"I'm listening. Go ahead. Let's see how convincing you are, Wyler."

"Okay. First, it gives me the opportunity to put some positive energy out there, and I'm one of those people who believes you get back what you put out in some way, shape, or form. They call it karma."

"Uh-huh," she responds skeptically. "I can tell you pretty for certain, chances be slim you getting anything back from Robert. You still want to work for free?"

"I sure do."

"Go on then. Why else?"

"Because just a little while ago, I met a nice girl with a lawyer whom I felt was going to short her, the way Robert's lawyer tried to short you guys. But she isn't as smart as you, Ethel. Even her doctor boyfriend isn't as smart as you, because they were going to take the money. I was able to prevent that from happening. It gave me a sense of doing justice, and that's the reason I became a lawyer. But I have to say, I'm not sure if I felt good because I stopped a wrong from happening or because she's extremely beautiful and I got the hots for her."

"That's honest," Ethel tells me. "Go on now, boy. I'm suspecting you're saving your best argument for last."

What great instincts she has. That's exactly the case.

"And because you don't trust lawyers and don't want Robert shortchanged, I can't do you any wrong if I don't take a fee."

"X marks the spot, X marks the spot with a dot, dot, dot. Now you reasoning soundly."

"Yes, Ethel, that's the right conclusion. It's a winning formula. And it's one that means Robert gets all the money to put toward his financial independence. You want that for him, don't you?" I'd been saving that one.

"That's what I'm staying alive for. To see that he can get on all by his own. For free, though? You'll do the lawyering for free?"

"The only thing I'll ask of you out of this whole thing is that, if I do a good job for Robert, in the future you'll refer your friends and family to me, should any of them meet with an unfortunate accident or get bad medical care. How does that sound?"

"Sounds like we have us a deal." Then she changes tone. "But Robert still got to do his collections on you, no matter what happens."

"Let him collect away. But I'm going to defend myself against it."

"We'll see how that one ends up, then, won't we now?"

"I guess we will, Ethel. Have you had any conversation with the attorney on the other side since taking over Robert's case?"

"Just one. He ain't bona fide, either, if you ask me. Calls himself Rich. What kind of lawyer calls himself Rich?"

"I agree. Rich is a stupid-ass name for a personal injury lawyer. But what did you say to him?"

"That my Robert deserves more money. That's about it. I had to tongue-lash the man to get it through his thick skull. Oh yeah, I told him Robert didn't cause no accident, either."

We chat a little more, and then I tell her I have to get back to the office just as she reminds me Robert has to resume his job. I like Granny. She's the right combination of gruff and concerned. And I give her full marks for being very aware of Robert's medical condition.

As soon as we click off, I send a text to Lily to set up an appointment as soon as possible. I don't want Robert's case to wind up dismissed because Ethel's unfamiliar with the procedures of the judicial system. Just by missing a simple appearance, you can blow everything.

Some judges are like that, but Ethel couldn't know it. She and Robert deserve better.

Stay Away from Her

So now I'm crossing Foley Square again. The giant black marble sculpture soaring way up into the sky in front of me is styled after an antelope-inspired African headdress and is mounted on a boat-shaped base. It was commissioned to memorialize the unknown enslaved Africans brought to America. It's called *Triumph of the Human Spirit*, and whenever I give myself the chance to think about it, I cringe at the knowledge that our country once allowed slavery. I hate that any one person could exert absolute control over another's existence.

As I'm on my way to get a dirty-water dog on the far side of the square before I hop the subway, a guy in oversize black plastic sunglasses and a mini trench coat gets up from a bench and starts walking behind me. His lockstep maneuvers lead me to believe I'm his target. Great. What could this be?

I take five more steps, confirming that his gait's keeping pace with mine, then stop. He stops, too. Damn! He's maintaining distance. That confirms it. Let me head this one off. I turn and begin closing the twenty-foot gap between us by walking directly at him the way a catcher goes at a runner caught between bases. At the ten-foot mark, he turns and starts walking away. Yep, he's for me, and he's really bad at what he does. I bet Robert Killroy could keep cover better than he can.

"Hold on," I say. "Let's get this over with." He stops and turns. "I'm pretty sure, although not certain, my wife believes in our marriage these days and didn't hire you. So what's up?"

He maintains silence.

"Come on. Out with it. Well?"

He takes his shades off and assumes a threatening stance. "Cookie," he says, "you know, the dancer. Stay away from her, Wyler. Seeeee." I'm immediately reminded of some cartoon character, a gangster type, but just which one escapes me.

"I don't think so."

He shoots me a nasty look.

I'm at least a foot taller, near double his weight, and can easily outrun him, but the real reason I don't feel threatened is because there's a cop fifty yards away.

"Listen, wise guy, you heard me. Just stay away from Cookie. Leave her case alone, that's all, seeeee. Got that? Walk away, and let Charles finish what he started. He's her attorney. That's all, seeeee."

"This is a first," I say in a tone of surprise. "I never had an out-going attorney dispatch his investigator or whatever you are to warn me not to take the case."

"Charles didn't send me, seeeee."

"Of course Charles sent you. He's the only one with interest. So tell him to get over it. She just signed the Consent to Change Attorney. Tell him to back off, or I'll have to seek judicial intervention to deem his discharge for cause, and he'll wind up with nothing for the work he's done. And clearly his efforts so far entitle him to something. Now run along."

His expression of contempt deepens. He's not ready to leave.

"If she signed the consent, then tear it up, seeeee. Tell her you can't handle her case, and then go about your business." His smirk firms and hands tighten, almost as if he's ready to go at it. No doubt he's one of those little guys who needs to overcompensate by acting tough.

Fact is, I don't want to tangle with this fist-clenching, wee man. I can just hear some smart-aleck now: "Hey, did you hear? Wyler got beat up by a twerp in front of the courthouse!" So it's not going to happen.

"Just take it easy," I say. "I'm not going to tangle with you. Let's be civil. First, you obviously know who I am, so why don't you tell me who you are."

"The name's Minotero, seeeee. My friends call me Mino. But you just stick with Minotero."

Minnow, I repeat in my head. That's an unusual name but very fitting. "Listen, Minnow," I say, ignoring his instruction, "let's just try to keep the peace."

"I'll keep the peace, seeeee. And you keep your distance from Cookie's case. You're through. You're out of the way. That's what you are. You got it, Wyler? Stay away or I'll beat you off!" His scowl transforms into a look of delayed realization.

He just threatened to beat me off.

"That didn't come out right, seeeee, but you know what I mean."

"Yes, Minnow, I know what you mean. Stay away from Cookie's case or you're going to beat me off."

He flexes toward me. The cop who's been taking a mild interest in our exchange now shifts his stance. Minnow looks over, clenching his fists and then releasing before he stomps away angrily, looking like a kid when the barbershop's out of lollipops.

"Hey Minnow!" I call out. He stops and turns. "Tell Charles not to be such a sore sport. Every attorney gets substituted out of at least one case during his career. It's unavoidable. But I'll make sure he gets something fair out of this."

"I told you, I don't work for Charles. Get that through your head, seeeee. And one last thing, this little meeting was between us. Got it?"

"No, I don't got it. You just threatened me with bodily harm— or maybe it was a hand job. I'm not certain. But, in either event, you're trying to scare me away from taking over a legal case. I'm pretty sure your tactics would get a thumbs-down from the bar association. You see that building over there?" I say, pointing. "I'm going in there to tell a guy named Henry Benson about our little exchange. He's going to be unhappy, and you know why? Because he has an interest in Cookie's case, and most of the people he affiliates with are either in jail, on their way to jail, or just out of jail. Are you drinking my sake, kemosabe?"

Minnow shakes his head. "Suit yourself," he says. "You, Benson, whoever. You'll all go down for taking part in it."

He resumes his departure while I watch intently, committing to memory every single aspect of him. Even so, I have to wonder: go down for taking part in what?

Before taking another step, I call Henry.

"Benson here," he answers—on the third ring, as always.

"I think we may have a problem with Cookie's outgoing attorney."

"Who? Charles? Nice guy. What gives you that impression?"

I didn't anticipate this response. "You mean you spoke to him already?"

"Just after Cookie and Major left. I reached him and explained the conflict, and he understood fully. I'm having the file picked up in the morning. He says most of the work's done, except that Cookie needs to be produced again for further oral deposition. She apparently took ill during her previous questioning. A bad headache. Charles also confirmed everything Major said regarding the defendant's position and offer. I told him we'd resolve the fee issue when the case concludes, and he agreed. Anything else?"

"You sure he wasn't harboring any bad feelings?"

"I have to say that, yes, he did, initially. As you know, Cookie spoke to him first thing this morning and told him she was coming here. She explained that she thought it was only fair that he knew because she didn't want to feel like she was doing anything behind his back. He tried to talk her out of it, persuading her to some degree. Then Major insisted they come see us. Why are you asking?"

"No reason, just curious. Charles told you all that?"

"That's right."

"Why?"

"Because I asked."

"Got ya. Let me know when you get the file."

"You'll know on your own. I'm having it delivered to your office." *Click.*

On the subway uptown, I think about why I didn't tell Henry about Minnow. He likes to be informed. On the other hand, he can also go overboard, and I guess I don't want to yell fire unless I'm sure there's smoke. The only way I may have compromised him by holding back was denying him the opportunity to decline the case. But I know Henry would never do that. Never.

Besides, we're not taking part in anything unscrupulous, so there's nothing for us to "go down for" as Minnow quaintly put it.

I will say, though, it's all a bit too mysterious for my liking.

7.

s I come out of the train at 28th Street, my phone vibrates. Please don't be Robert. Good, it's not. It's a message from my trusty paralegal, Lily. It reads, *Ethel and Robert Killroy are here waiting for you. When will you be back?*

I reply, feeling just a bit out of sorts, that I'm downstairs near the office on the way up. I quick-step it to my building, run for the elevator, though the door is closing, and thrust my arm in.

Just in time. It slides back open, revealing two super-tall models. There's an agency in my building, and the girls arc in and out all day long on Tuesdays. That's the open call day, which is a perfect stimulus for my occasional Tuesday night event at home. When it's not canceled that is.

I enter, gladly.

"Sorry about that, ladies," I say in my cheeriest voice. One responds with a polite smile. That's enough for me. The rule of thumb with models is: never try. They're obliged to fight off the dogs all day, so why set yourself up for rejection? But this one, she did acknowledge the acknowledging thing. So I gotta explore.

"Are you a model, too?" I ask.

"Yes. *You're* a model?" She's surprised. Why wouldn't she be?

"You bet ya." I look up at the floor numbers, straight-faced.

"What kind of model are you?" the other girl wonders, looking at me with an expression of disbelief.

"Fat-ass," I answer in a confident tone.

"Fat-ass?" she repeats.

"Yes. It's my niche." They look to each other, bewildered. An instant later the door opens. I go, giving my well-formed caboose an open-handed slap. Cookie and Major pop into my head as I think never in a million years would girls like that be interested in a guy like me.

At least I admit it.

I enter my reception area to find Ethel sitting right in front of me. She's in her midseventies with silver-blue hair. It's an interesting look, a black woman with blue hair. She's wearing glasses, is plainly dressed, and basically makes you think of a grandma—the kind you'd see sitting in a rocking chair on the front porch of a house somewhere down south where they still use a hand pump to access well water. When she smiles, I can tell instantly we're going to hit it off.

I step in and shut the door. This reveals what's hidden behind it: Robert. He's on the floor, looks about eighteen, and is heavy-set. He's wearing shorts, and his legs look like tree trunks. Overall, the vibe he gives off is definitely that of a young man who's mentally challenged. What he's doing is concentrating on a stack of magazines he obviously brought with him. He takes no notice of me.

"You must be Ethel Killroy," I say, extending my hand. She gets up with the energy of a young woman.

"I don't like lawyers," she says, "but I like you." Her grip is strong, just like she is.

"The feeling is mutual, Mrs. Killroy, the feeling is mutual. And I love your hair color." At this, she whips the wig she's wearing right off of her head and inspects it, turning the piece from side to side.

"This old thing?"

Robert looks over for an instant. Have I mentioned he's wearing a very large and shiny red bike helmet? "Granny's got the cancer. Granny's got the cancer," he chants.

"Hush, boy," she says, as she places the wig back on her head, adjusting it by feel. "Just a little setback, that's all." I nod toward my new pro bono client, recognizing her dogged courage.

Next, I squat down by her grandson so we can talk better. "You must be Robert." He nods without looking at me, absorbed in what he's doing. I note that on the floor beside him is a miniature recording device next to the magazines. One, I see, is titled *Investigator Weekly*.

"You owe Mr. Wang fourteen dollars and seventy-nine cents," he says suddenly, looking up at me. "He's a really nice man."

"You're all business, Robert." It's a compliment.

"Mister?" he continues.

"Yes?"

"It smells funny in here."

I straighten up and take a whiff. Nothing. My subtenants are *Toke* magazine, a competitor of *High Times*. They've got their weed-reeking runners coming in and out, but they're far and away the best tenants I've ever had. They always pay on time, prefer no signage on the door, and can be very entertaining. They also never mention a thing about my HIC clients, who might seem a little threatening should you happen to run into one unexpectedly.

"I'll look into it, Robert."

"I've smelled that smell before, mister." Oh man, Robert. Don't bring it to Granny's attention, please.

"Like I said, I'll look into it."

"I know what that smell is, mister."

I look at Ethel.

"Good, then you have it covered. Be right back."

I turn to go, but he's not done yet.

"Want to know what that smell is, mister?"

"Sure, I do," I answer, having no option. This kid has the nose of a bloodhound, because I can't even smell a hint of it today, unlike some other days when delivery is made.

"It's Glade Vanilla Plug-in." He points to the electrical socket on the wall behind him.

"So it is," I respond, "so it is."

Whew. He has, in fact, recognized Lily's solution to the olfactory consequence of renting to *Toke*.

"They gots the same flavor down at the collection agency. Where I had my interview. But I work from home—for now, that is. Until I proves that I can do the job."

"Listen, if you don't mind, could you give me a minute? I'll be right back out to get you." I'm a little annoyed at Lily for not telling me about this appointment sooner. When I close the door to the reception area and find her at her desk, she's just staring up at the ceiling.

"Hi, Lily."

"Give me a moment."

"Okay. But you're not doing anything."

"I'm doing something, I'm thinking. Just give me a minute." I wait ten or so seconds. Nothing.

"Lily, I have clients waiting. Please."

"Yes. They've been waiting for you. But you can see I'm busy, so just another second."

"I can see you're *not* busy."

"Was I doing anything?"

"Not that I could see."

"That's because you can't see thinking. Just like I told you. Just another second . . . There, I'm done. What do you want?"

"First," I inquire, as any boss would, "what were you thinking about?"

"If I wanted you to know, I would've been talking. Now, what do you want?"

"Why didn't you tell me sooner that the Killroys were going to be here?"

"Did you ask me to contact them?"

"Yes."

"Did you say to set up an appointment ASAP?"

"Yes."

"Did I set up that appointment ASAP?"

"Yes."

"Could I have set it up any sooner?"

"No."

"So you admit my ASAP was ASAP as ASAP could be?"

"Yes, I admit it. But why didn't you tell me about the appointment ASAP?"

"Did you not tell Ethel Killroy that you were going back to the office?"

"Yes, I told her that."

"And did you come back to the office by subway?"

"Yes."

"And can we agree that your phone doesn't receive service on the subway?"

"Yes, I get your point, Lily. Sorry. Remind me to stop bringing you to court to observe my trials. You're picking up some bad habits."

"What is it you say when you're done filling up the courtroom with your hot air? Oh, yes: I rest my case. Now your clients are waiting for you. They're not HICs, are they?"

"No, Lily, they're not."

"I didn't think so. That Ethel seems nice. But I think the boy has problems."

"He just might, Lily. He just might."

I head out to get them, feeling like one of my own cross-examination victims. Before opening the door that separates my internal office from reception—a door I call my spy door, because I can see in, but given the angle, it's difficult for anyone on the other side to see me—I pause to regard Robert Killroy in greater detail.

He has moderate skin folds at the corners of his small eye

openings, a short nasal bridge and a short nose, a small midface, and thin upper lip—all the classic signs of the syndrome. The only thing off is his head circumference. It's large—not small as one would expect—although it's difficult to assess because of the helmet. He's wearing Nike high-top basketball sneakers with his tube socks pulled all the way up just under his kneecaps.

Now, I open the door. "Let's go inside." I motion to them. "Please."

I watch as Robert gets up. He has some problems with that right ankle. Once he's standing, I note his foot has an obvious valgus deformity, meaning it's twisted outward. The odd thing is his muscularity. You'd expect some wasting or atrophy with his injury, but his legs are freakishly muscular. Not unlike a rhino. At roughly five foot nine, he's a wide, sturdy kid.

I watch as he drags his right foot behind him. It's a bad injury. Too bad I'm working this one for free.

At least I admit it.

"Robert, has walking been this difficult since the accident," I ask, "or is it getting worse?"

"I got no problems walking, mister. And I can ride my bike really, really fast."

Ethel, listening to us, now offers her opinion. "Been about the same, that ankle has." But she adds, "Robert loves riding his bike, took it up first in rehab. You know, a stationary bike. And ever since, he's been riding his own all around town. Like the wind, too."

What Robert Does Have

Once we take our positions in my office, Ethel begins. "First of all, Robert just got his collections job, and you happen to be one of a handful of debts they gave the boy. I want a promise that if you take over his case, it won't interfere one iota with Robert doing his job." Ethel, as we already know, is a woman of principle.

"As long as you understand that I do not intend to pay Mr. Wang that fourteen dollars and seventy-nine cents, we're cool."

"I understand all too well about the disputes in the world of debt collecting. So what's fair is fair. I just wanted to make sure you weren't going to try to use this to get out of what ya owe. Now, the next thing you should know is, I'm Robert's grandmother and court-appointed guardian. His drug-addicted mother died during childbirth, and my good-for-nothin' son never was much of a father."

"I understand."

"Good. Now, I like you and I also like that picture of you shaking President Clinton's hand up on your shelf. He a friend of yours?"

"No. I just met him at a fund-raiser."

"Oh, okay. It's a shame they tried to hogtie him for doing what comes natural to a man. Shoulda been enough having to deal with Hillary. That's a woman who's got a whole lot of patience. Smart, too. Anyway, maybe you can make a copy of that for me, and I could display it in my home. I'd feel honored other people knowing Robert's got a bona fide lawyer who shook hands with the best president this country ever had."

"No problem. I'll have Lily, my paralegal, make you a copy."

"I thank you for that. Now, enough politicking," she says, continuing to take charge. "I fired Robert's last lawyer and was gonna do his case on my own as you know. But the truth is, I'm getting tired of schooling myself in the law. Seems you come along at just the right time. I got his whole file here for ya." She removes a legal file folder from her double-layered plastic grocery bag.

"May I take a quick peek?" I ask politely.

"That's why I brought it." She hands it to me.

I open it up and go right to the police report. I want to see what their prior lawyer was talking about. Yep, there it is. Not good for the good guys. It puts blame squarely on Robert. And it's a double whammy—an unfavorable accident description and a skillfully penned diagram to corroborate it. But I've learned over the years that police reports may be less than accurate.

After a few more minutes of flipping through the file, inclusive of the medicals, I can see it's a big case, given Robert's injury. Unfortunately, there's only a hundred thousand in coverage from the Canadian insurer. Plus, there's no indication of activity in this file for over a year. A bad sign.

"Ethel," I say, putting the file down, "why don't we make a call on Robert's case now? There's only a hundred thousand in insurance, and they've offered near half. There's no doubt that Robert's injury has a value way in excess of that sum, but you can't get water from a stone. Do you understand what I mean by this?"

"Certainly, I do."

"Right. So maybe we can get this done on a call for the full extent of the policy. Sound like a plan?"

"Sounds like a plan, Wyler. Make the call." She looks over at Robert and gives him a warm smile. He returns hers with one of his own. They have a rich and loving relationship. If not for her, who knows where this kid would've wound up.

I dial up Cohen's office, the lawyer for the van driver. I don't know him, but maybe I can be persuasive enough. I put the call on speaker so Ethel can hear. It will foster trust.

"Ethel, listen carefully to our conversation," I say. I want to make her feel involved.

"Law offices of Rich Cohen. How may I direct your call?"

"Rich Cohen, please."

"Who may I say is calling?"

"Wyler, Tug Wyler."

"On what matter, Mr. Wyler?"

"The matter of one Robert Killroy, who didn't kill no Roy, and in fact, he didn't kill nobody. That's just his name." Robert and Ethel both smile.

"One moment. Transferring."

"Rich Cohen, here."

"Hi, Rich, I'm the new counsel on the Robert Killroy case. How are you today?"

"Fine. Please make sure to file, and send me your notice of appearance."

"Will do."

"Good. Now, what can I do for you?"

Time for some lawyering—I go with the only thing from the police report in our favor.

"Well, it seems your guy hit Robert with the front of his van. That puts him in a position to be seen, and since Robert has an injury in excess of your policy limits, I was thinking you'd tender."

"Well, you thought wrong. How long have you been on the case?"

I look at my watch. "Six minutes."

"What makes you think I'd pay the policy to you after six minutes when the matter has been in suit for three years and I haven't tendered to date?"

"Ego."

"Ego?" he questions. "What do you mean, ego?"

"I've got a big ego, Rich. I figured by this point in our conversation you would have seen my trial results on my website."

"I did, as a matter of fact, but I'm not convinced. There's more to this than just the points of contact. The police report clearly indicates that the accident was your client's fault."

"Was not!" Ethel yells out in Robert's defense.

Crap. I forgot to tell her not to say anything. I put my finger to my mouth giving her the international signal to keep quiet.

She waves me off, like I'm being silly. "You ain't no bona fide lawyer, Rich!"

"That you, Ethel? Sure sounds like it."

"As certain as your driver done my boy wrong."

"Okay, you two. That's enough," I intercede. "Ethel, I'm your attorney now, so please don't have conversations with defense counsel." She nods. "And, Rich, I know I don't need to say that to you. And sorry, I should've mentioned I have Ethel here while you were on speaker."

"Yes, you should have mentioned that."

"My bad. Anyway, is your position final?"

"According to the police report, Mr. Wyler, your new client ran in front of the van, so there was nothing my driver could do to avoid hitting him."

"Yes, I saw that, but the officer was documenting your client's version of the accident. That sentence begins: Driver of vehicle one states . . . there is no version of how the accident occurred from my client in that report."

"That may be true," Cohen acknowledges, "but look at the officer's detailed diagram. It's proof-positive your client was attempting to cross a major Brooklyn thoroughfare midblock between parked cars nowhere near the safe haven of a pedestrian crosswalk."

Who says *thoroughfare*? I think this guy's an ass.

"Cohen," Ethel blurts out, "I told you that dang diagram is wrong. That policeman didn't come to the scene until later when everything was all mixed up 'cause of all the commotion."

I quickly hit the mute button so Cohen can't hear me. "Ethel, please. We haven't had a chance to discuss Robert's case in detail yet, so I urge you to please try to keep quiet. This is just a preliminary call to see if we can get him to give us the policy." She nods again. I'm not convinced.

I take Cohen off of mute. "Mr. Cohen, even if we assumed for purposes of this conversation that Robert was fifty percent at fault for causing the accident, his injury still merits the hundred even with a comparative negligence reduction."

"Forty-seven five. That's it."

"Okay, Rich. I get ya. Listen, I should've asked this first, but is there any excess policy of insurance covering the van as it was traveling on this thoroughfare? I noted it was a commercial vehicle."

I hear Ethel mumble under her breath, "Excess . . . didn't know about that one."

"There sure is."

"Why didn't you say so before?" Ethel screams out. "You ain't no bona fide lawyer, just like I said."

"Ethel, please," I say.

"The excess policy was not disclosed because there was never a demand for its disclosure."

"Is that how you practice law, Mr. Cohen? It's pretty clear the State Insurance Department rules require you to disclose all policies as a matter of course."

"Then we also have different views on the law."

Now I'm certain of it. This guy *is* an ass.

"So now I'm asking, Mr. Cohen. What is the excess policy coverage over and above the one hundred primary?"

"It's a million, but it makes no difference because Robert darted out in front of the van."

"Did not!" Ethel shouts.

"Please, Ethel. Sit quietly."

"Sorry," she says to me. She then mutters loudly one more time for good measure, "Ain't no bona fide lawyer."

I shake my head at her. She shrugs, seemingly satisfied with having expressed her opinion.

"I think we're about done for now, Mr. Cohen. But I imagine you'll be hearing from me soon. Good-bye, then."

I hang up.

"What's this comparative negligence I heard you mention?"

"Okay, I'll explain. In the state of New York, when evaluating who was at fault—what lawyers call the issue of liability—you compare the conduct of the driver to the conduct of the pedestrian. So, if they can prove that Robert darted out in front of the van and/or crossed the street at an unsafe location outside a crosswalk and/ or from between parked cars, which can obstruct an approaching driver's vision, he could be found fifty percent at fault by a jury. Therefore, if that same jury gave him ten dollars, for ease of example, Robert would only collect five, it being reduced by half to account for his comparative conduct."

"I get ya. But Robert didn't do nothing wrong. I taught that boy correctly how to walk on the sidewalks and cross the street, for that matter. This accident was because that van driver wasn't looking where he was going. Plain and simple. That's why all vehicle accidents happen." Pronounced *ve-hic-ul*.

"Unfortunately, it doesn't say that in the police report."

"You saying you don't believe us, Wyler?"

"I've never believed a client more." She nods, appeased. "And you never know what the driver is going to say until he says it at the deposition." *If I can get one at this point,* I say to myself. "At accident scenes, drivers tend to lie to the police about what happened for a variety of obvious reasons."

She nods at this, too. "I got another question."

"Shoot."

"What's this notice of appearance he asked you for?"

"Proper procedure requires an incoming lawyer to file a document with the clerk of the court that lets them know who the new lawyer is on the case. That way they know where to send court notifications."

"Was I supposed to do that?" Ethel asks, concerned.

"Yes, you were."

"Dang it. I missed that one *and* the excess insurance. Better off leavin' lawyering to the lawyers. Too much stuff to learn at my age."

All of the sudden, I hear a faint clicking coming from Robert's direction. I look up, and his hand shoots down. He turns away as if minding his own business.

"Robert," I ask him, "did you just take a picture of me with that pen in your hand? Is that a spy-pen camera?"

He starts chortling.

"Yes, he did," answers Ethel. "He's technically a debt

collector, but his hobby is spying and investigating. He's also a process server who can start lawsuits, and the collection agency gave him full authority to use his investigating skills to collect debts. Right, boy?"

"Yes, Granny," he responds proudly.

We finish our business and agree to discuss things in detail after I've had a chance to read the entire file. That way, I can speak more intelligently. Ethel had gotten ruffled when Rich Cohen claimed Robert caused the accident, so it's clear she's a little excitable. I can tell, though, that our mutual dedication to justice, and to Robert, will enable us to work well together.

Ethel also volunteered that Robert had not sustained any brain injury in the accident. Rather, he'd been born "slow" because his mother was a crackhead during her pregnancy. Ethel actually stated that in front of Robert—in a very matter-of-fact way: "Robert's a little bit retarded because he was a crack baby." He then echoed the words *crack baby* under his breath as she said it, evidencing his familiarity with the description.

However, the truth of the matter is that Ethel is dead wrong. But it's not my place to say.

Back in the day, during the crack epidemic, when a pregnant woman exposed her fetus, it was thought that the baby would be born emotionally, mentally, and physically disabled. Upon further study, the scientific community has determined that no specific disorders or conditions have been found to result for people whose mothers used cocaine while pregnant.

What Robert does have, though, as confirmed by his medical records, is fetal alcohol syndrome, or FAS. It's scientific fact that alcohol crosses the placental barrier and creates the distinctive facial features that Robert has, also damaging the brain structures and resulting in both psychological and behavioral problems.

I walk the Killroys out of the building and put Ethel in a cab. I had to fight to pay for the ride, assuring her it wasn't some ploy to influence Robert away from collecting the alleged Wang debt.

Robert, after fastening his helmet, rode off on his bicycle, weaving expertly in and out of city traffic. Pretty impressive given his injury.

I'm now more than determined to help this woman's grandson attain financial independence. Feisty, but caring, Ethel Killroy isn't going to be around forever, given her age and diagnosis. Still, I'm not paying that dry cleaning hack, Mr. Wang, any money, no matter how nice a guy he may be. I tried his service that one time because his window sign reads: *EXPERT STAIN REMOVERS.*

Then he told me the large patch of discoloration that replaced the tiny rib sauce stain wasn't his fault because he sent it out for cleaning.

8.

For the past week Robert Killroy has called regularly, three times daily like clockwork. Each time, I tell him I'm not paying Mr. Wang, but it doesn't seem to be sinking in. I appreciate that this may not be his fault, and I will say he's getting better at his job. Now, he lets me know he's calling to collect a debt and is recording the conversation, and that what I say can be used against me in court. He told me the collection agency was going to provide the machine but agreed to give him the money instead because he wanted to order the one through *Spy* magazine that syncs with his computer.

So far, I'm the only debt he hasn't collected. He told me the others caved, attributing it to his persistence—although he didn't use the words *caved* or *persistence*. I think Robert may have found a way to make a living, and I'm happy for him.

I look at my watch—I've got time. So while I'm on the topic, I might as well have it out with Rich Cohen now. I dial him up on his direct line.

"Rich Cohen speaking."

"Hi, Rich. Tug Wyler on the Robert Killroy matter."

"Yes, Mr. Wyler. It's been a whole week. What can I do for you?"

"Rich, I'll be direct. Prior counsel on this file screwed things up. And although Ethel did her best, she's no lawyer. So the purpose of this call is to correct these problems like gentlemen. Are you open to that?"

"I'm listening."

"First, according to e-Law, the case was marked off the court's calendar for nonappearance at a compliance conference just three days shy of a year ago. Were you aware of that?"

"I sure was."

"Then you know I have three days to make a motion to restore it or else it will be deemed abandoned and the claim forever lost."

"I sure do."

"I thought so." As mad as I am at his tactics, the guy is only doing his job. "Okay then, so will you stipulate the case back onto the court's active calendar? We both know a judge will grant my motion should you make me go through the formal exercise. Ethel could not have known she missed a conference because she never filed a notice of appearance. I'd suggest, since she's a nonlawyer, that would constitute a reasonable excuse."

"So stipulated, Mr. Wyler. Case restored. Next."

"I need to take the oral deposition of your van operator."

"Prior counsel waived that, Mr. Wyler."

"This I know. But I need his deposition. Do I have to make a motion for it?"

"Isn't his statement in the police report enough for you? It's even in quotes."

"No. Am I making a motion to compel his testimony, or are you going to produce him voluntarily?"

"I'll ask the carrier what they want to do. Next."

"That's it.

"Okay, then. Good-bye."

That went pretty well. We didn't have it out after all. Maybe he's just half an ass. Time will tell.

It's a Visual That'll Catch their Attention

Lily buzzes. "Cookie and Major are here to see you. Shall I show them in?"

"Yes, thank you."

"Yes, thank you," I hear her echo in a mocking tone as the phone makes its way down. Nice. Moments later I can hear them approaching my office.

"Right in here," Lily says. They take their places in the guest chairs. Cookie sits at the edge of hers, with her back and neck held perpendicular to the floor by the halo. She looks unnatural, uncomfortable—and sexy as hell. I try not to stare at the pin insertion sites but, as before, the gruesome visual makes it hard to look away.

"I asked you both here to discuss your case and some of the things I've found and—well, not found—while going through your file and medical records." I sense that Cookie wants to nod, but her halo prevents this. She blinks instead, and the wince that crosses her face worries me.

"Are you all right?" I ask. "Is there something I can get for you?"

"Well, my halo's uncomfortable, but I'm okay, I guess. I do have a question, though." Major watches her but says nothing.

"Go ahead."

"They didn't take the money off the table, did they? I mean two hundred fifty thousand dollars is a lot. There're so many people who've helped me out over the last three years, and I know that money will cover it."

"I understand. No, Cookie, they haven't taken it off the table."

"Because it's been seven days and . . . ." She stops midsentence. Major now gets up, kneels down, and takes a hard evaluative look up at her. You don't need to be a doctor to know that her grimace means bad news. It's becoming more pronounced by the second. Major stands and turns to me.

"It's time for tap."

"Time for what?"

"Time for tap," he repeats.

I just look at them, baffled.

They both go into motion, propelled by an obvious sense of urgency. First, Cookie pulls the chair she was in away from my desk. She purposefully repositions herself backward on it, then gingerly steps off saying, "This will do." Me, I'm trying to figure out what's going on.

"I'm sorry about this," Major says apologetically, "but she needs an emergency spinal tap before things get bad."

It's perfectly clear to me that this probably isn't the best time to bring it up. However, it's happening right here in front of me, and I can't resist. I mean, it's the only thing in her file I can't figure out.

"Um . . ." I say, as he rolls up his sleeves. "So these spinal taps . . ."

"Listen to me," Major instructs, annoyed. "Dr. McElroy injured, that is to say perforated, certain structures during the surgery he performed on Cookie. The result is brain fluid building up inside her skull that, at intervals, must be evacuated, which is exactly what I'm doing here."

His tone, coupled with the evolving visual, leaves me no option. Mental bullet points:

- Even though I saw that claim in the legal documents—interval taps to prevent fatal brain compression from cerebral spinal fluid backup into the skull—I didn't find it as a working diagnosis in her voluminous medical records;
- There's not one entry recorded by her medical providers that documents Cookie's ever even having received a spinal tap;

- Tapping *is* mentioned in Cookie's medical history. But that history's only in forms she herself has filled in or penned by her treating doctors based on what she has told them.

In fact, there's a recent letter to Charles from defense counsel requesting he withdraw the claim that Major's just made since it's unsupported by medical documentation. Their next move will be a formal motion seeking the court to strike it from the case, which, based on the medical records I have here, will be impossible for me to oppose.

But I can't challenge Major on any of this right now. He's too busy laying out what looks like a travel-size spinal-tap kit on the edge of my desk.

"Moreover," he says, as if reading my mind, "I'm the one who made the diagnosis, and I'm the one doing the tapping. I have records, so don't worry. For each and every tap."

I'd like to share my gut response to this—which is incredulity—but there's something else going on that captures my undivided attention.

Cookie.

She's been undoing the buttons and now off comes her shirt. She's in my office, in front of my desk, standing topless except for the halo vest. Her breasts are just as perfect as they were a week ago. I'm trying, though not very hard, not to stare.

At least I admit it.

She catches me peeking, and a little smile briefly intersects with her painful grimace. I smile back, then quickly put on my serious face. Now, she addresses the chair again, placing first one knee, then the other on the seat cushion. Grabbing the back with both hands, she secures her reverse posture and arches her back. Once she assumes this position— one she's obviously taken many times before—her jeans ride down to expose a red G-string. I practically have to pinch myself.

"I'll leave the room while you do this," I tell Major.

"Not necessary," he reassures me. "It'll just take a sec." He begins to prep the area.

"When did you begin doing these taps?" I ask.

"Six months after McElroy's surgery."

"Wait a second," I say, seized by a sudden idea. "We have no formal documented medical proof from an independent, or should I say disinterested, medical provider that Cookie's been receiving spinal taps one to two times a week over the last two and a half years. We only have you two to say so, and since you're both interested witnesses—meaning a jury could infer you have an interest in the outcome of the lawsuit and weigh that against your credibility because of the inherent bias—we should video record the procedure. You know, for the purposes of proving damages."

There. Now I feel better. And congratulate myself on this very good idea. "Would you mind, Cookie?"

"No," she answers. "I'm not shy." She glances in Major's direction. He nods.

"Good. What I'd like to do is send it to the malpractice insurance company. It'll catch their attention, that's for sure. But it'll also facilitate their taking a hard look at coming up with a better number than two-fifty. That's because, I gotta tell you, right now they've got nothing else to go by, as far as this tapping is concerned, beyond what your lawyer claimed. Which doesn't count for much. I'm going to state in the cover letter that we intend to perform such a spinal tap in front of the jury as a piece of demonstrative evidence. That should give them cause for concern."

The truth is, despite my self-congratulations, I'm still not quite believing this.

"I always wanted to be in the movies," Cookie adds, half-laughing, half-wincing. "Although this isn't what I had in mind."

I opt for my ever-ready video camera over using my phone, to ensure better quality. "Major," I say, "tell us what you're doing as you go along. A judge may mute it at trial, but the adjusters at the insurance carrier will hear you." Then I begin watching through the viewer as I hold the camera steady.

After sterilizing and injecting Cookie's lower back with a local anesthetic, he takes out a large metal syringe. He holds it up to the camera. It's one formidable instrument. "This is a spinal tap syringe," he starts. "It's a three-inch-long needle"—he indicates—"specifically designed to enter the spine with a minimum of resistance and is hollowed to perform its function. I'm going to insert it between two vertebrae, which are the bones of the lower back, into a space where Cookie's cerebral spinal fluid circulates." He takes a deep breath.

"Cerebral spinal fluid, or CSF, is a clear liquid that circulates around and inside the brain. It also flows all the way down and around the spinal cord, occupying a channel known as the subarachnoid space. That's what I'm aiming for. The arachnoid mater is the middle layer of brain cover, formally called meninges, and the pia mater is the meninges closest to the brain. It's between these two layers that encase the brain where this fluid circulates, hence the term subarachnoid space."

"Hurry, Major, with your lecture. The pressure's building." Cookie says. Urgency is in her voice. He continues at a pace that indicates he knows exactly how much time he has before things might get messy.

"The function of CSF is to provide protection to the brain and cushion the spinal cord against jarring forces. It also distributes neuroendocrine factors, but that's beyond what we need to discuss here. In Cookie's case, she sustained an injury that penetrated through the dura mater or the outermost meninges, and through the arachnoid into this subarachnoid space at the C4 level of her neck. The C stands for cervical, which is the medical name for the neck, and the 4 stands for the vertebral level in her neck.

"Each vertebra in the stack of bones in the cervical spine has a corresponding number, beginning with C1 at the base of the skull and ending at C7 at the base of the neck where it meets the shoulders. Because of the surgical injury caused by Dr. McElroy's malpractice, Cookie's CSF no longer flows freely through that region. A partial damming effect has developed, causing it to slowly accumulate at the C4 level. The fluid builds and builds, backing up into her skull."

"Major! Hello?" Cookie's getting unhappier by the second.

"Rate the pressure, my dear."

"Four out of ten."

"Let's not go past seven. Is that satisfactory?"

"Fine. Just enough already with the detail."

"As we all know," he continues smoothly, "the brain is located in a self-contained housing, the skull. Inside, there's normal pressure that's regulated by Mother Nature. However, when spinal fluid backs up, it causes increased intracranial pressure. This is because the hard structure does not expand. So, as the fluid builds up, it slowly but steadily compresses the brain within the skull. As you might imagine, this results in the development of headaches, loss of balance, blurred vision, and other classic neurological signs leading to loss of cerebral functioning. It will result in death by brain compression if the pressure's not released and brought back to normal."

Trying to get a different angle, a better angle, I take a half step to the side and partially kneel. Perfect. Man, those lovely breasts now on screen are truly fabulous. Uncertain for an instant, Major pauses. Don't worry Major, I've been in the business a long time, and I know what's important to the future viewers of this video. A good lawyer always knows his audience. It's all part of the legal process.

"Hurry!" Cookie presses him. "Please!" He does.

"The only way to release the pressure is to drain the excess fluid by spinal tap. It's purely a mechanical release, and that's what I'm going to do now by inserting this needle into Cookie's spine to withdraw CSF into the collecting tube of this device. There are newer instruments that are now used to perform this procedure, but I'm comfortable with my old one."

Major now moves in to insert the big needle in her lower back, a tad left of center. I zoom in for a close-up.

"Easy, my dear," he says, "just a pinch, that's all."

He inserts the needle. Then, all of the sudden, without notice, bam! Cookie's left leg rockets back, kicking Major squarely in the gut. And I mean, her leg exploded backward in some form of hyper-reflex with a force like I've never witnessed before. It sends him flying as if he were a rag doll.

Major's flight ends when he slams into the base of my desk four feet away. Oh, shit! He's motionless. I'm thinking mild concussion and massive internal bleeding. Wait a minute. He shakes his head, the way boxers do after taking a hook to the temple. Slowly, he regains his composure and, with a confused expression, looks up.

Boy, is this crazy! But I've got it videoed and can't wait to share it with Mick and Henry.

"Cookie, don't move!" Major yells, fixated on her back.

"What's going on?" she asks. "What was that bang I heard?" She obviously has no idea what just happened.

I help him up with one hand, keeping the camera steady with the other and still aimed at Cookie. I don't want to miss one frame of this bizarre, highly unnatural moment. I zoom in. The large needle is hanging out of her spine. It's stuck in there.

Major straightens himself out in exactly the way anyone might after being mule-kicked during a spinal tap gone wrong. "Over here," he says, directing me to return the camera focus to him, as he grasps the syringe.

"What you just witnessed," he continues, earnestly eager for audience understanding, "is one of the risks and complications of a spinal tap. You see, this is a blind procedure, and as I was entering the needle to access the subarachnoid space, the tip penetrated a nerve root. These exit the spinal canal at each vertebral level and branch out to different parts of our body, hence the term peripheral nervous system. These nerves have two aspects, with one of those controlling sensory perception, or what our brain interprets from external stimuli. For instance, when Cookie kicked me, that was the stimulus causing the nerves in my abdomen to send a message of pain to my brain. The other aspect of the nerve controls motor coordination or movement. I obviously stuck the needle into the motor centers of Cookie's nerve, as evidenced by her violent kick."

"Major! Major! Please!" Cookie is losing her remaining composure. And justifiably so. "I'm at six, approaching seven. And, *what* kick? I didn't kick you! Did I?"

"Yes, in fact, you did. It was a reflex induced by my contacting your nerve, and, since your lower back is numbed, it's not surprising you didn't know about it. I realize it wasn't intentional."

"I really kicked you?"

"Yes."

"Oops." She frowns, suddenly more concerned about Major than her own increasing discomfort. "Are you okay? Did I hurt you?" I marvel at her solicitude. She's the one with the needle jutting hideously out of her back, a hair away from her spinal cord.

"I'm fine."

"Are you sure?"

"Remember," I interrupt, "we're still on camera here. I think we need to focus on the task at hand."

Cookie starts to say something, when a rictus of pain freezes her.

"Now, Major! It's got to be now!" she commands.

He resumes the procedure and completes it without further incident. Whew. When he's finished, he explains that the meter on the device is a gauge for measuring spinal-fluid pressure. The fact that her fluid is clear means there's no evidence of infection.

I've learned a lot in the past few minutes. And seen things I never imagined. Speaking of which, Cookie is still topless. I've never been near a woman so comfortable with her nakedness. She gives me one of her innocent smiles, and Major catches it.

Man, what's going on here? She's such a babe, and he's this

old dude who seems to command her total devotion. He appears resigned to the fact that my watching her get dressed is unavoidable at this point. However, I'm particular to keep a very professional look on my face. (I think.)

Incomplete and Filtered

Once we're all seated again, I clear my throat. "I have to say, I can't believe you've been doing that all this time. I've never heard of such an intervention. Isn't there another form of treatment?"

"Well, Cookie could have a shunt surgically sewn into her brain that would drain the excess CSF into a tiny tube implanted just underneath her skin running down her neck and around her shoulder with its spout ending in the peritoneal cavity in her abdomen, the most common site for fluid diversion. The fluid would drain through the tube and drip into her abdomen, then be reabsorbed naturally by her body. But she's against it."

"Why are you against it?" I ask her, thinking, Shit, yeah, I would be too.

"I'm against it because I could end up like a vegetable. The risks are off the charts. No way. Not for me. I'd rather be doing this than wind up brain damaged or worse. Besides, the shunt can fail, clog up, need adjustments, and worst of all, I'd have to totally give up dancing with one of those implanted in my brain." She pauses. "No way," she repeats. It's all I got left in my life. Oh yeah, and you, Major. Sorry."

She reaches over and takes his hand. But I can tell it's a guilty gesture and not a sincere one by the way she quickly lets go.

"Understood," I respond.

They look at me, waiting to hear what's next. I pick up the file. "Major, is there any reason why your medical records aren't in here? Or, for that matter, why Chris Charles didn't list your name as a witness or as a treating physician? You're obviously both, not to mention key to proving the tapping, which clearly is the largest element of damages."

Okay, Major, let's hear it, the voice in my head says.

"Early on," he begins, "I told Chris to try to keep me out of this, given the nature of my relationship with McElroy."

And this guy denied appreciating conflicts, I think to myself. Jeez.

"But, seeing how things are turning out, if you need to identify me as a witness or treating physician, please do so. Anything to help at this point."

"Good. I'll also need to provide defense counsel a copy of your medical records to go with the video."

"What about the clinic records, then?" Cookie adds. "From the day you saved my life." She's smiling again now.

"Clinic records?" I repeat, interested to know.

"Oh, he's so shy. When the headaches first came on, Major took me to his old medical clinic for evaluation. Two days of testing. It was there that he made the diagnosis and performed my first tap." She says it as if remembering a first kiss.

"Then I'll need the name and address of that facility, too," I point out. "Anyway, best now to finish the remainder of the agenda I had planned for our meeting today. Sound okay to you guys?"

"Sounds good," Major answers for both of them.

"Cookie, I've read your records and have seen for myself what you have to endure. Now I'd like to hear from your own lips how this injury has compromised your enjoyment of life, which is an item of noneconomic damage in the New York Pattern Jury Instructions. This will be important during negotiations. So I need you to proceed without holding anything back."

I can tell by the way she's looking at me that a gut spill is on the horizon. At the same time, Major's sitting next to her. She's going to tread carefully because of him. It's obvious by the way she's subtly just repositioned herself, adding a hint of distance. The inch tells the whole story.

Her eyes are filling with tears, but she won't let them run. It's Major, for sure: she doesn't want to worry him. Or hurt his feelings, either. Whatever she's about to say will be incomplete and filtered because of his presence, I realize. I'll have to speak with her alone to get it all.

She lets out a long, slow breath. "First of all," she plunges in, "I always wanted to be a mother, but because of this I can't have kids. The way I understand it is, if the pressure in my head increases too much during pregnancy or at childbirth, I could become brain damaged, die—or worse—compromise the health of my child from oxygen deprivation. Right, Major? I don't want to be brain damaged—I already said that—but more horrible would be having to live with myself if I caused any harm to my unborn child. No way."

She stops to compose herself. "So I'll never be a mother, and that's a pretty big loss, especially because I don't have any family of my own. Except for Major, that is." Time for another guilty hand pat.

"I grew up the only child of a single mother who died when I was twelve. I always hoped to start my own family, a big one with lots of children, but now that's never going to happen."

I say nothing, but it's a sympathetic nothing. Major clears his throat but also remains silent.

Cookie's eyes tear up again. "I can't do anything alone. I have to stay close to Major because I never know when my head pressure's going to get out of control. The normal tap cycle is every three to six days, but I've needed repeat taps as soon as twelve hours later. It's just not predictable. I had a tap the evening I met you, and that was two days ahead of schedule. And then there are times after the tap where I suffer from spinal headaches with nausea. They're awful. Besides, I've taken Major's life away from him, which I feel terrible about. He's got to stick around me, be close by at all times without any breaks, because . . . you just never know. I'm a big burden on him, and I hate myself for that. He deserves better."

Hand touch number three.

She's looking at him, wearing a sad smile and blinking back tears. "Then there's dancing. I don't care what any doctors say, I need to dance. It defines me. I won't give it up. No matter what. You have no idea what it's like doing the thing you love most in the world and having to do it in agony. But I can't disappoint all those guys who love me, 'cause I love them back. We're like family. And I won't give it up. Even though it hurts. It's who I am." Now she's got a defiant expression.

"Okay. I think I'm understanding the essence of this now," I tell her. "You've done a fine job of explaining your history and the toll it's extracted from you. I'm sorry I had to put you through it, but it was necessary. I'm going to start setting things up for settlement. This case demands it—from what I read in the file, from what I've now witnessed, and from what you've just said. I want to set the wheels in motion. You can consider the video we made today a big first step forward toward our goal."

I stand up, indicating our meeting's now come to its end. But what I'm thinking is: of course there's only a two-fifty offer. The insurance carrier never even considered the tapping. They had no records, nor the chance to question Cookie about it before she took ill at her oral deposition.

As they make their way toward the door, I realize one other thing I need to ask. "Listen, I know this is going to sound strange." They both stare at me curiously. I hesitate. Out with it. It's just that I don't want to sound like an idiot. Okay, here I go. "But do either of you know any reason why some person might not want me to handle this case?"

They give each other puzzled looks. "No," answers Cookie. I can tell she's confused by the question.

"What do you mean?" Major wants to know.

"What I mean is, would there be any reason why representing Cookie might make me unpopular? You know, like Chris Charles being pissed that he was substituted out or anything like that?"

Major studies me. I've thrown him a curve ball. "No," he answers.

"I spoke to Chris, and he understood the conflict. He wasn't happy, but he wants what's best for Cookie. We all want what's best for Cookie. Why do you ask?"

"Just curious, that's all. No reason really. It's just when you take a case over from another attorney they can get a little resentful, even start to act out. That's all."

"What's happened to arouse your concern?" It's reasonable that he should want to know.

"Nothing." I hate withholding information from a client, but I see no sense in sharing my Minnow encounter. Yet.

"All right then. If you say so." He resumes his solicitous escorting of Cookie from my office. After their departure, Lily buzzes.

"What's up?"

"Some guy called three times while you were in conference. He seemed real anxious. He's probably an HIC. But I couldn't get any info from him. He said just to tell you he called."

"So are you going to tell me his name or not?"

"Minotero. That's a strange name. Sounds like one of those masked Mexican wrestlers."

Speak of the devil. "Wonderful."

"Wonderful what?"

"Wonderful, nothing."

"Well, you said 'wonderful.' Did you mean it in a good way or a bad way?"

"I'm not positive, but I'm pretty sure it can't be good. Listen, I've got to catch up on some papers, so try not to disturb me."

"Okay, I'll give you the envelope later."

"Lily, what envelope?"

"The envelope someone dropped off on our reception counter."

"Who dropped it off?"

"I don't know. I went into the supply closet, and when I came back, there was an envelope sitting on the entry counter with your name on it."

"Bring it in, please."

"Now?"

"Yes, Lily, now."

She brings it in, flips it on my desk, and huffs out, sighing ostentatiously. Like you'd think *I* was bothering *her*.

It has one word on it: *Wyler*.

9.

What's with this Minnow character? The note Lily tossed on my desk an hour ago was a one-sentence warning: *Drop the case or you'll be sorry.* Highly imaginative. But it's hard not to be insulted by something so formulaic. I pick up the phone.

"Chris Charles," I hear a real person answer, not the voice mail.

"Hi, Chris. This is Tug Wyler, Cookie's new attorney. Do me a favor. Get over it! Can you call your guy off? I mean, I'm working this case for Henry Benson," I say, as if it were a mob threat. "And he's one guy you don't want to cross, believe me."

"I'm sorry, but what are you talking about?"

"I'm talking about Minotero, your investigator."

"Minotero?"

"Yes, Minotero, your investigator. He just delivered a note here, which I'm sure you're aware of."

"Really, I don't know any Minotero, and I don't know what you're talking about." He almost sounds convincing. "I can't afford an investigator. I work out of my basement, for God's sake. That was my big case you took, but I understand. I know who you are. She's in more experienced hands. I appreciate that."

End of conversation.

So if I believe him—and for some reason I do—then what school is this Minnow swimming with?

Tactic-switching time.

I pick up the phone and call Pusska, my private investigator. She took a course over the Internet and in less than a week became a licensed PI. The vibe she gives off is keep-your-distance. You could call her cold, but the better term would be *hardened*. On the plus side, when she decides to make an approach, she's always successful. She's thirty-three and gorgeous—tall, blonde, with killer blue eyes and full lips. She's skilled at connecting with guys, making her way in with the lure of sex, which, according to her, can be used to get anything, at any time, from any man. A useful skill set for an investigator.

She picks up on the second ring. "Vhat?"

"Hi, Pusska. How's it going?"

"Vhat do you vant? Don't bother me vith small talk. I busy."

"Sorry. I took over a case from another attorney and, not long after, this little turd started warning me to stay away—which, of course, I don't intend to. But I don't actually understand yet why I'm being threatened. I spoke to the lawyer I'm replacing, and he's adamant he didn't sic anyone on me. So I really don't know who else would have a stake in or be concerned with a run-of-the-mill personal injury case."

Then I remember little Suzy. And all the cutthroat stakeholders in that case.

"Put down and push *send*. Bye." The line goes dead.

That's how Pusska works. You just gotta accept it.

After I dispatch a detailed e-mail to her, I gather up my stuff and head for Grand Central. I walk uptown slowly, looking around for Minnow. I guess he's slithering around in other ponds.

Before getting on the train, I call home. The two troublemakers pick up at the same time. I say, "Hi, Penelope. Hi, Connor. Is Mommy there?"

"Hi," Penelope returns. "I told you I changed my name to Summer, Daddy. Now please respect my decision."

"Yeah, Dad, and I'm Dirk."

"Now both of you just stop it. You're going to get me into real trouble with your mother if you continue with that."

"No, we're not." This from Penelope. "Mom changed her name, too."

"Really?" I question. "What are you talking about?"

My son explains. "Well, Dad, you see, Mom always loved the name Amber, so she decided to change her name, too. Her new name is Amber Sizzle."

"Amber Sizzle? What kind of name is that?"

Summer—I mean Penelope—enlightens me. "Well, Dad, Mom was making bacon this morning and Brooks came up with it."

This is just great. I have a wife named Amber Sizzle, a daughter named Summer, a son named Dirk, and a new client named Cookie. My life sounds like it's turning into a low-budget porn flick.

"Okay," I say, sighing just the tiniest bit. "Just tell Ms. Sizzle I'm on my way home." *Click.*

My train ride, happily, is uneventful. My daily commute has comprised the only peaceful moments of the last seven days. I close my eyes and take in the multiple happenings since last Tuesday. The strange vision of seeing Cookie cartwheeling in a halo; meeting her unlikely boyfriend, Major; two of my children, and now apparently my wife, changing their names; having to defend my integrity and my law license in court after being accused of suborning perjury by a client who fired me after I procured a million dollars for her; little Minnow, the mystery man; videoing a softporn spinal tap in my office; and finally, Robert Killroy and Ethel, the ray of sunshine in my week.

I look forward to working hard for them and contributing toward Robert's financial independence. Helping and protecting the rights of people with fewer benefits in life—including those who might be shorted by the legal process, even by their own attorneys—are the reasons I became a seeker of justice.

The money ain't bad either. But I'm not taking a fee on Robert's case. It was clear from my interaction with Granny that there was no other way to gain her trust so her grandson could have proper representation. Good thing too because, among other issues, the case was just days away from final dismissal. I'd rather represent Robert for free than allow him to be another innocent victim of the miscarriage of justice. Don't get me wrong, though. If I had a choice here, I'd take a fee.

At least I admit it.

As I step off the train, I realize I never asked Ethel or Robert how the accident happened. But since Ethel is certain the police report is wrong, that's good enough for now.

As I walk to my car, I think how justice is something you shouldn't have to shop for, but it is. Meaning, different personal injury lawyers have different abilities. It could happen that Lawyer A resolves a case for one hundred thousand dollars while Lawyer B, a more able and skilled attorney, resolves that very same case for five hundred thousand. So choose your lawyer wisely.

When I walk in the door, my family's seated in the kitchen around our oversize round farm table made from antique wood planks. The day we bought it, I said, "Honey, why do we need such a big kitchen table?" I was expecting her standard irrational answer. Instead, she finally made sense with her explanation—"to keep the proper aesthetic proportion with our big teak island."

But Amber Sizzle didn't disappoint me when I asked my next question. "Why do we need to spend double the money for an antique table when a new one is half the price?"

"Because we do." It's her stock reply whenever I ask why we have to pay more for everything than seems necessary.

"What's up, everybody?"

No answer. Penelope is intently watching TV, tightly holding the remote in her hand for safekeeping. Connor is checking the sports scores on Tyler's laptop, and Brooks is doing something on his iPhone, the one I was against getting him for this exact reason.

I turn to Tyler. "What's up, honey?"

"The name's Amber Sizzle, remember? Until theirs change back. Everything's on hold until that happens." Crap. She's not gonna let this go.

"I'll have a talk with them." I offer a reassuring nod.

"That's a mighty fine idea you got there, Mr. Wyler," she says archly. Right. Then, in a change of tone, she sternly informs, "Your dinner's in the warmer."

I take out my plate and walk back to the table. Once I remove the tinfoil, I see my dinner: three burnt mini lamb chops, two string beans. I look up for an explanation. But I'm not going to make a big deal about it.

"Sorry, the kids were hungry." I nod. Connor looks up.

"Dad," he says, "when did you get home?" Brooks looks up from his device, "Yeah, when did you get home?"

"Just a few minutes ago. How was school today, boys?" Before I finish my question, their heads are back down into their devices. Something needs to be done about this technological home invasion before it gets out of hand. At the very least I'd expect my kids to notice when I arrive home.

"Oh," Tyler says, "I have my OB-GYN appointment next month. I made it the same day as Penelope's dance audition. It's near your office, so I'm going to drop her off with you, go to my appointment, and then you're going to take her for her audition. By the time I'm done, you'll be done, and I'll pick her back up at your office."

"Sounds like a plan to me."

"Well, then you better not forget this plan the way you have a habit of doing. I'm going to text and e-mail you the specifics to make sure you keep that morning free."

"I will. Not a problem." I briefly consider asking why she insists on going to her gynecologist in the city, given that we moved out over a decade ago. Oh, well.

The phone rings—once, twice—and nobody's making a move for it. On ring three, I say to the royal family of the round plank table, "Can someone answer the phone? I just sat down to eat."

"Dad." Brooks is using that specific tone denoting my having asked a stupid question. "It's not for me. I have an iPhone."

"Yeah," Connor chimes in, "it's not for me. But can you buy me an iPhone?"

Penelope is absorbed with the remote and SpongeBob. I don't even look at Tyler because it's clear she ain't making a move for it.

The answering machine intervenes, and the caller leaves a message. "Hi, this is Robert Killroy . . ."

Not long after this, I find myself brushing my teeth and getting ready for bed. I spit a swoosh of toothpaste-filled water, turn the faucet off, and enter my bedroom. Tyler's leaning on her pillows, strategically propped behind her at the perfect angle to comfortably play with her iPad. No surprise there. Once they install a vibrating mechanism into those, my marriage is over. But for now I have to contend with her current iPad game fixation: *Candy Crush Saga*.

"S'up, honey?"

"Quiet, I'm playing."

"I can see you're playing, but why do I have to be quiet? It's *Candy Crush*."

"I said quiet; this is important."

"What could be so important about *Candy Crush*?"

"I'll tell you what's so important," she says vehemently. "I turned Irma onto it last week, and now she's three levels higher than me, that's what's so important. She hasn't stopped playing for one minute. She's an animal."

"So what? She's three levels higher than you. Big deal." Tyler turns her head away from the game only for an instant. But it was way long enough to give me her crazy eyes. They have a tendency to slightly bulge when she's about to blow.

"Are you kidding me?" She fumes with her fingers moving a mile a minute, tapping her iPad. "There's no way I can let Irma beat me. We're competitive cousins. We've been competing about everything since we were kids. You know that."

"I guess I do."

Tyler believes everyone understands about competitive cousins.

"Shit." Man, she's really ticked.

"Shit what? Fail to get to the next level?"

"Yep. And I ran out of lives, so now I have to wait before attempting this level again." She puts her iPad down, required to wait the designated time period before the geniuses who designed *Candy Crush* will allow her to play this level again. She shakes out her hand a few times, up and down.

"What's the matter?"

"I've been playing awhile." Then she mumbles like some addicted computer gamer, "I need more lives."

"You know, while we're on the topic of *Candy Crush* lives, you have to stop sending friend requests to my Facebook friends who don't even know you."

"Why?" But not a warm and fuzzy, wifely concerned *why*. It's a hard, flat syllable.

"Well, I imagine the only reason you're sending them friend requests is in the hopes that they'll accept so you can then invite them to play *Candy Crush*, giving you a larger pool of people to send you lives, right?"

"Maybe."

"I'll take that as a yes. Can you stop that please?"

"No. I need more lives. This is an Irma thing. You don't understand."

I take a deep breath, then exhale in surrender.

"Can I ask you about something I think may be related, then?"

"What?"

"Yesterday I got several Facebook friend requests from a bunch of guys who were on my lacrosse team in college. I haven't heard from them in over twenty years. Then all in one day, seven teammates reach out to me. Do you know anything about that?"

"No. Maybe."

"I'm listening. Tell me about this no-maybe."

"I needed lives yesterday, badly. Irma was still one level behind me, and I didn't want her to pass me. I was desperate but had exhausted all my resources. I'd gone through all your Facebook friends, so I had to find a new pool. So I went down to the basement . . . which reminds me: you have to clean out the storage area this weekend. Anyway, I went through a few boxes until I found your Tulane yearbook, went to the athletics section, identified the names of your teammates, found some of them on Facebook, and then I blasted them."

"You're crazy. Stop that."

"You don't get this. Irma is sabotaging my resource of lifelines. We know all the same people, and they know she's my competitive cousin, and they're sending her lives and not me."

"Why would they do that?"

"She may have been a bit nicer than me when we were younger. I don't know."

"A bit?"

"Okay, a lot. But I wasn't going to be phony-nice to people decades ago in the hopes that when I needed *Candy Crush* lives from them in the future they would be there for me."

"But now you're making Facebook friend requests to people you don't even know so you can invite them to play *Candy Crush* and get lives from them. That's pretty phony."

"What's your point?"

"Nothing." I better stop now or I'll blow my chances. And this is definitely not the time to bring up all the money she's been spending on iTunes purchasing lives. Better make nice. "Honey, it's no big deal. Tomorrow you should pull out my high school and law school yearbooks and blast everyone in them. You might find yourself with a few new friends who will send you lives."

"Thanks," she responds cheerfully.

Now is my only shot. I get into the position that says it wouldn't be so bad if you lent me a hand over here. She takes notice and lifts a brow.

"What?" she asks. Unnecessarily, I might add.

"I don't know, honey," I say, trying not to seem too needy. "Last week you canceled TNHJ, and I was hoping for an unscheduled makeup event. It's been a rough week. You know what I mean?"

"What I know is Tuesday Night Hand Job has been suspended indefinitely until you get Connor and Penelope to change their names back."

I knew it.

"But I wasn't responsible for that."

"Yes, you were. And I couldn't take care of you tonight anyway."

"Why's that?"

"CCHC," she responds.

"CCHC?" I repeat in a questioning tone. "What's CCHC?"

"*Candy Crush* Hand Cramp."

10.

go to meet Mick at his place. Jingles, like before. But it's not the rain check I'd have preferred, since it's still about business, not entertainment. I'd normally feel uncomfortable going there because it's Cookie's workplace. But I know she won't be around because I made her promise that she wouldn't dance again until receiving medical clearance from her treating surgeon. Some injury lawyers direct their clients to stop doing what they normally do until the case is over in an effort to build up damages. But any lawyer who gives that instruction is telling you point-blank they can't be trusted.

"How ya doing?" I say, the way you do when you don't know the other guy's name.

"S'up, Wyler?" It's the same giant doorman. In this instance, I wish I were less memorable.

"Not much." I put my fist out there for a friendly bump. He looks at it hanging, then reluctantly obliges. "You know my name, what's yours?" Like I've said, doormen are a good source of cases for me.

"Nteekay."

"Nteekay," I repeat. "You African?" I ask, immediately wishing I hadn't.

"Nah, man. Brooklyn. *N-T-K*," he says, one hard letter at a time. "I give it on a need-to-know basis, Wyler."

Oops. My bad.

He flings a thumb back at the door. I meekly walk by him.

I take out my wallet as I approach the cashier's window. "Here ya go," I say, placing two twenties down. Just finishing putting on her lipstick, she gives a pucker into her compact, then stows it into her zebra hand pouch. I liked the leopard one better.

"Hey there, darling," she says in what I perceive to be a flirty tone. "You're comped tonight." She gives me a wink.

"Thanks. I don't get much consideration from beautiful women like you." Yeah, that's the play. Be humble.

"Darling, Mick paid for ya. Now run along before I forget he did."

This time Mick's at a table fifteen feet back from the edge of the stage. It's his idea of a location fit for business inside a venue that's clearly not. After he greets me, he wants to get right down to it. I give him the international hand gesture for "give me a sec." I signal the waitress.

"Sobieski orange vodka, please." That's my new drink. It used to be tequila, but now it makes me sick. Not the alcohol, the memory it brings back of being a coma victim. That's another story.

"We got Stoli O. Want it or not?"

"Yes, please," I tell her. "Go ahead," I say to Mick.

He takes a chug of his beer. "So, I've reviewed Cookie's case."

"Excellent. I love having a renegade doctor in my corner screening my malpractice cases for free. What do you think?"

"It's not a garden variety case."

"Yeah, I've come to the same conclusion. But I'm just a lawyer, you're the doc. Let me hear it."

Before he can continue, the house lights dim. "Now, for your viewing pleasure, on center stage, Jingles Dance Bonanza is proud to present, making her New York debut, all the way from Paris— L-O-L-A, Lolaaaaa . . . LaRue!" A few pairs of hands clap. It's a reception like this one that highlights how well-loved Cookie is.

The spotlight frames her. She's wearing a French cancan dress, petticoat, black stockings, and a large feathered hat. As the music starts, she does a Frisbee toss with her hat, sending it flying stage right. Then she pulls off her dress and tosses it left. Nice choreography. What can I say? I'm a dance dad, but, like I said, no pole for my Little Munch, Penelope. At this moment, I come to a distressing realization. *Pole* is spelled backward right in the middle of the very name I gave my daughter. Shit.

Mick and I turn back to each other after this brief distraction.

"So . . . Cookie's case," he restates. "I have my opinions, but why don't you tell me how you see it?" Always testing me.

"It's not what I see that's bothering me, it's what I don't see."

"Go on."

"Cookie's prior attorney, Chris Charles, claimed an injury compromising the flow of cerebral spinal fluid, requiring repeated spinal taps to keep her brain from bursting."

"Yes, I saw that in the legal document you sent me but not in any of the medicals. I've been meaning to ask."

"Yeah, well, that's what I meant when I said what was bothering me is what I don't see—which is any medical documentation of tapping. But I've got to tell you, I had them in my office, and I witnessed for myself our friend, Major, performing an emergency tap. He actually hit a nerve that triggered a kick that sent him flying. Cookie didn't even know she'd done it; it was involuntary." I couldn't help shaking my head as I remembered the scene.

"Anyway, it's why I called them in, trying to get this lack of documentation straightened out. Major explained it's not in the medical records because he's the one who diagnosed it and has been the one taking care of the procedure. Says he has complete records, which should be on the way to me.

"But here's what makes it more interesting. Dr. McElroy didn't document any injury to the structures responsible for the flow of CSF in his operative report, which is not uncommon when a surgeon wants to cover up something. Yet, at his oral deposition, he came right out admitting he *did* cause a penetrating injury into the subarachnoid space with a resultant CSF leak."

"Get out of here!" Mick says, disbelievingly. "We both know doctors never do that."

"Yeah, well, he also testified that it was self-limiting."

"Why didn't you send me a copy of his deposition transcript?"

"'Cause I wanted your opinion only based on the medical records."

"Unfair."

"You'll get over it. Anyway, given that any confession of error in the medical-legal game is unheard of, McElroy just rolled over and came out with it. And the way he did it was a bit odd."

"How?" Mick's definitely paying close attention.

"I'll tell you how. Cookie's former lawyer, Charles, asked, 'Doctor, did anything occur during the surgery that was not documented in your operative report?' Like a staged question—and then McElroy confessed, just like that."

"That's unusual."

"Yeah, I thought so, too. But maybe it's not as strange as it might seem on the surface. The guy knew he had a witness against him."

"A witness? In an operative case? What are you talking about?"

"I saw an unsigned statement by a nurse named Molina in the file, which laid the guy out for dead. They obviously had some difference in the OR regarding the handling of a 'leak' he caused. The statement indicates that Molina sought out Cookie before she was discharged and explained to her and Major what happened, knowing McElroy intentionally omitted the injury from his operative report."

"That's crazy. A member of the medical profession coming out against one of their own. It just never happens."

"Yeah, well, it happened—and *didn't* happen. Like I said, the Molina statement was unsigned. Maybe someone from the hospital's Risk Management Department got to her after Chris Charles did and created this draft copy."

"Maybe," Mick responds. "Anyway, McElroy did admit, against his interest, to the mechanism of injury necessitating the tapping, in the absence of medical records that would show whether Cookie had ever even received a tap. So what did *you* see in the medicals?"

"So," I say, "the medicals. The first post-op MRI taken of Cookie's neck the day before her discharge showed a moderate-size fluid collection in the area where McElroy admitted to injury. But there was no definite fluid invasion into the space where you'd expect to see a CSF leak. The radiologist said the differential diagnosis included a post-op blood collection, an infection, a CSF leak. He further stated at the end of his report, 'consider spinal tap if clinically indicated.'"

"Go on."

I gulp the last of my drink. "Now, the second post-op MRI was taken two weeks later and was read by the same radiologist. He did an interval comparison of the two and stated the fluid collection seen on the prior study had spontaneously reabsorbed, consistent with it having been a post-op blood collection. I have to agree with the guy because, if the fluid was a CSF leak rather than blood, you'd expect it to keep collecting, and there would have to have been a spinal tap within a week of McElroy's surgery. But that never happened."

"Keep going," Mick says, his expression resembling that of proud father. He swigs the last of his brew, then looks around for our server, holding up two fingers.

"Okay. Now, according to Major, he tapped Cookie for the first time six months after McElroy's operation—which seems too remote to connect to the surgery, despite the confession of injury."

Mick gives me a curious look. "I agree a temporal component seems to be missing," he says, "but nothing's black and white in medicine. Let's consider the big picture. Before the op, she'd never had a tap. Then, during it, she has a CSF leak from an injury to the structures that could compromise CSF flow, and the post-op MRI confirmed the presence of some kind of fluid in the area at question. And the radiologist raises the possibility of a tap. Six months later, she needs the first of many taps. That seems to work for me."

"Then how do you explain the absence of a fluid collection on the second post-op MRI?" I demand.

Mick's ready for this. And I know I'm about to play the pupil. But I like to learn.

"Here's the thing about MRIs; they show what they show on the date they were taken. The day before and the day after each could reveal different findings when you're talking about the ebb and flow of tiny fluid collections. Something as simple as the patient ingesting a vast quantity of water on the day of the MRI, coupled with her continued IV hydration, can influence the results because all an MRI is showing is the fluid in and around soft tissues." He takes a breath.

"Also, the injury that caused the CSF to leak could have been self-limiting at one point in time, just like McElroy testified. Then, it could have spontaneously begun to leak again at a later point. Remember, we're talking about an injury to a membrane here that has a very limited capacity to repair itself. So don't let that one finding throw you off. Besides, if there really was a tear bad enough to leak CSF, McElroy could've patched it up like a hole in an inner tube, with it reopening at a later date. "

"Well, we'll never know that because Charles never pursued that line of questioning with McElroy. He just accepted the self-limiting testimony. And I'd be crazy to ask him anything I don't know the answer to at the time of trial. Now, can we talk about the subsequent surgeries?"

"Sure."

I love my man, Mick. Just as I'm about to start, two drinks hit the table.

"This is a good place to conduct business," I tell him, lifting mine up. He nods in agreement.

"Okay," I continue, "not one op report mentions an injury into the subarachnoid space, nor did the surgeon dictate a repair to the structures that involve the circulation of cerebral spinal fluid. The first subsequent surgery was aimed at removing the surgical hardware McElroy'd improperly screwed into the joint space. The other was aimed at Cookie's healing insufficiencies; meaning the nonunion of bone, and then the donation of new bone to effect restabilizing the fusion that never took."

Mick shakes his head. "Yeah, now that you mention it, the surgeon never addressed the CSF issue other than making note of repeated taps by way of patient history. It's definitely mysterious. You're going to have to speak to the subsequent surgeon and get an explanation."

"I will."

"You're on top of it, Tug. Or should I say, on tap of it."

You can't be serious all the time, even when discussing leaking spinal fluids.

Just at that moment, scattered unenthusiastic clapping begins and ends just as fast. Lola from Paris is taking her bow. Now she's coming down the side steps of the stage. With dress and feathered hat in hand, she heads right for us in a determined manner. I take a sip of my Stoli O, wondering what's going on. She pulls up close to me and stops.

I lean back and look up. "*Bonjour*, Mademoiselle Lola from France," I welcome her. "I hope you're enjoying our wonderful city." Smooth, huh?

"I'm from Paris," she barks in an accent more Tommy's Trailer Park than Arc de Triomphe. "Paris, New York." She looks at Mick, then back at me. She puts her hands on her hips. "You two didn't catch one minute of my show. Yapping the whole time. That was rude."

Before I get a chance to respond—which is good, because I don't have a response—Mick takes charge.

"Lola, I can tell you are a lovely girl. And, yes, it is true. Mr. Wyler over here and I were quite rude to you during your solo by carrying on with our business instead of giving you the undivided admiration you deserved."

Her expression softens a bit. Funny that I'm paying attention to her face.

"For that, we apologize. Could I make it up to you in a bit? I'd be honored if you'd grace me with a private dance."

She smirks, jutting her thumb at Mick. "I like this guy. He's got class," Lola tells me.

"Sure, honey," she replies to Mick, "I'd love to give you a dance. I'll be around later when you two close up shop."

Mick smiles. They've got a deal. She puts her hat on, taps it down, and struts off with dress in hand, seemingly satisfied.

"You defused that pretty well, Mick. And to your advantage. But, listen, I've got to hop."

"You know what you need to do, right?"

"Yeah," I answer. "Have Pusska get all the MRI studies."

"Right. *All* of them. Not just the first two post-op ones from the McElroy surgery. And . . ." Mick adds, cuing me to end his sentence.

"Get them Ray-diated."

"That's right, get them Ray-diated."

Too Obvious

I walk out of the club straight into Minotero. This is far from coincidence. He's leaning against a Lincoln Town Car. The government-issued type with a searchlight attached just in front of the driver's side mirror. He's wearing that stupid trench coat again and seems even shorter than I remember.

Anyway, I'm glad to see him since I have something to tell him. I approach purposefully. "Do me a favor, Minnow," I say. "Never come to my office again, and don't involve yourself with my clients. You hear me?"

"Do you mean Cookie? Or maybe Robert Killroy? Which one?" What's going on here? How would he even know about Robert? I've only started his representation.

"Where are you getting the names of my clients?"

"That's what I do, know stuff. Seeeee."

I take a second to assess and collect myself. The names of my new clients are not public knowledge, so he's got some real source that, at the moment, I can't figure out. I realize I need to tone things down in an effort to appeal to his sensible side. If he has one. I mean, he did give me his name.

"I don't know who you are," I say kindly, "or why you're involving yourself in my business, and also in the business of my clients, but you're stepping over the line. I can't imagine what interest you have here. Don't you think it's time to explain?"

"You want explanations, I'll give you explanations, seeeee. I warned you off Cookie's case, and you didn't heed it. I investigate insurance fraud claims, and her case is one of my assignments, seeeee."

"What are you talking about? She has a solid malpractice case. Besides which, it's clear she's not the type of person who perpetuates insurance fraud."

"It's not Cookie we're investigating."

"What do you mean? Who else would be in the position to commit the fraud?"

"The doctor and the lawyer. It happens all the time, usually with medical facilities. But we've seen it like this, too, seeeee."

"Dr. McElroy and Chris Charles? No. I don't seeeee," I respond. "What fraud could they possibly be involved in?"

"McElroy commits the surgical error and Charles brings the lawsuit. Just like in the movies. Then they split the insurance payout."

"Wait a second. The money here isn't so large that any doctor would be enticed to co-conspire in such a plan with so little return. But something else makes the whole thing utterly farfetched . . ."

"Oh yeah, what's that?"

"If we accept that they're co-conspirators in this scheme, then it must have been set up beforehand. Meaning, they could only effectuate their plan if it was known that Cookie would retain Chris Charles. How do you explain that?"

"Easy, seeeee."

As frustrating as all this is, at least I got the guy talking. "No, I don't. Her boyfriend, Major, was the one who referred her to Charles and, come to think of it, to McElroy as well. Hmm, so are you saying Major's involved, too?"

"I'm not saying anything. We've been on this assignment a long time, and the end is just around the corner. You're interfering with an ongoing investigation, seeeee. So now that you know, get off the case. I got a job to do here, and you're getting in the way."

"Not so fast. I'm going to represent my client zealously to the end. Cookie did nothing wrong, based on what you've said, and in handling her action, I'll be doing nothing wrong. You know it and I know it. If she was injured, she's entitled to fair and reasonable compensation." I shake my head reproachfully. "You're the only one with something to lose here, if this story of yours is true." I mean, how can it be? Major seemed to be in support of Cookie switching attorneys. No way is he involved.

Minnow takes a threatening step forward. This guy loves intimidating gestures.

"You don't believe me?" he shouts. "What do you know? You don't even know these people! How do you explain McElroy testifying about the injury when it wasn't in his operative report? That's proof of his participation in this scheme, scccccc."

I will say this, Minnow knows his facts. He's definitely on the inside, somehow. But I've had enough of him and his annoying "seeeees."

"Listen to me. In fact, I view things just the other way." I pause, letting that sink in. "If this was the situation, then McElroy would've come straight out and documented his surgical error in his operative report. How do you explain that?"

"I'll tell you how," he quickly responds. "Too obvious."

"Too obvious?"

"Yeah, too obvious. These guys are smart. They're litigating the claim, making it real, seeeee."

"No, I still don't see. We're getting nowhere. I'm out of here."

I turn but not before taking in three numbers and three letters, and begin walking away. There's a remote possibility it all might be true, only because he's in possession of such detailed facts. Plus, I saw the movie Minnow was referring to with that plot—*Malice* with Alec Baldwin and Nicole Kidman. But it was the operating surgeon who co-conspired with his patient to commit the insurance fraud.

I feel his eyes on my back. He's pissed off.

I pull out my phone and start an e-mail. *To: Pusska. Subject: Various. Please come to my office at nine a.m. with the findings on your assignment. I also have something else for you.* I send her the make, model, and license plate of Minnow's car, stating, *I hope this helps. Thanks.*

Before I even have the chance to put the phone away, it vibrates in my hand. It's Pusska's reply.

"You know you vant to fuck me."

11.

et me know when Pusska gets here," I say as I pass Lily.

"No 'hello,' no 'good morning Lily, how are you today?' Just a command. That's a little disrespectful, don't you think?"

"Yes, you're right, it was. Good morning, Lily. How are you today? Could you buzz me when Pusska gets here, please?"

"I'm fine, and no. Why don't you get yourself a real investigator? And you're way too comfortable with me," she cautions.

I nod, continuing on. I think we don't have a normal lawyer-paralegal relationship. And she's right.

I enter my office and stop in my tracks. There's a surprise. Pusska. She's sitting at my desk with her feet up. There's an open bottle of red, and she's sipping from one of the wineglasses I keep stowed away in my private cabinet next to my mini wine fridge. To my further surprise, she's wearing a skirt suit, a first. However, her blouse is unbuttoned awfully low, lower than your normal suit-wearing woman.

Then again, Pusska is no normal woman.

"Shut door," she orders.

Having learned my lesson from Lily, I now greet Pusska accordingly.

"Good morning, Pusska. How are you today?"

"Vhat a nice vay to greet somevun," she responds, raising the glass of wine in her hand. "I'm good, but not as good as this vine. I'm connoisseur. It's magnificent. Pour yourself a glass before it's all gone."

I smile. "I try not to drink in the morning. It may lead to other bad habits that could play into my self-destructive tendencies. But thanks, anyway."

Pusska looks deep into my eyes. She's got something planned.

"Vell, okay then. I'll continue vith my drinking alone, if you don't mind, darling." She takes a large gulp and gives a long *ahhhhh* after she swallows. She's buzzed.

When this happens, watch out. I've seen Pusska like this on two or three occasions over the four years she's been my investigator. With each binge, she gets a little more revealing.

"No," I answer, "I don't mind. Enjoy your wine as long as it doesn't compromise your work product."

"I assure you, darling, it von't."

Two *darlings* so far. She's obviously got intentions. "So what do you have for me?"

"Right to business, so boring. Vhy don't ve sit on your couch and I tell you?"

"I'm good right here on this side of the desk. You can stay in my big comfy chair and sip your wine while you give me what you got."

She looks deep into my eyes again. Uh-oh. She swings her feet down and sits up. Taking a large authoritative slug of wine, she empties the rest of the glass. She leans forward. "You know you vant to fuck me."

I go with the truth. "Yes, Pusska, I definitely vant to. Who wouldn't? You're gorgeous, sexy, and there's no doubt in my mind that you know how to please a man. So what do you got for me regarding Minnow?"

"So vhat do you got for me! So vhat do you got for me! Is that all you have to say?"

"Yes."

"Suit self. Vhen you ready to vant me, I von't vant you."

"Yeah, that's basically how things go for me. Now, back to Minnow. What do you got?"

After a small delay, tears fill her eyes. Now what?

"There's no need to cry; it's not you, it's me." I've always wanted to use that phrase. Unfortunately, given my historical role in breakups, I've never had the opportunity.

"No, it's me," she asserts. "I hate myself."

"Pusska, why would you say that?"

"Because I do."

I can see I have no choice here. "Tell me why you'd say that, Pusska."

"Because I'm whore. No self-respect. I know this. That vhy I hate myself."

"First of all you're not a whore. Second—"

"I am whore," she interrupts. "I use sex to get vhat I vant. I learn this. My mother vas town whore. She had no teeth."

"You are not your mother. And using your sexuality to get what you want is pretty normal. Okay? Besides, you have beautiful teeth."

"I am whore," she restates in apparent distress. "Men in my country make me whorc. Old, fat man vith money have young sexy girl. Girl vith old man for money, old man vith girl for sex. It only vay for poor girl to have good life. Then I come to America and have chance to change. And vhat I do? I act like whore in vorse vay."

"Pusska, you've had two long-term boyfriends since we've been working together. Neither were fat, old, rich men. Give yourself a break."

"Yeah, my boyfriends. You don't know. Instead of fat, old, rich man, I go for skinny, young, rich. But both boyfriends married. Like I said, vorse. I use sex thinking they marry me vunce I break marriage. That never happen. They throw me avay to gutter like sick dog."

"Well . . ." I'm playing for time. "Did you really go after both these married men because they were rich?"

"Yes."

"And did you go after each one with the intentions of breaking up his marriage?"

"Yes."

"And you thought that after you'd used your considerable wiles to get them into a weakened emotional state, you'd eventually prevail and marry one?"

"Yes."

"And you were using hot sex to carry out this plan?"

"Yes."

"And you were going to marry them for their money?"

"Yes."

"Well, that kinda does make you a whore. And a homewrecker." She erupts, crying again. I roll my eyes. But she's too upset to notice. What did she expect me to say?

"Please," I beg, "stop crying. Don't be so hard on yourself. You were a young girl who had to survive some tough situations. You can't be blamed for that. Right now, it's time to move on, to clean up your act. You're a great person, so give a guy the opportunity to like you for you, not for the sex."

"Move forward, you say, like it so easy. Men vant only one thing. So I act like whore."

"All right, Pusska," I say, as if giving in. "If that's what you think, then just come over here and blow me."

"Vhat!" she exclaims. "I'm not going to do anything to you!"

"See," I say. "That wasn't so hard, was it? Consider *that* your first step toward being a respectable young lady." She smiles. "And you know I was just kidding when I asked you to blow me?"

"You can say you vere kidding, as long as we both know you vant me."

On the words *vant me*, Lily barges in like some overprotective buddy of my wife. They lock eyes. I'm sandwiched between the negativity that suddenly suffuses the room.

"Vell, vhat do you vant? This is private meeting."

"Not any longer," Lily responds. "And it's *well*, not *vell*; *what*, not *vhat*; and *want*, not *vant*. Get that right, already. You've been here long enough to know it's a *w*, as in *witch* and not a *v*, as in *vampiress*." Lily, having struck, defiantly puts her hands on her hips, ready for the counterattack. Can anyone say catfight?

Lily and Pusska are continually at odds with each other—and it's all Lily's fault. She dislikes everything about Pusska and has made it well known. Lily's a hard-working, single, *Puertorriqueña* mother from the hood who takes great pride in her achievements. She came from a family on welfare, was the first to graduate high school, went on to an accredited paralegal school where she finished at the top of her class, and has worked for me ever since.

She runs my small practice and knows more about law than most attorneys. As I think I've described, she also happens to be absolutely gorgeous. Think Penelope Cruz.

But unlike Pusska, Lily's never once used her looks to get anything. In fact, the mere thought of doing so repulses her. And when guys, failing to sense this, come on to her, she serves them a nut roast. The smart ones slink away, believe me.

"*Tsk, tsk, tsk,*" Pusska retorts. "You shouldn't talk with such anger and disrespect. But I'm glad you're here. Fetch me some coffee."

Lily comes up behind me and, by the sound of her footsteps, she means business. I look over my shoulder, and she smacks me upside my head. Not a hard one, but enough to rattle me.

"Hey! What did I do?"

"Oh, shut up, you idiot. I'm not going to work here if you're going to start cheating on your wife with this drunken—"

"Stop right there!" I command. "No one's cheating on anybody. What has to happen is that you two put aside your attitudes. I need both of you. You're both integral to the success of this law office, and I can't handle the friction anymore. Now I want you to shake hands and just get over it. Do you hear me?"

They look at each other. Neither is going to make the first move.

"Come on, ladies," I say. "It's in everybody's best interest that we all get along." I stand up, and Lily takes a step back. I walk around my desk and take Pusska's arm.

"Come on now," I coax. She reluctantly allows me to guide her. "Now shake hands," I insist.

They look at each other. "Come on now," I repeat.

Pusska, surprisingly, makes the first move. She reaches out saying, "Lily, I don't know vhy there's tension between us, but I am sorry there is."

They shake hands and share a sort of smile. I feel relieved.

"Great. I'm glad you guys finally got past this. Now, Lily, why did you barge in here in the first place? Were you just keeping tabs on me?"

"Your kids' principal is on the phone. He tried to call your wife, but she's most likely playing tennis and can't be reached. He's got Connor and Penelope in his office. He's on hold."

I sigh. "You should have said so right up front." Smugly, she walks out.

I pick up. "Hi, this is Connor and Penelope's dad. What's going on? Is everything all right?"

"Yes, everything's fine," comes the reply. Whew. "But both your children are refusing to respond to their teachers unless they're addressed by their new names, which we have no record of. If there's been a name change, we're going to need either you or your wife to come in and sign the paperwork to reflect that in Dirk's and Summer's official school records."

"I see. Well, there has been no official name change. They seem to be going through a phase. Could you put them on the phone for a second?"

"Certainly." I hear him tell them to share the phone.

"Hi, Daddy," they say.

"Guys, you've got to stop this."

"No way," Connor responds.

"Yeah, no way," adds Penelope. "We like our new names. I'm Summer and Connor is Dirk, and that's final. We need to show our independence."

"That's twisting what I said, and you can't change your names."

"Yes, we can," Penelope responds. "My friend Mark's dad, Mark, did it. Mark is his favorite name, so Mark's dad, Mark, changed his name to Mark. Then Mark's dad, Mark, named his son Mark too because, like I said, Mark is his favorite name. So I know you can do it because my friend Mark's dad, Mark, did it."

"Put the principal back on the phone."

"Hello."

"Yes, I'm sorry for any trouble this is causing," I say. "I'll try to get things back to normal. For now, please just deal with them in any way you see fit."

"I'll send Dirk and Summer back to their classrooms," he allows. Kids are his business, after all.

"So, do you vant to know vhat I got for you, or vhat?"

"Yes, Pusska, I actually do. I've been hoping to learn that since I walked in and saw you drinking my vintage wine. Tell me what you've got for me. Let's start with Minotero. Who does he work for, and what's his involvement with Cookie's case?"

"Ah, yes, him. Vell, I can tell you who he's not."

"Okay, who isn't he?"

"First, he isn't vorking for Chris Charles as you suspected. He isn't a government man, this is for sure. He doesn't vork for the DA, he doesn't vork for the FBI, he doesn't vork for Frauds Bureau, and he doesn't vork for any other state or federal agency. And, as far as I can tell, there's not vun such formal agency, government or private, taking any interest vhatsoever in Cookie's case or in Chris Charles or this Dr. McElroy. They're not on radar screens."

"Well, do you have any idea who he is and what interest he has in wanting me to step away from Cookie's case and return it to Chris Charles?"

"No."

"And the plate number?"

"Vell, I ran the Town Car plate you gave me and get info."

"Go on, I'm listening."

"Plate stolen."

"That's it?"

"Yes, that's it. I don't know vhat his interest is vith this case, but I'll find out if you vant me to."

"I do. But I'm not sure it's necessary this minute. We'll keep it on the side for now because I can't see how it matters to my properly representing Cookie. But McElroy? What did you find out about him?"

"Okay, him. Vell, he's been brought up on charges twice for performing unnecessary surgery. On vun of those occasions, Major submitted an affidavit on his behalf, stating the surgery was medically indicated. I have papervork here for you on both cases. Not too bad, eh?"

"No, not too bad, considering surgeons perform unnecessary operations every day."

"Ya, that vas my thought. I have Cookie's MRI studies vith me. I picked them up from Chris Charles on my vay here. He vas cooperative and say sorry for not giving you them vhen transferring file. He forgot."

"Great, thanks."

"You're velcome. May I make suggestion?"

"I'm listening."

"I vant to check out Major."

I think for a second. He's the tap-master. It couldn't hurt. "You're right."

"I'm alvays right."

I escort her to the door, thinking I should have come up with that. I must be off my game. She stops before walking out.

"I vant to thank you for your kind vords. I have low self-esteem, and that's vhy I use sex to get vhat I vant. I'm going to stop it."

"I think that's a good idea. I'm glad you were able to hear what I was saying."

"Thank you," she responds. "Vun more thing."

"What's that?"

"You know you vant to fuck me."

12.

The next morning, I meet Robert and Ethel at nine sharp to prep Robert for his oral deposition. I've read the entire file, but it contains no answers to the adverse police report. Still, I haven't had the opportunity to discuss the matter with them. Now's the time.

I'm looking forward to questioning the van driver. The carrier sensibly realized they had no choice but to produce the guy. A court would have ordered it despite prior counsel's ridiculous waiver.

"How you feeling today?" I ask Ethel. She knows what I'm talking about.

"Oh, pretty good. That cancer ain't taking me yet. We got business to conduct."

"You ready to pay your debt to Mr. Wang?" Robert wants to know.

"No, I told you I don't believe I owe him that money," I reply courteously.

"Mr. Wang says you do. He's a really nice man."

"Yes, Robert, but he ruined my new suit, and I'm just not going to pay him for that."

"I'm gonna have to serve you with papers if you don't pay him his fourteen dollars and seventy-nine cents."

"Oh, right, you're also a process server. I almost forgot that."

"Yes, he is." Ethel's pride is clear. "Bona fide, aren't you, boy?"

"Yes, Granny."

"Well, Robert," I say, "just as we agreed, business is business. If you have to sue me on behalf of Mr. Wang, I promise I won't dodge you." He looks at me now a little confused.

"Dodgeball?"

"What your lawyer is saying," Ethel explains, "is that he will take the court papers from you so you don't have to chase him around town. You won't have to use your investigation skills to find him."

"But I like using my skills, Granny. That's the way I can get money to be independent."

"Well, you'll have plenty of opportunity to use them, boy. Your lawyer here ain't the only one not paying his bills."

Ho, ho. Granny likes her little dig.

Robert, I notice, is wearing a spy watch. It's one I've seen advertised in the back of some of my kids' magazines. A Bluetooth receiver is in his ear, and he's wearing a utility belt with various gadgets attached. Across his T-shirt is the message *Live Free or Spy*. A secret agent he isn't.

"It's time to discuss your case, Robert—the van accident. That's why you're here. Today, a lawyer for the driver of the van is coming. He is going to ask you a few questions about how the accident happened and about your injuries."

He suddenly loses his look of aggressive confidence. Panic replaces it.

"There's no need to worry about anything," I reassure him. "I'll be sitting right next to you, defending your rights. You can count on me, okay?"

"Ooh-dat! Ooh-dat! Ooh-dat!" Robert abruptly screams out. He begins to chop at his ankle—karate style, one hard slash after another. Like I'd heard on the phone.

"It's his pains," Ethel explains. "They bona fide. When they come on, ain't nothing he can do but chop them pains away. You go at them, boy."

"Has a doctor told you why he's suffering like this?"

"Oh, sure, it's his neuroma, like we spoke about. Nerves all caught up together."

"Certainly," I say, "that can be painful. Have they proposed any treatment?"

"They did one of those nerve blocks, but it didn't work." I look at him and see he's vigorously rubbing the area. "The only other choice," she says, lowering her voice, "is surgery."

"No, Granny! No, Granny! I'm not taking no surgery!" he yells, hearing her.

"Don't worry, boy, I know that." She looks at me. "No guarantees with surgery. Could make things worse."

"I understand." I ask Robert, "Is it better now?"

"Yeah, it passed."

"Good."

He's cradling his right hand. I know I need to proceed carefully. "You ready to talk about the van accident, Robert? Lawyers call this prepping the client, what we're about to do."

He nods.

"I read your whole file, but why don't you tell me in your own words what happened?"

"He don't know what happened," Ethel breaks in. "Thought I told you this grandson of mine is a little bit retarded."

"Yeah, I'm a little bit retarded," he confirms.

I'm not going to interfere with their coping strategies. The hand they've been dealt isn't an easy one. Though I don't agree with their terminology, if it works for them, then I'll respect it. Besides, they're using the phrase descriptively rather than as an insult.

"Ethel," I say, "this poses a tough problem for us. If Robert doesn't know what happened and can't put fault on the van, it'll be difficult to get more money because the police report tells us that the driver's going to say Robert caused his own accident."

"Well, I know what happened."

"You?" I'm taken a bit off guard. How did I miss this? "I didn't realize that. I didn't see you listed as a witness in the file or the police report. What did happen?"

"Robert got hit by one of them Jew vans."

"What?"

"I said he got hit by one of them Jew vans."

That's what I thought I heard. I do some quick mental stocktaking as they watch me patiently.

Okay, this pair is given to using words and phrases commonly viewed as offensive. What's more, they live in Crown Heights, which is dense with West Indians and African Americans and is also the worldwide headquarters for the Chabad-Lubavitch Hasidic Jewish movement. So, there's the remote possibility that they harbor ill feelings toward Jews. No black community member can forget Gavin Cato being struck and killed by a car in the motorcade of a Hasidic Jewish rabbi.

When Hatzolah, the Jewish ambulance service, arrived on the scene, they took the rabbi's man away in the ambulance. Yet seven-year-old Gavin was still pinned under the vehicle that had jumped the sidewalk. Riots erupted in the neighborhood soon after, and a Jewish college student visiting from Australia, Yankel Rosenbaum, was murdered in retribution.

My take on it: Ethel and Robert have no agenda other than their own. This is simply the language they use, and what I need to do is listen, to get the facts of Robert's accident.

"That's horrible," I say. "How would you describe this Jew van, Ethel?"

"It was one of them big white Jew vans, stuffed all full of Jews."

"It was a white Jew van?" I ask. I am doing my job.

"Yes," Ethel answers, "it was a white Jew van."

"How many Jews would you say were stuffed in the Jew van?"

"'Bout fifteen, give or take."

"There were fifteen people stuffed into a van? Was this one of those extra big Jew vans?"

"Nah, it was a normal size van. But all them Jews were just

stuffed right in there, like sardines, with those little, round targets on their heads."

"Targets?"

"Yeah, you know, those little, round cloth targets they all wear on they heads, so you got something to aim for." I give her a serious look. She gives me one back, then she breaks into laughter.

"I'm just pulling on your leg there, Wyler. I know it's called a yarmulke. I live in Crown Heights, for God's sake." We share a grin.

"Very funny. Anyway, what was this van doing at the moment Robert got hit?"

"It was turning left."

"Turning left, you say?"

"Yeah, into one of them Jew driveways." Here we go again.

"Into a Jew driveway?"

"Correctly so."

"I see. Were there any witnesses?"

"Yeah, lots."

"How many?"

"Maybe 'bout a thousand."

"Ethel, are you telling me there were a thousand witnesses?"

"I'm not positive, maybe two."

"Two thousand?" I repeat, in a tone of disbelief.

"That's what I'm telling ya. Maybe more."

"Um, they wouldn't happen to be Jew witnesses, would they?"

"All of them. There were Jews crawling all over the place going every which way. Here, there, everywhere." For some crazy reason, I believe her. Anyone else—not a chance.

What soon becomes clear is that Granny herself hadn't actually witnessed the impact, but rather saw only the immediate aftermath. Therefore, the next two hours are spent on prepping Robert so he can make a case for himself.

In a personal injury lawsuit, it's up to the injured party to set out the elements of what's called a *prima facie* case. Meaning, he must say what the defendant did wrong that led to the accident and resultant injury. Despite what Ethel believes, Robert certainly *does* know what happened but is having problems putting the words together to describe the event in a coherent and comprehensible manner.

In short, the Jew van made a left turn into a Jew driveway as Robert was lawfully crossing the entrance to it on the pedestrian sidewalk—just like Ethel said. This version puts fault squarely on the driver.

All Robert has to say is the truth. That's it. I think Rich Cohen has problems if Robert can get these few facts across. And I think he's got problems even if Robert can't.

You Always Gots to Look Where You Be Going

We head toward my conference room for the deposition. We enter and join the court reporter, the driver of the van who struck Robert, and a young female associate attorney waiting there. The attorney has her brown hair up in a bun, and wears a blue pantsuit, a white shirt buttoned high, and a stern puckered look on her face, the kind she shouldn't have at this early stage in her career. The moment Robert sees the driver, his eyes slide wide-open, his jaw drops, and he thrusts his finger out.

"Mister," he says excitedly, "Granny told me it ain't polite to point, but you the man who gave me the ooh-dats." The guy looks at his attorney, confused.

"Mr. Wyler . . ." the attorney says. "It is Mr. Wyler, isn't it?" And I can tell from her intonation, along with her tight hair bun, she doesn't play nice with others.

"Yes."

"Could you direct your witness not to speak to my client? It's inappropriate to do so in such a proceeding."

"Um, may I ask your name, Counselor?"

"It's Ms. Kaufman."

"Ms. Kaufman, I agree. And I already instructed Robert not to speak unless he's being questioned by you."

"Well, he's not following your instruction."

"Yes. I have to agree with you on that, too." Lawyers hate when you agree with them. It undermines their sense of purpose.

"Well, don't you think you should—"

"Mr. Wyler," Robert interrupts, "I don't mean to bust in on you and Ms. Kaufman, but that's the man who gave me the ooh-dats. Sorry, mister, I don't mean to point, but you're sittin' right there."

"Yes, Robert. He is. But like we discussed in my office, we have to play the quiet game until this attorney begins asking you questions."

"Okay, but that's him, the guy who hit me with the van. He's sittin' right there." His tone is one of disbelief. And you can add three more finger points to the tally.

"Yes, he is, Robert. It's okay," I add, trying to sound comforting. At this moment, the full reality of a failure on my part hits me. Hard. I was so caught up in attempting to prep my client that I forgot to tell him the driver who gave him the ooh-dats would be here.

"Come, Robert," I say, "let's take our seats." I pull out a chair and guide him into it. He sits, keeping his eye on the driver as if it were a safety measure. The court reporter sits at one end of the oval table. Otherwise, it's us on one side, them on the other. Robert is sitting next to the court reporter, facing Ms. Kaufman, and I'm next to Robert with the driver across from me.

"Mister," Robert says to the driver. I look to Kaufman. She ain't happy. "I know you didn't mean to run me over, but you always gots to look where you be going when you driving a vehicle." Kaufman now has the opportunity for a directive.

"Mr. Wyler, would you tell your client—"

But Robert's not done.

"It's the same when you ride a bike. If I didn't watch where I was riding, I could run into somebody, too." The driver has no response, but Kaufman does.

"Mr. Wyler, are you going to instruct your witness to stop talking to my client?"

"Sure," I respond, as if it makes a difference. "Robert," I say, looking at him while he continues to mark the driver, "can you please not talk to the man who gave you the ooh-dats?" He hesitates, still looking across the table, then answers.

"Yes, sir."

"Thank you, Robert."

"You know, mister," Robert says, leaning forward in his seat, "I know you must feel bad about hitting me and all, but don't worry. Except for my ooh-dats that I can chop at, I'm okay. And I can ride like the wind."

I look to Kaufman. By now this young lawyer should realize that Robert is a special kind of kid. But it's clear from the maddened look on her face that she remains oblivious to this fact. She could be the greatest lawyer in the world, but she will never make it in this business—inside a courtroom—because she clearly cannot connect the dots. Trial work is about connecting the dots and connecting with jurors.

The deposition turns out to be an enlightening experience. By Ms. Kaufman's line of questioning, it's clear that, in addition to relying on the incorrect police report, defense counsel also intends to establish that there's no way the accident could've happened in the manner Robert describes. He would have been hit on his uninjured leg had it occurred the way he's claiming, given his route relative to the direction of the van.

I have to agree with her on that. He did make it seem like he got hit on his left side, which is highly unlikely given his right-leg injury extends from his knee, or bumper height, to his ankle. This clear inconsistency was something I could not have foreseen as it surfaced for the first time from Robert's answers.

However, Robert got it out, just barely, that the van was making a turn, "left or right, I mean this way or that way"—he points in different directions—when it hit him. He also said, about five times, "I don't walk in no street. I walk on the sidewalk, correctly." The first time was in response to the question, "What is your highest level of education?" I have to point out, this was a factor of my overprepping him.

In all, his testimony on how this accident happened was nearly incomprehensible. Bad for us—or is it?

What Robert did make completely clear was that New York Knick great Walt "Clyde" Frazier autographed his basketball when Granny took him to the game for his birthday. This basketball, which Robert was carrying en route to the park, went flying when he was struck. Where the ball came to rest is what's important here.

Anyway, despite Robert's shortcomings, he got the first question right. He answered, "My name is Robert Killroy, but I didn't kill no Roy, and I didn't kill nobody. That's just my name."

Not One Word

After Robert leaves the room to rejoin Ethel, I question the defendant. He's come to New York from his home in Canada just for this deposition. He's a Hasid in the usual long black jacket, with the usual long, curly sideburns, and the usual little, round target on his head. He's also wearing glasses.

He states that the first time he saw my client was at the moment of impact when Robert's cheek was, "smooshed, oy vey," against his windshield. Good for us. He testified that there'd been eighteen people from two different families stuffed into his van and that he was making a left turn into the temple parking lot at the moment of impact. There had been thousands of Jews roaming the streets that day, having come to Crown Heights to celebrate the Rebbe's hundredth birthday.

Granny—of whom I am more than fond—has been proven right: a Jew-stuffed van, a Jew driveway, and a whole lot of Jew witnesses.

On another note, the driver testified that he never spoke to the police. That's right, *not one word*. Rather, it was the father of the family he was traveling with, dressed in the same traditional garb, that did so. A clear case of mistaken Hasidic Jew identity.

I told the defense attorney it was time to settle the case. But she wasn't fazed, despite witnessing two bouts of Robert's ooh-dats. These people just don't know what's good for them. Given Robert's condition—and I'm not even talking about his ankle—I definitely have a jury charge on the law that will take them down. And the way Rich Cohen's young associate, Ms. Kaufman, found joy in relentlessly confusing Robert makes me believe she's missing a big point here.

My challenge is to persuade Cohen to bring his insurance adjuster to the mediation table so I can detonate this legal land mine in his face. Since Ms. Kaufman's ignorant about what's important, Rich Cohen will have to remain unaware too.

Lastly, I don't think I like Ms. Kaufman too much. Maybe it's because I dislike those who take advantage of others, even if it's their job. And especially so in Robert's case.

13.

After Ethel and Robert leave, I take out my phone. I'm looking for two e-mails in particular. I scroll down and find the one from Pusska. It reads, *Thanks for the other day. I haven't used sex since our talk. I vanted to, but I didn't.*

I scroll until I find the other I'm looking for. It's from Ray. It reads, *I'll be home all day, as usual. Come on by if you want.* She's my radiology expert—the doctor who reviews or "Ray-diates" imaging studies for me. Jurors love her quirky manner, and her credentials are unmatched. She's Yale-trained and board-certified in radiology.

Her real name is Dr. Reina Godfrey, but everybody calls her Ray. Short for X-ray, rather than Reina. The only drawback to using Ray is her insistence on doing her reviews from home. That means four flights of stairs. I grab the imaging studies and off I go.

She lives on Fifty-First Street between Eighth and Ninth Avenues, smack in the middle of Hell's Kitchen, which is on the western edge of Midtown and has a colorful history to justify its colorful name. Once the turf of a variety of urban gangs—the Irish being the best known—it's now all about restaurants, block after block, plus the usual gentrifying redevelopment.

I hit the rusted door buzzer of her brownstone, take three steps back, and look up to the top left window. Ray's fighting to get it open. Finally, she succeeds and sticks her head out.

"Be right down."

Ray reviews fifty imaging studies a day at a charge of two hundred fifty dollars per read. That's twelve thousand five hundred dollars per day, and she's on the job six days per week, fifty-two weeks a year.

Yet, despite her sizable income, her brownstone is dilapidated and unsightly. To illustrate how cheap she is, she struggles with her window and walks down four flights to get the door, instead of spending a few bucks to have the buzzer fixed. I could go on, detailing the broken handrail, the peeling paint, the cracked window panels, etc., etc., etc., but I think you get the picture.

As she opens the door, she steps out past me, looking down the street first one way, then the other. Surveillance. Like someone's out to get her.

"What's up, Ray?"

"You never know. Come on."

Whatever.

Once we're inside, she slams the door. The only upgrade she's ever made involved giant-size Master Locks and deadbolts. I smile at her as she secures her territory.

She smiles back. Her teeth are telling. She had a Spanish omelet with toasted, buttered seven-grain bread for breakfast, a ham sandwich with spicy brown mustard and tomato for lunch, and she snacked on a granola bar—my guess would be peanut-butter flavored—seventeen minutes ago. I can't wait to look at the images up close with her.

"Come on," she says, starting up the creaky staircase. I follow. The back of her bathrobe is hiked up. It's caught, somehow. Exposed are her legs, ghost-white from lack of sun exposure, and a hint of her droopy bottom. I mean, what's the protocol here? Do I say something?

At the first-floor landing, she stops. "Let's work here today."

"Okay, I've never been on this floor. We always work up top."

"I know," she responds, "but I got involved in some reviews and forgot to feed the cats on this floor."

"You have cats on this floor, too? Don't you have, like, seven cats upstairs?"

"Yeah. Well, I actually have twelve upstairs. On this floor I only have nine."

"You've got to be kidding me."

"Nope, nine more on this floor." She takes a ring of keys out, and the jingle incites a chorus of meows. We walk into a hungry pride.

"Why do you keep nine cats on this floor and twelve upstairs?"

"Because the Jets don't get along with the Sharks. It's your typical *West Side Story*."

"How did you discover which nine didn't get along with which twelve?"

She looks at me pityingly. "I asked them."

She begins filling dishes with cat food and setting them on the floor.

"Ready to start?" she wants to know, once the lower nine are locked onto their bowls.

"Sure," I answer, thinking I like Mick's workspace a heck of a lot better. The wide-open area, which comprises the entirety of this floor, is completely barren except for where we're obviously going to work. Also, there are no shades, no floor coverings, no furniture—no nothing. Bare, down to the exposed pipes and hanging lightbulbs.

"Good. Now give me those imaging studies, and don't say a word."

I hand her a stack of compact discs.

She prefers a cold read without any guidance. She says it gives her opinions greater credibility since they were formed without the influence of seeing the formal reports that come along with the studies.

I agree.

She places the numerous CDs on the tabletop, which has a heavily scratched white Formica surface. I'd say it was circa 1974.

Just so you know, we're seated on stools with cracked red vinyl cushions. These, I'd guess, are vintage 1960s.

She loads and ejects the CDs, one after another at a rapid-fire pace. Mixed in with Cookie's MRIs are a number of plain X-rays. After reviewing each study—zooming in and out on the pertinent anatomy—she takes the CDs and begins placing them back in their respective sleeves. The review takes eight minutes.

"I assume you don't want to show me anything?"

"Have you looked at them?"

"Yes."

"Well, after all these years, I'm sure I've trained you well. We both see the same thing, don't we?"

"I believe so."

"Well, what did you see?" she probes. She and Mick both love to do this to me.

"The first post-op set showed the surgeon improperly screwed hardware into an unintended joint space. It also reveals a collection of fluid at the C4 level. Subsequent study showed the fluid collection, whether it be blood or CSF, had spontaneously reabsorbed. The studies after her corrective surgeries show the removal of the offending screw and restabilization of the fusion that never took. Those images appear to be normal at the C4 level where there had been this fluid collection."

"That's what I see, too. Not such a big case, if you ask me, despite the prolonged course of treatment and multiple surgeries. Bone-healing insufficiencies, such as delayed and nonunion, are a known postoperative complication. The most recent studies show acceptable alignment and bone union where the nonunion was. She must be close to healed by now."

"Yeah, she's good enough to dance. But it's what's not imaged in the studies that's giving me the problem."

"I'm listening. Tell me what isn't imaged that you think should be."

"Okay. Here's the deal. According to the defendant surgeon, the patient sustained an injury into the subarachnoid space at the level of C4, causing an intraoperative leak. Now he didn't say this in his operative report, but he testified to such at his deposition."

Ray shakes her head. "That's unheard of."

"Yes. I agree." It's unanimous.

"But the first post-op MRI did image a fluid collection at that level, so maybe he knew he had to give that."

"I agree. Also, this nurse who'd been in the OR came forward and advised Cookie and her boyfriend while she was still in the hospital that Dr. McElroy had caused the injury. Anyway, about six months later, Cookie starts feeling pressure in her head, and Major, this retired doctor she lives with, starts tapping her on his own."

"Spinal tapping?" she questions in apparent disbelief.

"Yes. Spinal tapping. Privately. He's been doing it weekly, continuous to this day. It's sick. I've seen it. I've even made a video of it. He performed the procedure in my office."

"So what are you saying here? That these subsequent MRIs should show some form of defect in the arachnoid layer at C4 that's causing an obstruction of CSF flow and a backup of fluid to her brain?"

"That's exactly what I'm saying. Or at least an abnormal collection of fluid arising at that level if a defect is not visible."

"Well, other than the initial post-op MRIs from McElroy's operation—the first series showing the fluid collection at C4 and the second documenting the expected reabsorption of the fluid, neither having strong evidence of an arachnoid membrane tissue defect—none of the subsequent studies show a fluid collection at C4 or strong evidence of an abnormal arachnoid either. However on some of them, where the base of the brain was incidentally imaged, I did see the presence of increased spinal fluid that might require tapping if clinically indicated. But there was no visible explanation for it or anything indicating that it arose from lower down at the C4 level. So you know better than to ask me to come to court on this case, right?"

"Right," I agree. "I know better."

"Good. That's why it's impossible to cross-examine me. I say what I see, and no one could ever make me change my mind."

"I'm with ya." I put the CD sleeves together. While I'm doing that, a gray cat with yellow eyes and a patch of white on its throat jumps up on the table.

"That's Tinkerbell." She scratches her ears. "I found her barely alive on Fifty-Third and Eleventh. She was just lying there, and people were walking right on by. She's my favorite. Bright, affectionate, and understanding. But sometimes she'll scratch you for no good reason."

"That's nice of you, Ray. Are all of these rescues?"

"Every one."

As I'm at the door and she's throwing back the locks to let me out, I think about all that we've just discussed. "You've helped a lot," I tell her.

"I don't see how. I could talk about the screw extending into the joint and the initial fluid collection. Still, I understand there being no strong evidence of any defect at C4 impeding the circulation of the cerebral spinal fluid is against the interests of your client, if you're claiming that as an item of damages."

"Correct. But it's weird because, like I said, I actually saw him do it right in my office. 'It's time for tap,' Major said when he saw her taking a downward course."

"That's a dark expression, isn't it?"

"It sure is, and what followed was even darker." After the memory of what I witnessed skates across my brain, I realize I have another question for her.

"Several times you've used the phrase 'no strong evidence' with regard to whether there's a tissue defect at C4. Is there *any* evidence of an arachnoid membrane abnormality at that level?"

"There's a hint of something there. I almost had to convince myself I was actually seeing it. I'm just not confident in saying what it is or what it isn't with a reasonable degree of medical certainty.

It could easily be a normal anatomical variant. But I am certain whatever it is, given its miniscule size, could not cause a backup of CSF into the skull. May I suggest something?"

"Please."

"There are conditions other than a mechanical blockage from a tissue defect that can cause CSF to build up, requiring a spinal tap. These involve the overproduction of fluid and the failure of fluid to properly drain. You may want to explore such alternative explanations for the tapping."

"Sounds like a plan. Only thing is, I want the tapping to be related to the malpractice so she can collect for it. Can overproduction or the failure to drain be related to a surgical misadventure?"

"Highly unlikely."

"Why's that?" I ask.

"Because it's physiologic."

"Meaning?"

"In simple terms, on a chemical level the body just produces too much cerebral spinal fluid. Or something's going on that's interfering with the reabsorption of fluid."

14.

need to check in with Lily, make sure the office is still there. I'm also not too far from Cookie's part of town. No time like the present to discuss Ray's findings with them—or actually, with Major. As of this morning, by hand delivery, the tap video is in the possession of First Medical Liability, McElroy's carrier. So, no doubt, they're going to be reevaluating their two-fifty offer while also mounting a defense based on what they see.

Anyway, I want to hear what Major has to say about this—the lack of objective MRI evidence that could be responsible for the accumulation of cerebral spinal fluid. After all, he's the tap-master. I'll need to have something up my sleeve when First Medical claims it's unrelated to the malpractice.

On the fifth ring, Lily picks up. "Law office. We're on the side of truth and justice. May I help you?"

"That's an interesting way to answer the phone."

"What can I tell you? I'm bored."

"I can think of a few things for you to be doing."

"Never mind that. What do you want?"

"Pull up Cookie's phone and address, will you?"

"Yeah, but I think there's something you should know."

"On Cookie's case?"

"That's who we're talking about, right?"

"Yes, Lily. But what should I know?"

"It's not good news. You got a letter from First Medical Liability today. They pulled the two hundred fifty thousand off the table. It said the time period within which to accept the offer expired, so now you'll have to litigate the case."

"You're right, that's not good news. When is the letter dated?"

"Two days ago."

"No worries. You delivered the video this morning, right?"

"I did, along with a copy of Major's medical records, as instructed."

"Good. They'll have a change in position. A big one."

"Okay. Listen, I'll text you her contact information. I'm busy."
Click.

Well, is she bored or busy? Whichever, Cookie's contact information magically appears on my phone. I give her a call, letting it ring off the hook. No answer. I hop in a cab uptown, thinking I might as well head over there, imaging studies in hand, in the event Major wants to review them himself after I share Ray's interpretation.

Within a few minutes, I arrive at the impressive high-rise building. One white-gloved guy opens the door for me. Another one's standing behind a black marble reception counter. Yet a third fellow, also white-gloved, is seeing a trio of women onto the elevator. "May I help you?"

"Yes, you may. I'm here to see Cookie and Major."

"Really?" He's clearly surprised.

"Um, yes, really. If they're here, that is. Why?"

"Only because they don't entertain visitors."

"I'm sure they've had guests occasionally."

"Actually," he says, "no." Then for emphasis: "Not ever."

He seems pretty confident about this. I could question how long he's worked here, his hours, point out the fact that maybe one person may have visited when he was off, or ask some other lawyer-type question aimed at trying to prove that it could be possible that someone once came when he wasn't on duty, but then I'd be just like the rest of the have-to-be-right lawyers I know. I take the high road. "Well, let's give them a buzz and see what happens. Wouldn't you be curious to know if they'll accept a visitor?"

"Now that you mention it," he confesses, "I actually would." He picks up the phone and rings their apartment. "I know Major's out," he says, as he waits for a response, "and I think you got a better shot at getting upstairs without him there, anyway. In fact," he continues reflectively, "since Cookie moved in, not even Jimmy the super has been in their apartment. The truth is, Major even comes down to pick up any deliveries."

Remember what I said about doormen?

He's listening to the phone now. "Yes, Miss Cookie." He nods at me. "There's a gentleman here to see you." He listens to her response. "No," he says, "I forgot to ask him. We were talking about something. Hold on."

Taking my cue, I say, "Tell her it's Wyler. Tug Wyler, her lawyer. I was in the neighborhood and have something I need to discuss with her."

"Miss Cookie," he says, "Tug Wyler, your lawyer, wants to talk to you."

He waits for a response. I can tell he's anxious. A few seconds pass. Time enough for her to have answered him. But nothing. A minute passes. Still nothing. The doorman's just holding the phone to his ear, giving an occasional wave to the tenants coming and going. At the ninety-second mark, he shrugs. At a minute forty-two, he responds, "Okay, Miss Cookie, I will."

"This is a first," he states, shaking his head. He seems shocked, even. "Go on up to thirty-four B. I can hardly believe it. What kind of lawyer are you, anyway?"

"I'm an injury lawyer. You know, construction accidents, car accidents, slip-trip and falls, or strip-slip and falls as the case may be; people getting hurt when it's someone else's fault. But I specialize in brain damage injuries and medical malpractice."

"Oh, man, my auntie got messed up in the hospital just yesterday."

I hand him a card from my wallet. As he goes to tuck it away, I say, "Hold on." Taking out a pen, I hand it to Wilson (as his lapel tag reads). "Write your name, address, and phone number down on the back of the card," I tell him. "Also write down your aunt's name, address, and phone number, and what hospital she's in. Give me the name and number of her closest relative, too."

He complies and I take the card back from him. "I'll call ya tomorrow," I say, returning it to my wallet. Thirty-four B, here I come.

"Thanks," he says. He's trying to figure out why I didn't just give him a card. I leave him still wondering.

The reason I didn't simply give Wilson my card is because I'd never be certain what happened if no call ever came. By getting the information, if I don't lock up the case, I'll know the reason why. In the injury business, where you have to wait for an unfortunate mishap to occur, you never leave the signing to chance.

I step out of the elevator on her floor and mosey down the hallway to Major and Cookie's door. I press the buzzer and hear a faint yelp. The door opens a crack and Cookie looks out over the chain.

"Are you all right?" I ask. "I thought I heard a scream."

She laughs.

"Yeah," she says, giggling, "that was me. I'm fine. I just never heard the buzzer before. It startled me. Come in." She shuts the door, undoes the chain, and reopens it.

I enter the apartment, which is gorgeous. "Let's sit over here," she says. I follow her into an open-plan living room with breathtaking city views all around. It's wall-to-wall windows. Wow.

"Nice view," I say, playing it cool. But I'm impressed.

"Thank you," Cookie says. It's clear from her tone that she's a little embarrassed to be living in such an apartment. "Can I offer you anything to drink?"

"No, but thanks. I'm okay."

She slowly moves closer and prepares to sit next to me on the oversize sofa. She bends at the knees, puts here rear down on the edge of the couch keeping her spine straight, then slowly shimmies back. She turns her stiff upper body toward me, scratches her head with a finger where one of the halo screws is penetrating her skull, and smiles encouragingly, prompting me to start.

"I came here to update you on your case. I hope I'm not imposing or interrupting anything, but I was in the neighborhood."

She giggles again. "Um, I really don't know how to respond to that." A hint of confusion crosses her face.

"Meaning?"

"Well, it's just that no one has ever come here before. Major's a private man and, although he's never said so, it's always been understood visitors aren't really welcome."

"Not even your friends?"

"Not even my friends. When I first moved in, I'd ask about having people over, and Major would just tell me maybe another time. I kept trying until I realized another time was never going to come. I guess that's why the buzzer scared me. And when it buzzed, the truth is, I felt sad because I realized I've never had a visitor." She takes a deep breath, then lets it out in what I'd call a reflective sigh.

"Anyway," she continues, "I tried Major on his cell when Wilson said you were downstairs. When he didn't pick up, which is unusual, I just told Wilson to let you up. I hope Major doesn't get upset with me."

"I don't know him that well," I respond, "but I'm sure he'll be okay with this. Besides, it's in the interest of your case. So let me update you."

As I say this, though, I realize she's uneasy. "What's wrong?" I ask.

"Could we wait 'til Major comes back before we go into my case? We shouldn't have to wait too long. He never leaves me alone for more than a little bit. That way you won't have to do it twice."

"Sure. I'm good with that."

"Thank you," she says, and then the conversation stops. What follows is an uncomfortable lull. It's not that she's uncomfortable with me, or that I'm uncomfortable with her. What's obvious is that she can't stop being worried about what Major's reaction's going to be when he finds me here.

"Don't worry," I reassure her. "I'll make him understand why I dropped in. It'll be fine."

"No, I know, it's just that . . . oh nothing, forget it." She has something she wants to tell me. The incomplete and filtered stuff I sensed she was leaving out at my office is my guess. Should I make it easy? Or should I let her come out with it on her own, hoping she'll be able to muster the strength to do so.

I'm sensing she wants to spill her guts, but that's my trial lawyer's intuition. I could always be wrong. It might just be the fact that she's never been alone with anyone long enough to share how she really feels about what's happened to her.

"It's just," she continues, "having a visitor here, even though it's only you, no offense . . ." She pauses. I wait encouragingly.

"Well, Wilson calling to say someone's here, my own doorbell scaring me, having a real live person in my living room, and being nervous about Major's reaction, well . . . I just have no life!" Cookie exclaims. The tears make a bursting arrival. Holy crap. I didn't expect this.

"Easy, Cookie," I say, thinking under normal circumstances I'd move to comfort her, despite lacking skills in that department. But under these circumstances, such an act is definitely a bad move. I could just imagine Major entering, only to find his first-ever visitor in an embrace with his prized jewel. Better to keep her talking. She wants to vent, anyway.

"Cookie," I say, "what do you mean you have no life?"

"Look at me!" she exclaims. Everything about her suddenly radiates an intensity I didn't know she had in her.

"I'm looking. You're a beautiful, wonderful woman who met with an unfortunate accident. Remember, I was at the club the night you made your comeback, and I saw how well loved you are.

You're the queen of the place. They love Cookie the person, not just Cookie the exotic dancer. You'll get past this situation. I'm sure you will. And Major's . . ."

As soon as I say his name, she falls apart further.

That's it. It's Major she's talking about when she says she has no life.

"Things are good with you and Major, right?" What she's harboring is a repression I need to understand.

"Major's a wonderful man. I'm lucky to have him in my life." Her weeping now intensifies, a behavior inconsistent with her assertion.

I say nothing, preferring to wait to see where she's going with this.

"I love him. But I'm a prisoner. He's too old for me. Don't you think I know that? Don't you think I know that every person who sees us together thinks the same thing? That I'm a kept woman. I mean, why else would a girl like me be with a man his age? Right? Why else? For the money. And then there's the fact of what I do— the stripper with the rich old guy! I know what people think."

Then, suddenly, she's spent from the shock of saying all that aloud. I can see it. But her crying continues. It's the first time I've ever seen her other than cheerful, accepting, excessively polite.

She swallows hard. There's more to come.

"Are you going to tell me you didn't think that the night you met Major and me?" Man, oh man.

I'm going with the truth. She deserves it, and anything less just isn't going to be believable. I don't want her thinking her lawyer's a liar.

"I have to admit, that's what crossed my mind when I first saw you two together."

"See. I told you!" She bursts out, "But, that's not it!" It's so loud that if Major had been outside the door, he certainly would've heard.

"Of course, that's not it," I say consolingly.

"But if that's not it, then aren't you wondering why I'm with him?"

"Um, well, now that we're into this conversation, yes, I do wonder, actually. So, tell me, why are you with him?" She looks at me.

It's the look one person gives another when they're about to confess something deep and dark.

The suspense is killing me, but I need to give her a way out. "Listen," I say, "you don't have to do this. We hardly know each other and—"

"Because he taps me!"

"Because he taps you?" I repeat.

Why am I not surprised? Maybe because my instincts had locked onto this already. "Time for tap." It makes perfect sense.

"Because he does it when I need it. And that's, like, all the time. Do you know what my life would be like if I had to run to a hospital every time? And hope to get there before my brain bursts? That's what keeps me here. Not his money, not this apartment, and even though he's a lovely man, I'm not with him because of that. And the thing is, I'm my own prisoner. It's my condition. I'm a slave to it, yet I resent Major because I'm so dependent on him. It's twisted, I know."

Her crying now reaches epic proportions, indicating it was well overdue.

"Here, let me get you a tissue. Please."

"No, I'll get it." She starts a labored shimmy to the edge of the couch.

"No," I say, "I'll get it. You just relax. Where's the bathroom?"

"Over there," she responds, pointing behind her, finger over her shoulder. I look and see two doors. I walk back to check. "This one?"

"Yeah, that one." But she isn't, in fact, looking.

I open the door and it's a bedroom. A female bedroom. "In here?"

"Yes, in there." She's still not looking.

I enter.

Pretty Far-Fetched

So they definitely don't share a bedroom. This is Cookie's alone. Suddenly, the edge of my jacket gets caught on a decorative plant holder, tipping it forward. I catch it before it topples over but not before several pots fall and crash to the floor. Shit. Now there's a bunch of depotted prickly plants surrounding my feet with soil dust mushrooming up.

"What was that?" Cookie calls out.

"Um, I accidently knocked a few plants off your plant stand. It was top-heavy and—"

"Plant holder? You've got the wrong door," she corrects me.

"Sorry. No worries. I'll take care of it." I'm hoping I can restore order before she has a chance to see what a mess I made. And even more importantly, before Major arrives to find me in her bedroom. I slide the plant rack back into position, then quickly pot and reshelve four of the strange-looking thorny flowering plants. The soil is dry and dusty, not moist. As I reach down to finish repotting the last three, I hear the front door open.

Holy Aphrodite! Crap! Major!

"Cookie! I'm home!" he yells. "Everything okay? I saw I missed your calls and rushed right back. My cell had run out of battery . . . and I understand we have a visitor."

"I'm fine," she says. "Don't worry." She's pulled herself back together. Thank God. I'm now shoving dirt into the next to last pot as fast as I can, ignoring the dust permeating my nostrils and the lenses of my contacts.

"Hey, Cookie," he says, "Where's . . ." Starting to ask where I was, he's suddenly distracted before completing the sentence. "Hey! What's your door doing open?"

This question has a troubled tone. I hear determined footsteps approaching. Uh-oh. I have one plant in hand and one still to go. Plus the dirt I have to wipe up.

Tell me this isn't happening.

As he enters, I'm on my hands and knees in mid-scoop. I look up.

"Hi."

"What happened here?"

Even I can't wait to hear what my explanation sounds like.

"Well, Cookie needed a Kleenex, and I mistakenly thought this was the bathroom. My jacket got caught on the pointed metal leaf on this iron thing and tipped it over, and I just . . ."

"I see," Major says, seeming sympathetic to my plight. "You can put that plant down, and I'll take care of the rest later." I do as I am told. I walk out past him, and he closes the door with authority. He doesn't slam it, merely closes it with a firmness, as if to say, "You stay shut."

We walk over to Cookie. She's miraculously herself again and looks as if she hadn't just broken down feeling the strains and conflicts of her situation. However, since she obviously wouldn't want Major to know what we were talking about, let's hope he isn't interested in exploring why she needed a tissue.

I feel like a kid who got caught with his hand in the Cookie jar, if you'll pardon my pun.

"So, what brings you here?" he inquires. Reasonably, I might add.

"Well, I was in the neighborhood after meeting with my expert radiologist to review the case. So I didn't think you guys would mind if I dropped by and gave you an update."

"That's fine." Good, he's not mad, and I'm in the clear. "Do you drop by all your clients' homes to update them on their cases?"

Hmm. Maybe I jumped to the wrong conclusion.

"No, I don't, actually. But there's something here I'm still struggling with. And since you're a doctor, in addition to everything else, I'm hoping you'll be able to offer guidance. I just know I'm going to hear from the insurance carrier on the issue," I add.

I'm also thinking that at some point during this meeting, I'm obligated to tell them about the withdrawal of the offer. But not now. I have to set it up first.

"The thing is, I'm going to need a good counter to what I anticipate as their position."

"Well, I'll do the best I can. What, specifically, did you go over with this radiologist?"

"Cookie's imaging studies. What they show and what they don't show."

"Then let's see if I can help. However, as you know, I'm not a radiologist."

"Yes, I appreciate that," I answer. "But do you read MRIs?"

"Not to any degree that I'm comfortable with."

"Okay, well here's the deal. We're claiming there's a mechanical obstruction at the C4 level that's acting like a dam, causing CSF to back up into Cookie's skull. Right?"

"Yes, I believe that to be the mechanics. But don't forget McElroy put a screw into an unintended joint space, as well."

"Yes, of course. This I know, and it was imaged—meaning, we have objective proof of this. Yet, according to the subsequent surgery report, that error was corrected. So the largest part of the damages here is the permanency associated with lifelong continued spinal tapping. Correct?"

"It would certainly seem that way."

"Okay. Now it's a given that McElroy caused an injury and a CSF leak at the C4 level at the time of his surgery. And it's also a given that there was a fluid collection at this level on the immediate post-op MRI. The presence of fluid imaged at C4 clearly supports our position. But the thing that troubles me," I go on, "is that none of Cookie's studies to date, inclusive of this first MRI, show strong evidence of an arachnoid membrane tissue abnormality at this level that could cause such a backup. So, to me at least, it's kind of a mystery as to what's causing the need for the spinal taps."

"I see what you mean. Is your expert a neuroradiologist?" This is a brilliant inquiry.

"No."

"Is there *any* evidence of a tissue abnormality at this level at all?" Brilliant question number two.

"The answer is yes. There's a hint of an abnormality at C4, but my expert cannot say what this finding is with a reasonable degree of medical certainty. And whatever it is, she doesn't believe it could cause a backup of fluid into the skull, given its small size."

"I see. Did any of the MRIs image an unusually large collection of CSF within the skull?"

"Yes, but my expert couldn't identify the source or reason for the excessive amount of fluid."

"I see. Then why don't we just wait and see if the insurance company makes an issue of it?" This question is almost, but not quite, a reasonable one.

"That's one approach. But I'd rather be fully prepared right from the start in the event it does get raised. It's my nature. Besides, putting the lawsuit aside for a second, let's focus, instead, on Cookie's health and well-being. My expert, although not a neuroradiologist, is the best reader in town. When she became board certified, there was no such subspecialty, but she possesses the same qualifications. She allows that there could be alternate explanations as to why this problem is occurring. Maybe it would be in Cookie's best interest to have a full workup. You know, cerebral spinal fluid culture and a bunch of other stuff to see if this is an overproduction or a failure-to-drain issue, rather than mechanical blockage."

"That's an excellent suggestion," Major replies without hesitation. He turns to Cookie. "I'll send some of your fluid to the lab after the next tap and have it analyzed as a first step. Then, we'll take it from there."

She nods and he continues, "I guess we should be thankful that we have such a thorough lawyer on our side. The issue was never even raised by Chris Charles. But, quite frankly, it's not such a mystery, as you put it."

"I'm listening. Educate me. I know when they view that video they're going to go balls-out in denying any causal connection to the malpractice." I'm choosing my words carefully but, given that I framed Cookie's perfect lovelies, it ain't easy.

"So, let's hear it," I continue. "Oh, and before I forget, it's my obligation to inform you of any material developments, and so you need to know that they have withdrawn that two-hundred-and-fifty-thousand-dollar offer."

There, it's out. The idea was to gain a bit of advantage by telling them the MRI evidence isn't supporting their case, and implying that fact accounts for the withdrawal of the offer. Even if there's no relation between the two. To further distract, I then was asking this retired doctor, a guy with no expertise in reading MRIs, to present an alternative explanation.

I'm not proud of taking this approach, but I had to do something.

Cookie doesn't look happy. She hops right on it.

"Did you just say they took the money off the table?"

"Yes, yes I did."

"Um, Mr. Wyler, when did they take the money off the table?"

"I received the letter today. But not to worry. I also delivered our tap video today, together with Major's records. So, before this morning, the only thing they had relative to our largest item of damages was a mere statement in a legal pleading, and a medical history of recurrent tapping documented in the medicals. Now, with the exchange of Major's records and the video, it is very real to them. I'm confident the money will flow and will flow big."

"Are you sure?" she asks. Her tone is one of disbelief.

"Positive, don't worry." I don't blame her, though. Her prior attorney works the case for three years and achieves a two-fifty offer. I'm on the case for just a short stint and that money's now gone. Not to mention that, in the last ten seconds, I've told her defense counsel will go balls-out in denying a causal connection for the tapping, yet at the same time promising the money will flow big. The rules of evidence call this prior inconsistent statements. The legal inference is not good. Talking out of both sides of my mouth to my clients is something I promised myself I'd never do. But I do it now.

What's worse, it's in my own defense, and that makes me a shithead.

At least I admit it. But this admission gives me no solace.

She's not done.

"The thing is, I remember Mr. Benson saying their threat to pull the money off the table was just a negotiation ploy, that it never happens, and that the money would always be there—and you agreed. Twice."

I feel like a heel. Such a sum probably represents more than she's earned in her entire life. "But not to worry. I assure you that video we made tells a chilling story."

I turn back to Major, hoping to move away from this sore topic and the guilt I'm trying to ignore. The only way I can remedy this is to fight hard and achieve a large recovery for her. "So, picking up where we left off"—I'm now addressing Major—"tell me why the MRI finding isn't such a mystery."

Like Cookie, he's not happy. But he clears his throat. "Well, first, the MRIs could be false negatives. You have to appreciate we're talking about a microscopic injury, so it could be present but just not imaged. You see, the only definitive way to identify the abnormality would be to do a study while her syndrome was in progress—in real time. And that cannot be done without substantial risks, given the technical difficulties presented in performing an MRI during the course of evolving cranial pressure and tapping. Do these explanations help you out any?"

"Yes, they do. But it'd still be nice to have a recent objective test confirming the injury I'm claiming has occurred."

"Well, she has the clinical manifestations of her injury. That's pretty objective, as you've seen for yourself."

"That's true. But, like I said, what's on my mind now is our little homemade video. It should set the scene for a big payday, but at the same time it will undoubtedly also trigger an aggressive defense. They may even seek to compel Cookie to have further medical examinations at their behest. The best way they could defend this horrible aspect of the damages would be to claim that the repeated and continued tapping is unrelated to the care Dr. McElroy rendered to her. A black-and-white causation defense.

"In a medical malpractice case in the state of New York," I

begin to explain, "you have to prove both that the doctor departed from good and accepted medical practice in his care and treatment of his patient, *and* that this departure was a substantial factor in causing injury to the patient."

Major gives me a look. "I'm not a lawyer, but a causation defense sounds pretty far-fetched." For emphasis, he even gives me a snort of contempt. "Before McElroy's surgery, Cookie never had a tap. He cut into the arachnoid membrane causing a CSF leak at the time of the surgery. A fluid collection is imaged at the level of injury in the immediate MRI. Within a short time after, she began to require weekly tapping. Your own expert finds a tissue abnormality at C4, albeit, just a hint. It seems pretty open and shut."

"I admit you share the opinion of another of my experts, who came to the same conclusion. But, all I can say is: welcome to my world. In a malpractice case, the use of a causation defense is the best way to disassociate the malpractitioner from the worst of the injuries. Here, according to my radiology expert, a causation defense would involve Cookie somehow overproducing CSF or there being a compromise in her ability to drain the cerebral spinal fluid, both unrelated to McElroy's operation and both arising from some other trigger."

"That seems a bit out there." Major, I sense, is just a little uneasy.

"Out there, maybe. We'll just have to wait and see what happens." I look at Cookie and see she's still upset about the two-fifty.

"Um," she says to me, "the details are a little beyond my understanding. But are you really saying my tapping might be necessary for a different reason and not my surgery?"

"It's possible. How probable, I can't say. But it's definitely within the realm of medical possibility."

"And do you think there could be a cure if we found out why this was happening?"

"That, too, is always possible." A glimmer of hope flashes across her face—the prospect of freedom, no doubt. Major catches it and cuts in.

"Cookie, dear, I intend to send your fluid to the lab as a starting point, and then we'll begin to investigate things from there. I don't like feeling I've overlooked anything. It's only that I never would have considered alternate explanations, given what I know. Still, it's always good to get a fresh look at things, and so we are fortunate to have met Mr. Wyler. Nonetheless, I continue to have my reservations about an alternate explanation."

Having delivered this little monologue, Major hands the floor back to me.

"All I wanted to do is bring the weak radiological evidence to your attention as soon as possible and ask you to consider that more may be going on here than we're aware of. Understood?"

They nod.

I continue. "From a legal strategic point of view, any attempts to discover an alternate explanation for the tapping should be undertaken on the down low. Meaning you should pay cash for the medical services. Don't put any medical costs associated with this undertaking on Cookie's insurance. If it becomes documented there, McElroy's attorney will see it and obtain the records. So, if we're able to come up with an alternate cause as to why this is happening to Cookie that's unrelated to McElroy's malpractice, I don't want his attorney to know about it. The insurance company will not consider or pay on our largest item of damages if it's unrelated to McElroy's care."

Cookie's now listening carefully. I feel like a scumbag for saying any of this. But the truth is it's up to the defense attorneys to disprove our claim.

"They pay only for damages they are responsible for or cause," I explain. "So you see, we're straddling the line here between getting Cookie cured, if that's possible, and at the same time keeping the insurance company out of the loop. I'm pretty sure that's legal. Anyway, that's about it for now. I'm sorry about their withdrawing the offer, though I'm expecting it to be only temporary once they view the video. I also apologize if I imposed myself on you two."

"Not at all," Major says.

"No, not at all," echoes Cookie who, while still upset about the money, now has the unexpected hope of a cure to think about. I leave the apartment wishing I could hear the conversation after I'm gone.

On my way out of the building, Wilson sees me. "Well? What happened up there?" By his tone, I'm pretty sure he wants to share something. I slip him a twenty.

He leans toward me, "Major wasn't very happy when he heard you were upstairs."

"And?"

"That's it."

"That's it?"

"Yes, sir."

"That ain't no biggie, Wilson." He looks around and leans in.

"You got another twenty?" I fork it over.

"Listen, I've known the guy for seven years," he says. "Even when his mother died, he showed no emotion. But I will say it again—he was a very unhappy camper when he learned you were in his apartment. Very. Something's up."

"Got ya." I walk out the door, thinking if he says "something's up," then something's up.

After all, he's a doorman.

15.

ince dropping in on Cookie and Major two days ago, I can't get them to return a call. I've left a total of six messages—three each day—asking them to contact me. This is not a good sign. I take a deep breath and stretch, having slept late this morning, which almost never happens. My internal alarm clock hasn't gone off. It's 7:42, according to the digital one. My wife's up and out. I didn't even hear her leave.

Before getting out of bed, I note I feel a little lethargic. Maybe that's why I've dozed too long. My chest feels tight, too. I've felt this coming on over the last twenty-four. It's no time to get sick.

The kids are seated around the kitchen table. They're watching the birds on the feeder out on our patio. Why did it have to be imported bluestone? "Because."

"Dad," Penelope says, "how come the boy birds have so many colors, and the girl birds don't?" I follow her line of sight. There's a male rose-breasted grosbeak pecking for sunflower seeds. He's regal, with his black-and-white markings contrasted by his red-feathered chest. On the other side of the feeder is his mate. She's gray and could be mistaken for the female of about ten other types of birds.

"Well, Penelope . . ." I begin.

"It's Summer," she corrects me, "and that's the last time I'm going to tell you."

"Do you really want me to call you Summer?" Before she answers, Connor looks at me, trying to determine if, in fact, I mean my question. I show him a poker face.

"Yes, I do."

"Then I'll respect your wishes and call you Summer until instructed otherwise." She beams. I look to Connor. He can tell I'm not happy about giving in.

"Dad," he says.

"Yes, Dirk," I say, understanding I'm obliged to play along with his name change, too.

"You don't have to call me Dirk anymore. You can call me Connor again."

"Okay, Connor." Summer seems a little surprised at her brother but looks back at me, still waiting for an answer to the bird question. "It usually has to do with their mating or courtship, meaning how the female chooses the male as her partner."

"You mean in the bird world the girl chooses the boy?"

"I'm pretty sure of that, yeah."

"That's weird; it's just the opposite with people."

"What do you mean?"

"You know," she says, "the boy chooses the girl."

"Is that what you think?"

"Yeah."

"It won't be long before you know otherwise," I say, feeling an unpleasant sense of pressure in my chest.

"Dad?"

"Yes, Summer?" She gives a thanks-for-calling-me-Summer look.

"Nothing."

I head out the door wondering why the kids are home on a school day and my phone goes off. *Private Caller*.

"Hi, Robert," I answer.

"This is Robert Killroy, but I didn't kill no Roy, and I didn't kill nobody."

"Thank you, Robert. I know that already. First let me ask, is this call in connection with your own case or is it a collection-related call?"

"I must advise you that I am calling to collect a debt." His delivery is choppy. "This call may be recorded and anything you say—"

"Robert," I cut in, "I know the drill by now. How can I help you? Please, make it quick. I'm late this morning. And I say that talking to you the bill collector, not you my client, since you wear two hats here."

"I'm not wearing no hat, Mr. Wyler."

"It's a figure of speech. But go on, just finish, please."

"I must advise you that if payment isn't made within the next seven days, I will have no choice but to . . . I can't read this part; give me a second . . . Granny! Granny!" I hear him call out.

"Robert!" I yell. "Robert!"

"Yes, Mr. Wyler."

"Is the next word spelled *I-N-S-T-I-T-U-T-E*?"

"How'd you know that? You done bill collecting before you started lawyering?"

"No, Robert, I just know. And the words after that are 'formal legal proceedings,' correct?"

·"Seems so. But I still got to check with Granny. Never got this far in bill collecting before. Everybody else done paid their debts, 'cepting you that is. That Mr. Wang sure is a nice man. I don't know why—"

"Robert, listen to me. If you were calling about your case, I'd stop what I was doing, but since you're not, I'm not. And I'm *not* paying that bill. I told you why. And tell Granny that I'm going to need you two to be present at a mediation that I was able to schedule. Got that?"

"Sure, I got that. But I never did no meditation before. I'll be seeing ya. I got to start this here lawsuit against you. I take my investigating seriously."

Click.

You Know I'm in Here Crying

I get to the office late. "Good morning, Lily," I say in a cheery voice, then proceed to have a violent coughing fit into my hand. I give myself a chest pat and take a deep breath. I hear a wheeze. Not good.

"You sound sick. And you're not going to like what's on your chair."

"What?" I say. "No 'good morning, Mr. Wyler? How are you today?' That ain't right."

"Go look on your chair. This is not a good morning for you."

"Give me a hint." I watch her consider this.

"Okay, one of the letters on your chair is an offer of settlement for two million dollars on Cookie's case."

"That doesn't sound so bad to me. And that wasn't a hint, by the way." She rolls her eyes, "as if it matters" being the clear message.

"It's the other letter you're gonna hate. It was hand-delivered by an attorney, Chris Charles." No playful Lily there. She's right, I fear. I hustle to my office, wheezing all the way. I'm concerned about why Charles would be delivering me a letter. Really concerned. I didn't push Lily because I could see she didn't want to tell.

This is bad.

I pick both envelopes up off my chair and sit down in the same motion. The top letter is the offer. Perfect, two mil. I guess all my worrying about the spinal tapping being unrelated to Cookie's claim was wasted energy. Just trying to be a good lawyer. First Medical Liability, the insurance carrier, references the tap video as the basis for the offer. No fucking kidding. It's a chilling procedure to watch, and they'd have to be crazy to go to a jury when I have that in my front pocket.

They go on to say that they had provided insurance coverage to Dr. Major Dodd and his clinic for over thirty years and that they respect his opinion on the matter. I wonder if they'd feel the same way if they knew Cookie and he are an item. A peculiar one, but an item nonetheless.

I turn my attention to the envelope delivered by Chris Charles. It's actually three different correspondences. The top one is handwritten. It reads:

> *Please take no further action on my case. You are hereby discharged as my attorney. Do not attempt to contact me. Please arrange for the prompt transfer of my file back to Chris Charles.*
>
> *Cookie*

Holy shit! This can't be happening.

I turn to the next page. It's a formal Consent to Change Attorney, substituting me out and Chris Charles back in. Damn! There goes a large chunk of my share of the attorney fee. Just like that. In one mail delivery.

Lily was right. She's always right.

The last page is a cover letter from Chris Charles referencing Cookie's handwritten letter and the Consent to Change Attorney. He adds that I should call to arrange for the transfer of Cookie's file, reiterating that I am not to contact her. He was also nice enough to give me the reason for my discharge, something that's never done in letters like this. But he's putting me on notice that my discharge is 'for cause.' Meaning, I get no fee, as I caused my discharge by conduct unbecoming an attorney.

Not this again.

The last and only other time a client claimed I was discharged for cause was the morning Cookie retained me. There, Josefina's dirtbag attorney, Wilbur, alleged I suborned perjury. In the hearing before Judge Brown, I preserved my fee by establishing Josefina's lack of credibility.

Now Charles is stating that I violated several codes of conduct by advising Cookie the two hundred and fifty thousand would never be pulled off the table. I don't know about "several," but he has a good argument on at least one—that's all he needs. It was the two *agreeds* Henry prompted out of me that are coming back to bite my ass. Hard. Still, I did it, albeit reluctantly, so I own this conduct.

At least I admit it.

The letter goes on to further state that Cookie directed me to accept the two fifty, and I refused to communicate her acceptance to the insurance carrier against her wishes. That part is an outright lie. But he'd written it believing that the money offer was gone, in order to set up a claim against me for legal malpractice. My, my.

But what I can see from here and he can't is now the circumstances have changed with two million on the table. I wonder how it's all going to play out. I'm discharged for alleged cause with two fifty on the table. However my efforts after the money is withdrawn yielded two million. I'd like to suggest it's a novel legal question. One that's going to be decided in my favor because Charles committed his basis for discharge to paper. The guy is a novice.

Lily buzzes.

"What's up? You know I'm in here crying." *Cough, cough.*

"I guess now would be a bad time to ask for a raise then."

"That's not funny, Lily."

"I guess you're right. Sorry." *Click.* My click, not hers.

Lily appears at my door and enters cautiously, knowing how upset I'm certain to be about losing Cookie's case. But I'm not going down without a fee-fight. It was my video and sending them Major's medical records, after all, that sparked the big offer. Charles handled it for years and snagged only the paltry two fifty. Me—I get it, do the one obvious thing that needs to be done so the largest item of damages can be properly evaluated, and two mil is thrown at me without even giving a settlement demand.

Dammit, he's going to have to fight it out in court for our respective shares. It's not necessarily the quantity of work performed;

the court also considers the quality and who was instrumental in getting the case done—and that would be me.

"Hello? Hello? Hello?" Lily says, standing in front of me. "Anybody in there?"

"Oh, sorry. I was just thinking about something." She tosses an unopened box of tissues on my desk.

"Let me guess," she says. She doesn't even have to spend time thinking. "How much of the fee you think you can keep on Cookie's case?" That's my Lily.

"You know me as well as I know myself. What are the tissues for?"

"Your fee-loss bereavement, your cold, either/or."

I'm feeling terrible right at this moment, emotionally and physically. "Listen, I've got to get outta here for some fresh air. I'm going down for tea. Want some?" *Cough, cough.*

"No, thanks. You better take care of that. I don't want you getting me sick."

"I appreciate the concern. That's what the tea is for."

Kau Cim

I enter Chicken-Wing Deli and smile as I always do, because the name brings up some nice childhood memories. "Ain't no big thing, chicken wing." I approach the register girl who doubles as the coffee girl.

"Usual?" she inquires.

"No. I need a tea." *Cough, cough.* "Feeling under the weather. How about a green tea with peppermint?"

She studies my face, mixes my brew.

"Thanks," I say, giving her the same good-bye smile I've flashed for a decade. But this time, it takes an effort. I'm not used to feeling sick, so I'm not very good at it. Plus, there's this Cookie business.

"What your problem?" she asks.

"What do you mean, Chi Chi?"

"Just asking, what problem? You got problem face."

"Just business, Chi Chi, just business."

"No. Chi Chi know you long time. You need see Betty." I admire her stripped-down, highly focused English, I must say. It'd cut my workday in half if I could talk like Chi Chi in court.

"Who's Betty?"

"Betty my mom. She have parlor on second floor. You see Betty." I know exactly who Betty is and what she does. Every Wednesday through Friday, there's a line running halfway down the street that forms at the entrance door to the second floor. They wait all day to see Betty, the Chinese psychic, whose neon sign blinks in one of the second-floor windows.

"Betty's your mom?"

"Betty Chi Chi mom. Call me Chi Chi after fortune sticks. You go see. Give advice, so you no worry. Maybe though, you worry more."

"I'll wait in line Wednesday, thanks."

"You go now."

"But today is Monday."

"Moment." She yells out, "Walter! Walter!" The deli order-taking counter guys all lean back, creating an unobstructed channel of communication. Standing at the end, watching over the operations, is an old guy who's worked at Chicken-Wing since the day it opened.

He screams something back. Chi Chi goes into overdrive, speaking a mile a minute. Eventually, after a great deal of excited back and forth, he pulls his phone out.

"What was that all about?"

"I ask Dad if Mom upstairs. He say yes."

"That's what your whole conversation was? Come on, Chi Chi. What else did you say?" *Cough, cough.*

"Nothing. You go upstairs. Take two apples. Give to Betty. No say from me. From you. Go."

"But the neon sign isn't lit."

"You go. She in." How can I refuse this? I always wanted a Chinese psychic reading and now's as good a time as any. Maybe she can tell me if I'm going to get a fee on Cookie's case.

"Thank you. I'm on my way up."

I walk out one door, take two steps, and look into the other door that provides access to this brownstone. It's dark. A second later, a light comes on. A second after that, an old Chinese lady, one whom I've seen many times, appears descending the steps. A man walking on the sidewalk stops and looks in. He moves behind me as if forming a line. He's wearing a dark blue suit and an ultra conservative striped tie. I've seen all types of professionals waiting in line to see Betty. Even a diplomat one time, as identified by the plates on his car.

"No," I tell him, "she's not open. Today is Monday." But before he can say anything, Betty opens the door. She steps out and dismisses him. Then she looks at me and nods.

"You come," she orders.

We walk up the stairs. "Oh," I say, "these are for you," handing her the apples. She takes them. "Chi Chi give you for me?"

"Uh, no."

"Good," she says, seeming satisfied. "You loyal to Chi Chi, but lie to me. Now, you loyal to me, too. Okay?"

"Okay," I answer. My chest is getting tighter by the second.

"Sit," she directs. She places herself opposite me. "You lawyer."

"Yes, I'm a lawyer. Right at first guess. You've got some skills."

"You funny. No guess. Chi Chi tell me you lawyer. Chi Chi tell me you have problem on face. Chi Chi right. She good student."

As I watch, she begins getting down to business. She picks up a bamboo cylinder half the size of the blue kaleidoscope I once had as a kid, purchased from the Museum of Modern Art. She shakes it a few times, and it rattles like a percussion instrument.

"What's that?" I ask.

"Kau Cim. Kau Cim."

"What's that mean?"

She shakes her head. "Be patient, lawyer. Stick inside make prediction. Stick inside tell future. Stick inside give you guidance." Now she shakes it seven or eight times, and I can see little pieces of wood jut out a hole in one side, then slide back in. On the tenth or so shake, a stick falls out, landing between us. I look at the four-sided piece of wood. It's about three inches long, red-tipped at one end, with Chinese characters running down its sides.

"Listen carefully," she begins. "You have much going on. All good, but you think bad. You in danger. Be careful. But you no die. Very funny, hee, hee, lawsuit save lawyer life. You live long time. You sick, take care of self. You have woman you help. Special message for special woman—no, girl. You teach her lesson. She learn good. You no worry. You mom get big worry, but you no worry."

I lean forward to hear more, but she's stopped. "That's it?"

"That's it."

"Well, what's good about the bad things? What am I in danger from? Take care of myself how? The woman I helped was Cookie, but who's the special girl? My daughter? And what's my mom worried about that I shouldn't worry about?"

"Answer inside." She points to my heart and then my head. "You go now. Today, Betty day off."

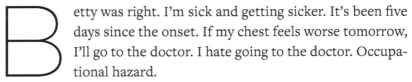

16.

Betty was right. I'm sick and getting sicker. It's been five days since the onset. If my chest feels worse tomorrow, I'll go to the doctor. I hate going to the doctor. Occupational hazard.

I arrive right on time at Adjudicate Services, Inc., the mediation company chosen by the defense counsel on Robert Killroy's case. A mediation is a nonbinding settlement conference, usually before a retired judge, where the rules of evidence don't apply. Therefore, I can say basically anything I want in an effort to get the case resolved. Stuff I'd never say before a jury. I was happy Rich Cohen chose Adjudicate because they know me there. *Well.*

The law charges a driver with the obligation to see what is there to be seen. The Jew van operator failed to do so. This, I assume, along with the mystery that Robert's basketball solved, have given rise to this quicker than usual mediation, despite his problem with testifying.

Regarding his ball, Robert testified it ended up underneath the van, which had stopped midturn within the entrance of the driveway. Just after impact, he popped up onto his uninjured foot and yelled at the driver to back his van up so he could get his signed ball, a gift from Ethel. The driver reversed out into the street until

Robert could see it under the front bumper. He hopped over in pain to get his cherished ball, sitting down next to it in the road-way, unable to move one more inch because of his injury.

His location there must've led the police officer to erroneously conclude that Robert had darted out into traffic from between parked cars.

Robert's case went from nothing to a big something simply because I did what I was supposed to do. I listened to my client, took the driver's deposition, and ascertained the full amount of insurance coverage. Had their prior attorney done this, in all likeli-hood, he would have earned a hefty fee, as well as the respect and gratitude of his client, not to mention becoming a poster boy for integrity in an area of law that's filled with schlemiels.

Anyway, I imagine Cohen and his insurance adjuster are here in an attempt to save money on their one-million-dollar excess pol-icy of insurance. That ain't happening—I've got Robert's financial independence to consider.

Before I walk in, I pull out my phone and speed-dial a favorite contact. I should've made this call the moment I left Betty and her fortune sticks.

"Hello."

"Hi, Mom," I say. "Is everything okay? Are you worried about anything?" *Cough, cough.*

"Yes. I'm worried my daughter-in-law is not properly taking care of my son by the sound of that cough. A little less tennis and a little more chicken soup wouldn't hurt."

"I can tell you're feeling fine."

"Yes, under the circumstances. Anything else? I'm on my way to Lenox Hill for some blood work."

"Nope. That's it." Her circumstances are a prolonged battle with breast cancer. She's a fighter, a real tough one.

Robert and Ethel are waiting in reception. He's sitting on the floor, legs wide-open, with five small bags of pretzels and three packs of chocolate chip cookies in between them. (Adjudicate provides courtesy snacks.) He's also wearing a fully loaded Batman-type utility belt and has his Bluetooth in his right ear.

"Morning, Ethel."

"Morning. You sure you doing this for free?"

"I meant what I said. But, remember, the deal is that you refer me to anyone you know who's been in an accident or who received bad medical care, right?"

"Right."

"Hey, Robert."

He looks up. "You owe Mr. Wang fourteen dollars and seventy-nine cents. He's a really nice man. I'd have sued you by now, but Granny ain't had the time to help me with the papers. You my first lawsuit. You gonna pay or am I gonna sue?"

"Sue me Robert, just sue me. I'm not paying." He frowns.

"Listen, guys, just sit quiet in there, please. Follow my lead, if need be, but let me work the room. Got it?" *Cough, cough.*

"Got it," Ethel says. I look to Robert.

"Fourteen dollars seventy-nine cents, plus filing fees. And I get fifty dollars directly for getting my serve in." I understand what he means is service of process.

We're shown into a large conference room. Sitting at the head of the table is the mediator, Allen Joseph. He's a retired New York State Supreme Court judge and is the number-one guy here. On the other side is attorney Rich Cohen. Gray hair, three-piece suit, midsixties, and a know-it-all air. The woman sitting next to him, I assume, is the adjuster. Mid-thirties, blonde, attractive.

We take our seats across from them. Normally, I have my clients sit in the waiting area while the negotiations take place. But not this time.

Allen Joseph looks to me to get started. "So, what's this case about? Given the short notice, both sides waived submissions, so I'm in the dark here."

Before I get a chance to answer, Rich Cohen makes himself

heard. "There's no way this accident could've happened in the manner the plaintiff testified." At this, he nods at Robert across from him. Robert's taking his cell phone apart on the table. There are roughly ten little pieces arranged in a straight line.

Judge Joseph now looks to me for rebuttal. The thing is, I'm not supposed to be rebutting. I'm the plaintiff. The plaintiff has the burden of proof, so in any form of legal proceeding the plaintiff speaks first. This is why Joseph posed the question to me. What's up with that, Rich? Feeling the need to be heard and to take control is the answer. That's my favorite type of defense counsel. The ones that walk right out into the middle of the quicksand. They sink the fastest.

"He would've had to be coming from the opposite direction," Rich states, "for the accident to have happened in the way the plaintiff testified." He nods at Robert again. His expression is both vehement and righteous.

Joseph looks to me, but I'm not fast enough.

"His opposite leg would've been the one struck if the accident happened in the way he testified," Rich states, relentless in his pursuit of justice. "I tell you, there's no way this accident could've happened in the manner he describes."

Robert's phone now is completely dismantled.

I'm not certain Rich is done big-mouthing, so I inquire, "Are you done yet, Rich?"

"Yes, I'm done. But this accident could not have occurred in the way your client testified," he repeats. "His opposite leg would've been closest to the van, and hence the one struck. He would have had to be going in the direction opposite to that testified."

"Rich, you can't say you're done and then continue on. That's not being done. That's being almost done. So are you finished now?"

"Yes."

"Could you say the words that confirm this for us, please?"

"Words? What words are those?"

"'There, now I'm done.' That's the phrase. I'm waiting until you say it." I look at Ethel, who grins. Rich, on the other hand, is annoyed. We wait a second as he decides.

"There, now I'm done," he says, grudgingly. I look to Judge Joseph, who shrugs.

I briefly consider starting with the fact that his driver didn't see Robert until impact, or that he failed to yield the right of way to a pedestrian on a sidewalk. Or even that, with the driver's acknowledgment, he backed out into the roadway after the accident so Robert could get his basketball, thus offering an explanation for the erroneous police diagram. But these are facts this lawyer and his insurance adjuster already know from the testimony. I mean, that's why we're here—they both realize they have a problem.

I plan, however, to start with something they don't know. It should cut things short and dismiss their silly notion of saving money. I pat my chest and clear my throat, beginning midlung. It hurts.

"So, Rich, are you stating that you accept and believe the testimony my client gave?" He snickers like he's got me on the ropes.

"Of course I believe it. Since the accident could never have happened that way, it makes the rest of his testimony also unbelievable. So, yes, I believe it. Don't you? He's your client."

I find this confusing. He accepts and believes Robert's testimony because he knows it's unbelievable? Isn't he *not* accepting it?

"I understand he's my client, but I also understand my client has a disability." The word *disability* catches the ear of the adjuster. Her posture changes from confident to uneasy. If there's one thing insurance adjusters hate, it's being involved in an injury case where the injured is mentally challenged—in short, the R-word that Granny and Robert have no qualms about using in daily conversation.

Insurance companies understand such victims can't fend for themselves and that this heightens the potential sympathy factor. Besides which, a special jury charge exists to help protect them.

Thus, they're not held to the ordinary standard of care of a reasonably prudent person but to a lesser one. That standard fluctuates to embrace the nature of the disability, and I'd suggest it may be a bit low here.

"So what are you saying here?" Rich wants to know.

"I haven't said anything yet, really. I've just been listening to you state your position, i.e., that the accident couldn't have happened the way Robert says. At the same time, you're relying on what he says to win your case. It doesn't make much sense to me. And I find it interesting that a defense attorney with your experience would be relying on my client's near incomprehensible testimony. I recognize the fact that it wasn't you yourself who took Robert's deposition, but certainly your associate, Ms. Kaufman, must have made the appropriate report regarding Robert."

Rich looks unsure of himself. The blonde is looking at him to save the day. I don't think so, honey. As for me, I think Rich is about to pose the one question a lawyer should never ask. The one you don't know the answer to. The one you especially don't raise in front of the person paying your bills.

"What's this boy's disability?" Rich asks. Thank you, dumbass.

I look at Granny. "Tell him, Ethel."

"Be glad to," she says. "My grandson over here is a little bit retarded." Robert looks up from his assemblage of electronic bits and pieces. His red bike helmet is on crooked.

"Yeah, I'm a little bit retarded. Ooh-dat! Ooh-dat! Ooh-dat!" he yells, as if on cue, chopping at his ankle in obvious pain.

Case settled.

Ethel was right. Rich ain't no bona fide lawyer.

Spit in This

Right from the mediation, I took Ethel and Robert downtown to the offices of Structure Solutions. There, we had a three-hour meeting with my structured settlement consultant, Brian Levine.

A structured settlement is where a portion of the proceeds is used to purchase an annuity that pays Robert in fixed sums, at specified intervals, over his lifetime. Guaranteed. Not only does the structure have tax benefits and cost-of-living increases, but it also does away with Robert attempting to manage his own money.

One thing I did insist on was immediate up-front money so he and Ethel can do a few things they haven't had the resources to do. They wanted only enough to buy a new bike for Robert and a new wig for Ethel. One she's had her eye on. It's purple. I persuaded them to take a small chunk more.

After cleaning things up at my office, I meet Mick at a gentlemen's club that just opened on Twenty-Third and Eleventh. It's called Boner's. The retired pro-football player and celebrity personality John Bonner opened it up. The second N in his name is hanging down below the other letters on the sign out front, looking like it's about to fall off. (I don't think this is on anyone's list to fix. Trust me.) We're meeting here in order to have the night out that keeps never happening.

I'd suggested The Palm for steaks, but Mick insisted the evening involve live entertainment, and we couldn't meet at Jingles. I didn't want to risk seeing Cookie. I intend to honor her directive not to contact her, even if the contact would be incidental.

Anyway, I feel like crap—a lot worse than I did at Robert's mediation this morning. I'm sick. Really, really sick. My chest feels like it's about to explode, and I've had horrible pressure headaches coming and going all afternoon.

When I walk in, after noting that the doorman and cashier here have friendlier dispositions than those at Jingles, I see Mick sitting alone at a table closest to one of the tips of the five-pointed star stage. At each of these points a tall dancing pole is affixed to the ceiling, and beautiful girls are performing sensual maneuvers on them. It reminds me of two things, both related. One is my life goal to keep my daughter, Penelope, off the pole. The second is that she's got a big dance audition coming up in the city right near my office, a commitment Tyler's now reminded me of twice, since it involves my participation.

I take a couple of steps, then have to stop. My chest. It hurts. My joints hurt, too. Maybe I have Lyme disease or something. Mick, seeing me hunched over with my hands on my knees, comes to check. He bends down, imitating my position, creating a two-man huddle.

He's tilting his head. I do the same. We lock eyes.

"What's the matter with you?"

"I'm sick. Probably a bad cold." *Cough, cough, cough.* "Let's sit down. I've got to give it a rest." We move toward his table. We began together, but he arrives three steps before me. I have a longer stride. You draw the conclusion.

"You look like shit," he says from across the tiny round table.

"Thanks. A Chinese fortune-teller predicted it."

"What?"

"Never mind." *Cough, cough, cough.* I look up at the girl on the pole three feet away from us. She's hot. No halo. *Cough, cough, cough.* And quite skilled. *Cough, cough.* Prior to meeting Cookie and witnessing how she connected with so many men in a very genuine way, I would have objectified and trivialized this pole dancer now before me.

At least I admit it. *Cough, cough, cough.*

"That sounds bad," she comments, looking down at me as her bikini top flies off.

"Yeah, that sounds bad," Mick agrees. "You're right," he adds, to her, not me.

To me, not her, he says, "I need to put my head on your chest."

"Maybe later," she says to Mick.

"Oh, sorry, I was talking to him, I need to hear what's going on in there."

"Suit yourself," she responds, then does a triple twirl on the pole. Mick slides his chair around the star tip next to mine and puts his ear on my sternum.

"Get those queers outta here!" yells a rowdy homophobe. Mick ignores him. He knows and I know that it'd take too much effort to explain I don't feel well and that Mick's a doctor.

"Take a deep breath," he instructs.

"Aw, that's cute," chimes the busty server on her arrival. "Can I get you boys anything? A blood pressure cuff, maybe? Or how about a rectal thermometer?"

Everyone's a comic.

"No, thanks, just two beers." *Cough, cough.* Mick continues to listen to my chest, and I appreciate it might look a little funny.

He picks his head up. "You got lower lung rales. They're starting to crackle. That's bad. Cross your right leg over your left for me."

"Mick," I tell him, "no need to keep going. I'll go to the doctor tomorrow."

"Cross your right leg over," he repeats, not taking no for an answer. He gives a tiny karate chop just under my kneecap. My foot shoots up, kicking the undersurface of the table, sending it flying over.

"Good thing we didn't get our beers yet." Just then, a large swiftly moving object comes at us from the right. It's an oversize man in a black suit with a communication device in his ear, CIA style. Robert would love that. He weaves around the scattered tables, moving agilely for his size, while Mick uprights our table.

"What's your problem?" he roars. I look up at him from my seat. When Mick turns around, he's a full head shorter than our new companion.

"He's hyper-reflexive," Mick answers. "That's the problem. It's not a good neurologic sign."

"Then take some motherfucking blood pressure pills," the bouncer prescribes. "But I'm telling you, you either settle down or you're out." He adds an extra growl for emphasis.

Mick regards our new friend. "Don't I know you?"

"Nah, man. You don't know me."

Mick nods knowingly. "Yes, I do. Crush Hampton. How's your neck?"

"Oh, shit! It's Dr. Mickey Mack! Yeah, man, you do know me. My neck? All better, except for a few kinks here and there. You said it would take time and it did. You got rid of the pain with those injections. I owe you, man. Surgery wasn't for me."

"Think nothing of it. But you really shouldn't be doing this. You could reinjure yourself."

"Nah, man. No worries. Take a look at these guys. They come here for the attention they ain't getting at home. Needy mofos. Some of them think the girls are for real with them. Anyway, they don't want no part of me."

"I guess you're right." Crush is still grinning, so I decide I might as well add my five cents.

"Crush Hampton," I say. "Middle linebacker for the University of Arizona Wildcats. I remember the hit that earned you your name. I was a big fan. I had high school buddies who were Wildcats."

I turn to Mick. "I didn't know he was a patient of yours."

"I did my training out in Arizona. In fact, took care of him after that very hit."

"I didn't know that. Nice to meet you." *Cough, cough.*

"Better take care of that," he cautions. "Doesn't sound good to me." Hearing loud voices across the room, he's off with a wave. "Later, guys! Have fun!"

Mick resumes his exam. "Do you have flulike symptoms?"

"Yes." *Cough, cough.*

Mick reaches for one of the beers now on the table and chugs it. He takes a napkin and wipes down the inside of the now-empty plastic cup. Shoving it at me, he commands, "Spit in this."

"I'm not spitting in that. I'll go to the doctor tomorrow, like I said."

"Spit in it. I don't like your lung crackles and that hyper-reflexia. I'll have it grown out. No big deal. It gives me an excuse to see the old boys in the lab. Now spit in it. There's nothing more definitive for a chest infection than a sputum culture. Spit!"

I take the cup, bend down under the table so no one can see how disgusting I am, and I hock a loogie while Mick chugs the other beer. I sit up.

"Give me that." He takes the second empty plastic cup and slides it into the specimen cup as a cover. Gross.

Once this has been taken care of, I update Mick on my being substituted out of Cookie's case. Right after, I go home—on doctor's orders.

A Known But Unspoken Rivalry

I fall asleep on the train home. That's never happened. But I just don't feel well. If I had spoken that last sentence aloud, it would have sounded like a whine. Men are such babies when ill. I turn into the driveway and watch my garage door as it opens. Before pulling in, I check my phone. There's an e-mail from Pusska: *Almost finished my snooping on Major. Interesting background. He's son of army doctor. Not a doctor that makes you better, but kind that do experiment. More to tell when I see you.*

Crap. I forgot to call her off Cookie's case. And crap, that's how I feel. I think tonight would be a good night to avoid Tyler Wyler.

When I get inside, she's nowhere to be seen. Good. As I head toward the den, I'm summoned from up above.

"Is that you?"

"Yes"—*cough, cough*—"it's me."

"Come upstairs."

"Do I have to?"

"Yes."

"Can it wait until morning? I'm feeling terrible."

"No. Come up." Crap. I hike up the stairs one slow step at a time, losing my breath before reaching the top. I pause, inhale a few deep ones, then enter our bedroom.

"Where are you?" *Cough, cough, cough.*

"In my closet. Come in."

So let me tell you about this closet—her woman cave—where Tyler spends a bunch of time. It's bigger than Penelope's bedroom and is filled with clothing, shoes, handbags, and accessories, organized in a very particular way with specific departments like Bergdorf Goodman. Many of its contents have tags on them, too, just like in Bergdorf's. Oh, and one entire wall is stocked with shoeboxes from top to bottom. Eight shelves, ten boxes per shelf.

Time to say hello.

"What's up, honey? What are you doing in your closet . . . with just your bra and thong on?" It's her red thong with black lace. On the back, centered just under the elastic band, the script lettering reads: *Friday.* I should have that shit customized to say *Tuesday.*

"I'm trying on outfits for visiting day."

"What?" *Cough, cough.*

"Visiting day. You know, camp, where our children spend their summer."

"Yes, I know. Camp. I seem to remember writing out large checks to this organization. But why are you trying on outfits? Camp is months away."

"I always start thinking about my outfit around this time. I want to look good."

"The kids don't care if you look good, honey. They want junk food. You bring tons of junk, you'll look good."

"Not for the kids, you idiot. Who cares what they think? I want to look good for the other parents."

"The other parents?"

"Well, not parents exactly. I want to look good for the other moms."

"Why do you want to look good for the moms? You thinking of playing for the other team?"

"No, you moron. I want to look better than the other moms."

"Better? Why?"

"Because it's a competition."

198 / ANDY SIEGEL

"What's a competition?"

"Which camper has the hottest mom—that competition."

"What are you talking about? I've never heard of this." *Cough, cough.*

"No one has. It's just a known but unspoken rivalry among the moms."

I take this in as I watch the show. Tyler goes about her business as if she hadn't said something absurd.

The crazy thing is it's probably true. She steps into a pair of cutoffs. Short shorts. They highlight her tiny little bottom, which is almost peeking out. She slips on a white tank top that has an extremely low neckline exposing a tad much for the day in question. Her arms and shoulders are well toned yet feminine. She looks at herself in the full-length wall mirror, rotating from side to side. She goes over to the shoebox wall and runs her finger left to right across the top shelf, then repeats the procedure moving down shelf to shelf. She stops on the fifth row, pulls out a large gray box, and puts it on the floor just in front of the ottoman stationed in the center of her closet. She takes out a pair of sexy brown boots with three-inch heels, sits, inserts her feet, laces them, pops up with confidence, and goes back over to the mirror, turning this way and that again.

"Well," she says, "how does Amber Sizzle look?"

"Like a slutty camp mom."

She smiles, then responds. "Perfect."

17.

After a restless night's sleep owing to a major breathing issue, I hardly make it through my morning routine. I avoid Tyler, and I don't say good-bye to the kids— which I always do—since, I have to say, I don't think I could handle it.

During my commute in, there are moments on the train where I feel my head is literally going to pop off my neck. And the coughing doesn't ever stop. The only thing positive about the ride is that no one dares sit next to me.

"Morning, Lily."

"That's a good boy," she answers. "Now that wasn't so hard. Pusska's here. She's waiting for you in your office." I nod, then head there. I turn in and there she is.

"Vhat's up?" I ask.

"Vhat's up? I tell you vhat's up. You gonna pay me for my investigation on Major. I don't care Cookie fire you."

"No problem. Chillax. I'll pay you."

"Good. You also going to listen to vhat I find on him."

"No need. I'm not handling the case anymore. What's the point?"

"Point is, Pusska proud of effort. I vork hard on this and find lot out. Difficult to find out because involve US military."

"Fine. I'll listen to whatever you've got, as long as you promise me you didn't go off and bone some general in exchange for the information."

"General?" she repeats in a questioning manner, as if searching her brain for the rank of whatever informant she'd banged. "No. No general."

"Well, did you use sex on anyone of military rank to obtain this info?"

"Does that include retired military? I just kidding. I vas good girl. Ready?"

"Ready."

"You see, Major is son of army doctor, like I told you. Major's father spent many years in California vith armed forces developing chemical varfare. He name son Major because he make career in army. Okay, that not part of investigation, that educated guess. Anyvay, like I say, Major's dad experiment in developing biological veapon. It receive military symbol O.C., but I don't know vhat O.C. stand for. Okay, anyvay—"

"Stop right there, Pusska. Please. I really don't need to know about Major's dad. You were going to investigate Major, not his father. Come on now, I'm really not in the mood, since I'm off the case." *Cough, cough.* "My lungs are ready to collapse."

"You say you listen, so listen. Interesting. Anyvay, so Major's dad vas developing O.C. to use as spray like nerve gas so people can't move. But too dangerous, have too many problems vith general population. You know, unintended victims vith also environment effects. So army—how you say?—abandon."

"What does any of this biological weapon development have to do with Major?"

"Major and father have same interest. Major vork as army doctor in same place dad vork."

"Well, did they work there at the same time?"

"No. Major dad retire before. But interesting, because Major vork on team that make vaccine antidote to O.C. father developed, just in case fall into enemy hands."

"Well that is interesting. But again, not relevant." I need a time-out. I suck in a deep breath of air, which hurts as it enters my lungs. I hock up some green phlegm and spit it into the wastebasket.

"Okay, last thing." Pusska's patience with me is unusual. Maybe she's actually sorry I'm feeling lousy.

"Go on."

"Major and Cookie make bad couple."

"Really? How'd you find that out?"

"Just my opinion. I don't know how she have sex vith him. I make good personal progress, no?"

"Yes, you've made good personal progress. Anything else?" *Cough, cough, cough.*

"One thing, unrelated."

"Go on."

"Your dogs. They give you kennel cough."

18.

t's two days since my doctor told me I have a bad chest cold. I explained to him my neurologist friend heard rales in my lower lungs, but he said he didn't. Anyway, I'm expecting Mick to get back to me about what my sputum culture grew out. So I let my guy slide. Besides, he took a chest X-ray and read it as negative.

I didn't even want to come into the city today, but one of my referring attorneys has a new client for me to meet this afternoon so I had to. I can't rely solely on representing HICs.

Now sitting at my desk, I decide I'm just going to chill for a while. I recline and up go my feet. I buzz Lily.

"What do you want?"

"I need to relax. I'm not feeling well. Hold all my calls."

"Hold all my calls, what?"

"Hold all my calls, please." *Cough, cough.*

"I will after this one. Pick up line two."

"But I don't feel up to speaking to anybody."

"It's your mom. She says it's an emergency."

Mom's been battling cancer for two decades. Every time she calls me, it's an emergency. Not to sound insensitive, but after all these years her crying wolf has become quite unnerving. One time, for example, the crisis was a can of dog food that had gotten stuck on the electric opener. But since she was hospitalized after getting the results of her latest blood work, there's always the chance it's truly bad news she has to tell me.

"Hi, Mom."

"I'm not going to die. Come pick me up."

"Glad to hear it. You thought you were this time." *Cough, cough, cough.*

"Well, I'm not. Come pick me up. Now! And keep your distance if you're sick."

"I will. So it's not an emergency?"

"Don't be cute. Come pick me up. Hurry."

"When were you discharged?"

"Stop asking questions and get a move on. I'm not one of your witnesses."

"Okay."

"Now! Let's go!"

"Easy, Mom. I'll grab a cab."

"Well, grab it now!"

It's not long before I'm stepping onto the sidewalk in front of Lenox Hill Hospital on Seventy-Seventh Street.

But just before I enter, a familiar sight catches my eye. It's Robert Killroy. He's pedaling up to me super fast on the sidewalk. His thick legs are pumping up and down but freeze as he hits the brakes. He skids several feet sliding up to me, stopping six inches away. We're face-to-face. That was impressive biking.

"Hi, Robert," I say as he launches into his usual spiel.

"But I didn't kill no Roy, and I didn't kill nobody." He's panting and seems excited.

"Thank you for reminding me of that, but what are you doing here?"

"I told you if you didn't pay Mr. Wang his fourteen dollars and seventy-nine cents, I'd have to sue you, so that's what I'm doing." He takes out some papers and thrusts them at me.

"You are hereby served with . . . um, I forgot the word. It ain't no good unless you say the right word, and I can use that fifty dollars I get to help Granny pay the rent."

"Process, Robert, served with process." *Cough, cough.*

"Okay, thanks. Served with process." I look at the papers without taking them. I'd meant it when I told him I'd accept service, but right about now I'm not feeling that. Right now, I'm not feeling anything but sick. I can't shake this thing, and my morale's in the toilet from singlehandedly losing one giant legal fee on Cookie's case.

"Robert," I ask with admirable patience, "do you have your process server's license on you?"

"No," he answers.

"Then you can't serve process on me. You need to carry your license with you when serving someone. Just like a driver of a car has to have his license on him when driving. If you serve me now, it will be no good. It's called improper service."

Of course, none of that's true. At least I don't think it is. I just don't have time for it now. "You come down to my office tomorrow, and I'll accept service. Or better yet, no need to make a special trip. Come in twenty days when your settlement check has arrived on your up-front money."

He doesn't seem to understand. No surprise. He puts the legal papers back in his carrier bag and pulls out some kind of manual.

"What's that?"

"It's my directions." He opens it up to page one and starts reading. Out loud.

"Robert, what are you doing?"

"Reading my directions."

"Why?"

"To see if you be dodging service. I'm gonna look for that license thing." I could advise him to go to the index to speed up his search if, in fact, such a rule actually exists. Then again, it might not be so bad if he begins from the start.

"Robert, how did you know where I was?"

He looks up. "My investigating skills."

"I see." A sickly older man is wheeled out of the hospital past us. *Cough, cough.* I pat my chest.

"You come here 'cause you sick, Mr. Wyler?"

"No, Robert. My mother has the cancer just like Granny."

"Oh, man. I'm sorry. I hope she feels better."

"Thank you, Robert." He returns his focus to the manual.

"Good luck, then. See you around." I leave him standing there, bike between his legs, with his finger moving slowly across line three. I didn't think it would come to this: that Robert's collection agency would pay him a fifty-dollar service of process fee on top of filing and legal costs to collect on a fourteen-dollar debt.

I enter the hospital and go directly up to seven. I walk past the nurses' station, which is emptier than normal and down the hall. I approach Mom's room and walk in. First thing I notice is her roommate's been discharged.

Mom's sitting in a wheelchair, with her overnight bag on her lap. Hanging off the handgrips are two triple-layered plastic grocery bags filled with the stuff she's stealing. Standing behind her is a uniformed orderly holding onto the handgrips, waiting for instruction. White skin, chiseled masculine face, and a crew cut. Eastern European's my take. His tattoo-filled arms ripple with muscles as he squeezes the grips.

"Hi, Mom."

"Let's go. Now."

"I see you wasted no time, huh? You got"—I take another step forward to read his name tag—"Branislav over here ready and waiting for an immediate departure."

She looks up at Branislav. "Lawyers talk too much." She looks back at me. "Let's go."

"Branislav," I say, "for two decades I've been Mom's wheelchair Sherpa so no need to depart from tradition now." He gives me an uncertain look.

"I'll wheel her out." *Cough, cough.*

"Cover your mouth!"

"I did."

She turns to him. "Good-bye, Branislav. You're quite a gentleman."

He's about to leave since he's no longer needed.

"Wait," Mother says. He stops and turns stiffly like a robot. "Remember what I told you."

"Yes, ma'am. Zabar has best gefilte fish in city. *Dovidjenja*."

"*Dovidjenja*." He turns and leaves.

Mom looks up. "That means 'good-bye' in Serb. Let's go."

"We're going. Do I have to race you out of here?"

"Yes."

"Why?"

"That's not important. Let's go."

"Okay. When did you learn to speak Serb?"

"There are a lot of things you don't know about your mother. Now wheel me."

I shrug and begin wheeling her down the hall past the nurses' station. When I press the elevator *down* button, Mom looks anxious.

"What's the matter?"

"Nothing. I need a smoke." Her addiction to cigarettes has kept her alive this long. *Ding.* The elevator arrives.

"Come on. It's the one over there." She points. I wheel her over as a guy pulling a big cart carrying all sorts of food trays comes out of the elevator. We wait just to the side, and he engages us.

"Sorry, you can't use this elevator. It's the freight elevator."

"Okay, thank you," Mom says as he clears the entry and continues on his way. "Push me in."

"You heard the guy; we can't use this." She juts her foot forward. The closing door hits it and retracts.

"Push me in or I'll make a scene."

"Okay, okay. We'll go freight. No scenes please."

As we descend she asks, "How's business?"

"Good and bad. I resolved one pretty big case but was fired from another with a large offer on the table."

"People don't fire their lawyers without good reason. I hope you learned your lesson."

"I did. Thanks for your support."

"No problem. But at least you did good on the other."

"Yeah, I did good." A good deed—no need to tell her it was pro bono. She has this idea I'm a good businessman, but I'm not. I'm a committed lawyer, that's all.

At this moment, I attempt to clear my throat starting way down in my diaphragm. The tightness goes that deep. Mom looks up as I'm *um-humming*. The glare says don't get me sick.

When the doors open on G, I turn my mother toward the main exit. She says, "No, that way," pointing in the opposite direction.

"Mom, the front entrance—"

"I said *that* way."

You have to pick and choose your battles when dealing with a terminal cancer patient. Besides, there's an exit sign hanging from the ceiling in the direction she wants to go. I wheel her down the hall into an open area where nurses are standing, sitting, eating, drinking, and talking. It's clear this is where they gather for breaks.

"Shit," Mom says. "Back the other way."

"Listen, I'm not going back the other way. The exit's right there." I nod to the doors just past the collection of nurses.

"Back the other way or I'll make a scene."

"So make a scene," I say, as I wheel her forward. She leans down and shields her head with her left arm the way people do when they don't want to be discovered.

"What are you doing?"

"Germs. Nurses have germs. You know that. I have a depressed immune system. You know that, too. So stop coughing, for God's sake. You want to get me sick?"

"I didn't cough."

"You did before. And you sound like you should be home in bed having a bowl of hot chicken soup. She knows how to make soup, doesn't she?"

"If by 'she' you mean Tyler, then the answer is yes."

"Well, that's something. Are you dating anyone?"

"No, I'm married."

"Well, just keep your options open, that's all."

Once outside, Mom takes a deep breath, which turns into a sigh of relief. "Ah, fresh air," she says. Glancing to my right, I see Robert in the exact same place where I left him, his finger still moving slowly across the page. Mom catches my glimpse.

"Who's that?"

"The client whose case I just resolved."

"The big one?"

"Yeah, the big one."

"How injured could he be if he's riding a bike?"

"Oh, he's injured, believe me. It's just that he won't let it get in his way."

"Admirable."

"Very," I say. I feel the same about how my mother has handled her diagnosis.

"What's he doing here?"

"He's attempting to serve me with process."

"He's suing you?"

"Yep. It's a long story."

"You'll tell me some other time. Let's go." She points to the left. But after I've wheeled her five feet, she says, "Hold on. Stop."

"I'll stop up ahead." There's a guy down on his luck sprawled on the sidewalk leaning against the wall with all kinds of bags littered around him. The same type of bags Mom has hanging off her wheelchair, which I realize at this moment is also stolen hospital property. I continue forward.

"I said stop. Here! Now!"

"Mom, I'll—"

"Here!" I stop. In front of the homeless man. She leans down. "Hey, buddy," she says to him. "Hey, buddy."

He looks up, struggling to focus, then zeroes in on her face. He's confused.

"Yeah, you," Mom says.

"What? Me?" he questions.

"Yeah, you. Can I bum a cigarette off you?"

"Huh?" he responds.

"You got a cigarette for me, buddy, or not?"

He looks at the hospital entrance as if to say "Are you sure you should be smoking, having just come out of there?"

"Well?"

"Yeah, I got one. But . . ."

"No *buts*, except the kind you can inhale. Let's have it."

He reaches into his sport jacket. Yeah, that's right, this street guy's wearing a grubby navy blazer and pulls out a pack of high-nicotine cigarettes. Chesterfields. No filter.

"Ah, perfect." That's her brand.

He shakes it and one pops up. He extends his arm as Mom leans farther down and puts her lips around the end of a cig. He withdraws the pack as it slides out.

At this moment I acknowledge my head is pounding, I'm in a hot sweat and feel just terrible. Still worse, now my mother's going to fill the air with her noxious smoke.

"Gimme a light," she says, still leaning over. He pulls out a yellow Bic and gives it a flick. The flame ignites, and Mom draws her start-up puff the way I've seen her do a million times before. Satisfaction permeates her face. She tilts her head back and exhales a giant cloud of smoke, which plumes right into my face. *Cough, cough, cough.*

"Thanks, Mom."

"Sorry about that. It was the nicotine high," she says. After all these years, she continues with this filthy habit. I remind myself it's her only comfort.

"Hand me that plastic bag," she says, indicating the one she wants. I do as I'm told. She looks in it, nods, then hands it to her new friend. "Here, take this."

He complies and looks in it. His eyes light up. He reaches in with his grimy hand and takes out a roll, resting it on his dirty lap. Then he takes out two more, a shiny metal knife and five butter packets.

"Really, Mom?" I question. "Rolls, butter, and a knife. Really?"

"It was for my bum. But this guy's a good sharer."

"Your bum?"

"Yeah, near my apartment."

Lastly, he takes out a small white vase with a red carnation in it and sets it down on the sidewalk. He proceeds to butter up his roll as Mom enjoys her cig. They both seem pretty satisfied.

A moment later, we're distracted by a distinctive hearty laugh in the close distance but coming our way.

"Oh, shoot," Mom says, "oh, shoot. Wheel me that way, quick!" She takes a long last drag and tosses the cig. It lands next to the bum. He picks it up, puts it into his mouth, and takes a hit while still chewing a chunk of buttered roll.

"But we're heading this way."

"Turn me around and wheel me that way! Now!" I look to see who's approaching—it's a trio of nurses.

"I said turn me around. *Now!*"

I slowly begin turning her, making sure the nurses can get a glimpse of Mom.

"Faster," she demands. "Faster!"

I get her pointed in the other direction. Then she barks another order. "Push!"

I obey.

"Adele! Adele, is that you?" It's the hearty voice.

"Push!" Mom says. "Faster!"

I stop. "But that nurse wants to talk to you. Maybe she wants to say good-bye." I know for a fact by the tone of that nurse's voice she clearly does not want to say good-bye.

"She's annoying," my mother responds. "Push! Hurry!"

"Not a chance. You think everyone's annoying, so there's something else going on here."

The nurses reach us, and I pull a one-eighty. Mom looks up.

"Well hello, Adele," the nurse says snidely. She's a large black woman, over two hundred pounds, and she speaks with confidence and authority. Mom must love her. She loves health care providers with high self-esteem.

"Hi, Anita. How was your lunch?"

"Don't give me that, Adele. You can't play me. Now, did I see you smoking a cigarette?"

"No."

The big nurse offers a stern look. "Are you sure I didn't see you take a big puff just a few seconds ago and toss it down to Montgomery over here?" she asks, nodding to the bum who looks up upon hearing his name.

"Wasn't me," she responds.

"Was!" They give each other a momentary stare down.

"Big deal," Mom finally says, breaking the tension.

"It is a big deal, Adele. You heard what the pulmonologist said."

"Yeah, I heard what he said. I have twenty-four percent of my lung capacity left and, as far as I'm concerned, that's plenty."

The big nurse rears back and squints her eyes. She's mad. Then she turns to me.

"Who are you?"

"I'm her son."

"Oh yeah, the lawyer with the bossy wife and rhyming name."

"Tyler Wyler," Mom offers. "Ridiculous."

"Yeah, Tyler Wyler," the nurse repeats. "I heard about you. And her."

I look at Mom. She shrugs.

"Well, you ought to know better than to let her smoke," Anita chides me.

"It makes her happy."

Her face softens just a bit. She gets it. "Well, turn her around," she orders. "Wheel her back inside."

"The hospital?" I question.

"Yeah, the hospital, dummy. That's where she came out of, right?" The two other nurses with her giggle at this.

"Why would I do that? I'm taking her home."

"Oh, you are?"

"Um, yes." Somehow though, I'm not so sure of that answer.

"Nobody discharged your mother. She played you for a fool. Step aside. I'll wheel her back in."

My mom gives Anita the look one gives when their big getaway plan has been foiled.

"Mom, don't ever do this again, understand?" *Cough, cough.* I keel over and churn out three more deep, painful coughs. On the last one I see lightning bolts flashing inside my head. Leaning back, I try to conclude my reprimand, but it's lost its force by now. "You understand?"

"No promises."

"I can tell you this," Anita says to me. "You sound like you should step inside, too."

"I'll be fine."

Just before she wheels Mom back in, she pulls me aside to explain what it's all been about. The woman in the bed next to her died unexpectedly last night. It freaked my super-brave Mom out, and that's hard to do.

At this point, Robert's still exactly where I left him. Still straddling the horizontal bar of his bike, book open. I walk over to say good-bye. I love this kid.

"Hi, Robert."

"Hi. There're no pictures in here. I don't like books without pictures." I'd say he's three-pages deep.

"Me, neither. But did you find what you're looking for?"

"I think so." Suddenly, my vision becomes blurred, then doubled. Robert's helmeted head rises above itself.

"Are you okay, Mr. Wyler? Why you looking up like that?"

"Robert, how tall are you?"

"Five feet nine plus one inch."

"Do you mean five foot ten?" I ask, as my focus returns.

"No. Five feet nine plus one inch."

"I understand, Robert. Why don't you just go home now and come see me in twenty days when your check's ready, like I said? You bring your process server's license and I'll accept service." He doesn't need to be standing there all day. But it's no use. When I start walking away, he resumes his scrutiny of the process server's manual. Best to let Robert be Robert.

I walk down the block to the subway on Seventy-Seventh Street near the hospital but don't go down. My chest is on fire, my head is throbbing, and my lungs are filling up with green gunk. I lean against a building, looking at a hot dog cart across the street. Since I don't want a dirty dog, something must be seriously wrong—despite the opinion of my internist.

My phone vibrates. It's Mick.

"What's up?"

"Been out of state lately?"

"I think you know the answer to that."

"How's your head feeling?"

"Killing me."

"How are your joints?"

"Achy."

"Your chest?"

"Getting worse."

"Got any neck pain?"

"Recent onset."

"Your vision?"

"Was blurred and doubled just a moment ago."

"Your culture came back. You're positive for something that you couldn't have been in contact with."

"No kidding. Go on, I'm listening. What do I have that I haven't even been exposed to?"

"Cocci, buddy. You need to get to a hospital. Pronto!" I look across at Lenox Hill.

"Hold on. You're way ahead of me. What's cocci?"

"Coccidioidomycosis."

"What the heck is that?"

"It's a fungal infection."

"Like athlete's foot?"

"Hardly. Listen, I'm ninety-nine percent sure that's what you got. But you need a particular blood test that evaluates your serum to see if your body has produced the antibodies to this specific antigen."

"All right," I say in a tentative tone. "But can you tell me why exposure occurs outside of New York?"

"Sure. Because *Coccidioides immitis*—which is the mold that causes the fungal infection—only resides in the soil in the Southwest."

"Then how did I get it?"

"I don't know how you got it, but typically the mold has long filaments that break off into airborne spores. Your infection was caused by the inhalation of those particles. That's about it."

"I see. Could my sputum culture be a false positive?"

"Could be if you had some other fungal disease, but highly unlikely in your case."

"Why?"

"You got all the classic clinical features. You also need a chest X-ray."

"Just had one. It was negative. How does that factor in?"

"I want to see the film, that's how. I very much doubt it's negative, given your constellation of symptoms. Who read the film? A radiologist?"

"No, my primary-care guy."

"He wouldn't know what to look for."

"How do you know about this condition?"

"My training in Tucson. Some of the convicts from the local penitentiary would come down with it from time to time. Our hospital provided medical services to the inmates."

"Okay." *Cough, cough.* "I'll get to a hospital."

"Go now," he insists.

I look at Lenox Hill Hospital for the third time. Pedestrian traffic into the ER has been light since I started monitoring it.

"Hey, you're worrying me. It's a fungal infection, right? You spoke about antibodies, so there must be a treatment for the condition. Am I correct on that?"

"Yes, there is. But the way yours sounds is troubling me."

"I'm listening. Go on."

"Your cocci presented as a pulmonary infection. That's why you're coughing so much. But it sounds like it's also disseminated into other systems. Your joints hurt, your head hurts. These are bad signs. Signs of an advanced disease. This could lead to a brain insult if you don't get treatment soon. And by soon I mean, like, *now.*"

"What are you talking about? A brain event, from a fungus?"

"That's right. I've seen it. When it gets to the brain, there's a high risk of mortality if not promptly treated."

"You're freaking me out. I don't feel like I'm about to die. All I've got is a bad cough, plus achy joints and terrible headaches that come and go."

"It's the etiology of the headaches that poses the risk. This fungus has disseminated through your systems and into your head. It causes inflammation of the tissue layers that surround your brain, meningeal disease with hydrocephalus being the most disastrous complication."

"You've got to be kidding me, right? Hydrocephalus?" I'm stunned. "Water on the brain?"

"Well, it's not water, it's cerebral spinal fluid."

"I know what it is—so, please, spare me your corrections. How do these spores cause it?"

"It's a combination of factors. Overproduction of fluid is the main culprit, coupled with obstruction of the drainage routes. The fluid's overwhelming your brain's absorption capacity and the buildup of CSF is causing increased pressure inside your head. That's what's happening. This is serious stuff. You got a bad case of Desert Fever, buddy."

"Okay, okay. I get ya."

"No. I don't think you do. Listen! And listen carefully. You need to understand the seriousness of this. The spores of *C. immitis* were being developed as an agent for chemical warfare at one time. That's how serious this is. Now get yourself to a hospital right now! No, better yet, where are you? I'm coming to pick you up."

Mick's words resonate in my fluid-filled head. I'm formulating and assessing, and, although my concentration is off, my executive function is off, and my recall—yeah, that's off, too—I quickly realize this is not about me.

"You there?" I hear Mick ask. "You there?"

Holy shit!

"I gotta go, Mick!" *Click.*

Some No-Contact Directives Require Direct Contact

As I scramble-scroll through my phone, thoughts flash across my pounding head. The MRIs showed no evidence of a surgical injury at C4 that could be responsible for the backflow of CSF . . . no one ever came up to their apartment . . . Major and his father both worked on chemical agents out West . . . dry desert plants confined to Cookie's separate bedroom. Ones I knocked over. Exposing myself.

Major is poisoning her!

The guy's a psycho. He's inducing the overproduction of fluid and creating the false need for repeated and emergent spinal taps. Setting up a dependency, so he can keep his dancer prize to himself. Who'd ever believe it?

I hit the *call* button. Come on, Cookie, pick up, girl.

"Hello?"

"Cookie, it's me, Tug Wyler, your old attorney. Is Major there?"

"Um, uh, I don't think I'm supposed to talk to . . . um, no, he'll be back in a few. I'll tell him that you . . . to call you."

"No!" I shout. "Don't tell him to call me! Listen! You've got to get out of there! Now! Major's poisoning you! Do you understand me?"

"Not really." Justifiably, I have to say. "Um, I like you and all," she continues, "but I'm pretty sure you're not supposed to call me or contact me in any way since I switched back to Chris. I mean, he just got the file back, and they've offered him two million dollars."

Oh, man! This is no time to set the record straight.

"Cookie! You have to listen to me!" Some no-contact directives require direct contact. And this is one of them. "It's not about your lawsuit. I promise I know what I'm talking about. Major may be manipulating Chris, too. He could even be part of the fraud scheme."

"Fraud scheme? What are you talking about?"

"I was contacted by an investigator, from where I'm not sure, but while I was handling your case a fraud investigator approached me. A little fish named Minnow."

"A little fish named Minnow?"

"Yes, listen, I'll explain everything to you. I promise. Wait a minute, Minnow's not actually an investigator. I mixed it up. Pusska said she couldn't find anything on him. Oh, that's not the point. Anyway, right now, it's you I'm concerned with. Your health and well-being. I'm on my way over. It won't be long. I'm close by. Meet me across the street from your building. Hurry!" I add with a sense of urgency, "Please! This is very real. And stay away from your plants!"

"My plants?" she repeats.

"Yes, your plants. They're poisoning you."

"That sounds totally crazy. Are you sure you're feeling all right?"

"No. I'm feeling horrible. I've got headaches. Pressure headaches . . . from the spores . . . headaches just like yours! Separate rooms . . . keeping your door shut . . . no visitors! Don't you get it?"

"Not really."

"You told me when I was there that you had no life and felt like a prisoner. Remember?"

"Yeah, and . . ."

"Well that's because you *are* a prisoner—Major's prisoner! Just get out of there! You've got to trust me on this! He's inducing your headaches so that you need him! He's the tap-master and you're his slave."

Silence. I hear silence on the other end. I struck a nerve. I need to know one more thing to be sure, though. Before I turn her world upside down.

"Cookie, when did you move in with Major?"

"About five months after McElroy's surgery."

"When did the tapping begin?"

"Almost a month later."

"Were those plants in your room when you moved in?"

"No."

"When, in relation to your first tap, did you get those plants?"

"Less than two weeks before."

"You need to meet me now! I'll explain everything so you understand. Or else you'll be Major's high-rise hostage forever."

Further silence. Jesus, what more does she need?

"Cookie! Major took you to his medical clinic downtown when he saved your life doing that very first tap, yet you guys live closer to three major hospitals. Don't you get it?"

"Okay, I'll meet you across the street from my building in five minutes. But you've got a lot of explaining to do." *Click.*

My wife! I hit the speed dial as I race as best I can to Cookie. I'm in a slow jog but finding it difficult to put one foot in front of the other and increasingly difficult to breathe.

"Hi, honey," she answers. "Oh, before I forget to tell you, your doctor's office called. The practice radiologist read your chest X-ray and has some concerns. They want you to come in."

"I already know the problem."

"What is it? And why are you breathing so heavy?"

"I have Desert Fever, and I'm out of breath because I'm running down the street sick as a dog, trying to talk on the phone."

"Desert Fever? I don't know what it is, but I assume you have to go to a desert to get it. And why are you running?"

"I'm running to go meet Cookie. I got it at her apartment and—"

"Cookie, the stripper who fired you?"

"Yes, that's the only Cookie I know."

"Why did you go to her apartment? Doesn't she live in the city? And isn't your office in the city? Why couldn't she come to your office? I mean, you pay rent to conduct business there, don't you?"

"Which of those questions do you want me to answer first?"

Click.

I embrace her reaction and forge ahead. If she didn't care, the click would've preceded the inquisition. I turn and give Lenox Hill, now in the distance, one last look, thinking I'll just circle back there with Cookie. People are moving left and right out of my way as I labor down the sidewalk, in my suit, out of breath and starting to feel off-balance. I turn onto Seventy-Ninth Street and see Cookie standing there, up ahead. She's looking sweet as ever, halo and all.

My pace slows as I pull up. I can't breathe.

"Are you okay?" she asks with earnest concern.

"Fine. I mean, no, not really." I sway off balance.

She steadies me. "Careful," I warn her, "don't move like that in your brace."

"Oh, I'm not worried. I had an X-ray yesterday, and I'm finally fused."

"That's great news. Listen, we've got to walk and talk. I don't want Major to see us. You're not going to believe what I have to say to you."

"Okay, let's walk and talk. I like that. It rhymes. Where to?"

"Let's go to Papaya King on Eighty-Sixth," I suggest. No way can I make it, but I'll be done with what I have to say in two blocks.

Then it's back to the hospital.

"Fine, let's go. I love their dogs." Figures. She's such a catch. I attempt a step and realize I can't achieve a proper toe lift. So I lift my shoe off the sidewalk straight-footed, only to realize I can't manage a proper heel strike.

"What's the matter with your foot?"

"Nothing, but I have Desert Fever. And so do you."

"What's that? And why did you do that with your foot?"

"Um, what did I do with my foot?"

"I don't know, you kind of kicked it out in a jerky motion.

"I didn't realize. Is it getting dark out here?"

"No, it's beautiful out. What's the matter with you?" She's getting more worried by the second, and with good reason.

"I don't feel good. It's your plants, they're . . . Cookie, where are you?"

"I'm right in front of you. Hello. Hello in there. You're just staring at me. Move or something. What's the matter? Hello? Hello?"

I feel my legs collapse. I go down, on my back. I use every orbital muscle I have to get my eyes open, if those are the right muscles. At this point, I'm not sure. Cookie's standing over me, I think. Lenox Hill Hospital was right in front of me. Damn!

"Shit!" she cries out. "Oh my God, what do I do? I don't know what to do. I'm not good in emergencies." Her words sound all garbled. I'm fading. I'm searching for the strength to tell her to call 911. Everybody knows to call 911, don't they?

I'm doing everything to summon all that's left within me, but I can't speak those three important numbers. And just as important, I can't tell her how Major conceived this whole unbelievable thing once Nurse Molina told him about the spinal fluid leak. He parlayed that knowledge into something only *he* could have, given his background. He's truly one mad scientist.

She takes out her cell. Finally. Although I'm certain it's only been a few seconds since I went down. Good girl. Call 911. She dials. Good. Hurry up, I'm paralyzed down here.

"Hello," I hear her frantically call out. "I need help! Please!" Good girl. When they get here, just tell them what I told you—that I have Desert Fever. Her lips are moving, but I don't hear her saying anything. And then, an instant later, I do.

"We're on the corner of Seventy-Ninth," I hear her say. Perfect. "Hurry, Major!"

No!

19.

uring my journey to wherever I am, I think I hear Minnow. Those distinctive, *seeeees*. Or maybe I just imagine it. One thing is for sure, the image of the giant black marble sculpture in Foley Square memorializing the enslaved Africans brought to America flashes across my mind during my ride. That was the day I signed up Cookie.

My next sense of awareness is the sound of a voice. Major's voice. I hear it clearly.

"No, Cookie," he says, "that's not a good idea. You shouldn't have had contact with him in the first place. I'll tell him of your concern. Yes, dear, we're still at the hospital. No, nothing serious at all. He's just one of those overworked lawyers who possibly drinks a little too much. They also found his electrolytes to be low. No, that's not serious, either. I'll explain it all to you later. Yes, I told the doctors here about Desert Fever and, no, he doesn't have that. No one in New York does.

"That stuff he was saying to you was just part of his dehydration dementia. What's that you say? Oh, dementia is when you imagine things because of sickness. Here, it's from lack of fluids in Mr. Wyler's system. They're giving him IV fluids now to help that out."

I know for a fact that there is no IV in my arm, hand, or

elsewhere. Unless that's what's sticking me in my lower back. Which would be an unusual access site.

"When people are in that condition," he continues, "they hallucinate and have wild fantasies. He'll be just fine. I spoke to his wife, and apparently it's happened before, on more than one occasion."

I vehemently deny that allegation. Deny, deny, deny. But I can't say a word, since my mouth seems to be covered.

"His wife's coming for him, dear. I guess we learned our lesson about hiring a lawyer who frequents the club, with all due respect to your profession. You know I support it entirely. Good-bye, dear."

For the record, Major, I was only meeting my friend for a drink at Jingles. I don't *frequent* strip clubs. But anyhow, at least you got me to a hospital, and my wife's on her way. I certainly don't feel, though, like I'm in any hospital bed or even on a gurney. However, my thoughts are still scrambled, and I'm just now approaching semiconsciousness. What I need is to be patient.

Major walks over the floor, which creaks underfoot, and stops in front of me. He slides up whatever's been covering my eyes, holds first my right, then my left eyelid open, and flashes a pen light in each eye. He slides the cloth back down and walks away. That wasn't very thorough.

There's something hot poking me in my back. No way is that the access point. Wait a minute. I'm not in a hospital. Hey, my arms are taped to my sides. And my mouth—that has tape on it, too. Crap, I'm blindfolded. That's what he slid up and down.

What the—? Where did he take me? To the psych ward?

My feet are flat on the floor, my crotch in a spread eagle and my inner thighs separated by I'm-not-sure-what. It feels like I'm sitting backward on a chair. But I have to say, despite the restraints, my headache is completely gone. I haven't felt this good in a while. In fact, I feel a great sense of relief. It's like night and day without the pressure. This must be how Cookie feels after her tap. I get it now, why she'd stay with him.

Let me see if I can somehow stand. I think I saw some guy break free that way in a movie once. I press down on the floor with the soles of my feet. The chair lifts up a bit and crashes back down.

"I wouldn't do that," Major admonishes. I'd say he's about ten feet away. "You have a spinal needle sticking out of your back, and if you fall over, it will penetrate your spinal cord, and you'll paralyze yourself or worse."

That settles it—I'm not in a hospital, nor am I in the padded ward of some bin. I'm a captive. I've been held against my will before, and this is exactly what it feels like. This Major likes to do that to people. Thanks, Henry, for landing me yet again in a predicament. I don't think I'll accept any more HIC referrals. They ain't worth it. Although, technically, Cookie's not one of Henry's injured criminals, a distinction that seems inconsequential at this moment.

The floor lets out another creak. "I'm going to take your gag off," Major cautions. "You can scream all you want. Nobody's going to hear you. We're in an abandoned building in the middle of nowhere." He rips the adhesive tape off my mouth.

"Fuck, man," I say. "What the fuck is going on here? And take my fucking blindfold off." I feel him unknotting it from behind. Behold, I'm staring at a dilapidated wall with paint chips and punch holes. He steps in front of me. I look up.

"What the fuck is going on here?"

"You know, you say the word *fuck* a lot."

"Oh, I'm sorry. Does that bother you? Let's make a fucking deal then. Take the fucking needle out of my spine and unfucking tie me and I'll stop saying *fuck*. How does that fucking sound? Sounds like a fucking plan to me."

"Curse all you want. It doesn't bother me. It just confirms that you're an uncultured lowlife."

"Oh, let me get this straight. You poison Cookie with those plants . . ." His eyebrows raise. "That's right, I know about the spores your father worked on to develop chemical weapons. Then you kidnap me so your little codependent thing with her won't get ruined—and *I'm* the lowlife?"

"I see you did your homework. My father was a good man."

"I don't give a crap about your father. But I can't imagine him being a good man with you as his son. Now, unfucking tie me, like I said."

"I can't do that."

"Then what the fuck are you going to do with me?"

"I don't know. I didn't plan for this. Your meddling has made it all very complicated."

"Well, if you think it's complicated now, just you wait. You're going to do jail time for this kidnapping. And for your enslavement of Cookie."

"No, I don't think so. I'm not interested in going to jail."

"Good. Then untie me, and I'll ask the prosecutor for leniency."

"No, I don't think so. You know, I saved your life."

"You saved my life, Major? You mean, after I was exposed to your fungus and developed systemic cocci that's ravaged my central nervous system, causing my CSF to go haywire, you were nice enough to tap me and save my life? I never looked at it that way. But you're right. Thank you for saving my life. I guess Cookie should be thankful, too."

"She is."

"You're messed up in the head. Tell me something: How do you keep Cookie from dying? From the infection disseminating into her organs?"

"That's an intelligent question."

"Well, fucking A, man. The lawyer who uncovered your sick and twisted poison-plant scheme asked a smart question."

He smiles, but it merely distorts his face. He's uncomfortable with this, I can tell. Uncomfortable with the situation he created and uncomfortable with the fact that he has no clear solution. This could be very dangerous for me, but I sense he doesn't have it in him. The killer instinct, I mean. Me, I intend to keep him irritated and distracted from any solution I might not like by the further overuse of the F-word. It's my only option at this point.

"So," I say, "are you going to answer me or not, fucker? Fuck, fuck, fuck."

"I give her a pill," he says, hesitating. "She thinks it's a multivitamin, but it's an antigen that keeps her condition at a manageable level, so she doesn't get hurt. That's how I do it."

"That's really nice of you not to hurt her. I'm sure she'd appreciate it if she knew you were manipulating her cerebral spinal fluid to prevent her head from exploding, you batty old fuck."

"Stop your cursing. It's making me uncomfortable."

"Well, I'm really fucking sorry about that. I wouldn't want you to feel uncomfortable, given the high level of comfort I'm experiencing right now—with a spinal needle piercing my nervous system."

"You shouldn't talk to me that way. I'll just leave you here . . . to starve."

"First of all, I'm not concerned with death. Betty, the fortune-teller, with those sticks of hers predicted I'm going to live a long life, and so far she's been pretty damn accurate. And I shouldn't talk to you this way as opposed to what? Speaking to you nicely? Are you that twisted that you expect I should speak to you courteously under the circumstances? Well? Are you?"

"Um—"

"Um? Is that it? You know what I think? I think you don't have the guts to do this, that's what I think. You're running scared. Best of all, you're scared Cookie's gonna find out and leave you. Then what?"

"Be quiet!" he snaps. "Be quiet, I tell you!"

Now who struck a nerve?

He moves in angrily. He reapplies the blindfold, then retapes my mouth. He begins pacing behind me, eleven steps each way. On steps nine, ten, and eleven he enters my peripheral vision on each side. I can see him through the slit created because he put the blindfold back on too high.

"Don't ruin this for me!" He sounds about to lose it. "Do you hear me? Don't ruin this for me!" I'd say the F-word ten more times but for the gag. He walks around me, once, twice, three times, like a shark circling its prey. Not a great white, but some timid kind that swims away at the first sign of danger. He doesn't have it in him to kill, and we both know it. He stops a foot from my nose.

"Cookie's perfect, and she loves me! Don't ruin this for me!" he reiterates, with the passion and the desperation of a man whose world may collapse at any minute. She doesn't love you. It's that she can't live without you. You biologically assaulted her, you sick lunatic.

"Stay here!" He yells this into my face.

Let me see . . . Okay. I'll stay here tied and bound to this chair with a spinal needle in my back that will result in quadriplegia if I make a wrong move. I hear the floor creaking as he walks away. He slams the door without saying good-bye.

That wasn't very nice.

20.

'd estimate it's been about twenty minutes since Major left. And no escape is foreseeable despite my hearing the door squeak open from the rebound of his slam. What a tease. I feel the needle in my back, reminding me of Cookie's tap and also of my wife's epidurals at the births of our children. Not exactly a matched set of memories.

By the sounds outside, I know I'm near the East River. I can't hear the water, but rather the faint hum of motorboats in the distance. Not little ones, but barges and tugs. I'm near downtown Brooklyn. I'm certain, because I also hear the familiar chime of church bells I listened to while attending Brooklyn Law. They're way in the distance, though, coming from the industrial area of Greenpoint.

The bells somehow remind me of the evening when this all started—because they make me think of the leaflet lady who warned me that the end was near as I walked into Jingles Dance Bonanza. Maybe she'll turn out to be right, but I'm hoping for Betty's take on things. Anyway, I'm pretty sure I'm in a deserted part of town, because there's no street noise.

I hear the hinge of the door squeak again. Crap. Major's back. I hope he didn't rush because of me. And I was having such a nice time without him. I hear him approaching. He must be carrying something heavy, because the pitch of his step and the creak of the floor sound different—deeper or heavier. The tone of his walk is different too, like he's struggling with one leg. Maybe he stubbed his toe on his crazy way out.

He stops in front of me, breathing heavily like Taz, the Looney Tunes character. He starts at the corner of the tape, lifting it off my cheek.

Good. I can't wait to curse him. He rips it away.

"Ouch! Take it fucking easy!" He grabs hold of the blindfold, from the front this time, and harshly pulls it up over my forehead.

Robert Killroy! Bike helmet and all.

"Mr. Wyler, Granny says it's not nice to curse. It's offenseful."

"She's absolutely right. Now what are you doing here?"

"Serving you with process."

"Okay, great, we'll talk about that later. Hurry up and untie me."

"Nuh-uh."

"Robert, please, untie me. We've got to get out of here!"

"Nuh-uh. You got a dart in your back, Mr. Wyler. But I don't see no dartboard up around here. I like playing darts."

"That's not a dart. That's a spinal needle. Now, please, untie me."

"Nuh-uh."

"Why not?"

"Because you tricked me."

"I didn't trick you! Now untie me this instant!"

"Nuh-uh. You told me I couldn't serve you because I didn't have my license in my pocket. I knowed what I read on page five, paragraph two."

"Okay, so I may have been wrong. Not a big deal. Just untie me!"

"Nuh-uh."

I can see if I want to get out of here, I just better do what he says. Don't resist what is. I'll give it one more try, nicely. "Robert, please untie me."

"Nuh-uh. I got to serve you first. I don't want to chase you again, dodging service."

"When did you have to chase after me?"

"Before."

"Before when?"

"When I finished my reading after you came back down. You turned the corner and I was gonna come after ya, but my chain fell off. Got stuck. Had to take the back wheel off to get it on. I raced around the corner, looking all over, and when I found you two blocks away, you were passed out on the street. Page four, paragraph three says you can't serve nobody if they not, con . . . con . . ."

"Conscious?"

"Yeah, conscious. So I waited there 'til you came to, but you never did. Some nice man picked you up. That's when I had to chase ya. On my bike. Broke my speed record following that Town Car ambulance. Never seen an ambulance like that, black with no lights. Hit thirty-three. I can prove it. Got it in my digital speedometer. Would've lost ya, but for bridge traffic. Followed you here and waited 'til your friend that helped you left. I came up 'cause I didn't want to chase ya again, even though Granny says not to trespass. So it'd be good if you didn't tell her."

He looks around the place. "This ain't no hospital."

"No, it's not, but don't worry. You won't have to chase me again. Just untie me, so we can get out of here."

"Nuh-uh. I got to serve you first."

"Okay. Then serve me."

"Something ain't right. Service is where you hand the papers to the guy, but you all tied up. Let me check that."

"Robert, please . . ."

"One moment," he tells me. He takes the manual out of his bag.

"Robert!" He looks up. "Just untie me, and I'll accept personal service. That solves the problem."

"How do I know you ain't gonna trick me or run again?"

"I promise, I'm not going to do that. My legs are tied to the chair. I can't run." He looks.

"Cross your heart and hope to die?"

"Cross my heart and hope to die."

"Stick a needle in your eye?"

"Yes, Robert, stick a needle in my eye."

"Okay, then, seeing as you crossed your heart . . ." Just then someone appears at the open door.

Robert looks over. "Uh-oh," he says. Out of the corner of my eye I see it's Major.

Then, stepping in around him is Minnow. Now it all makes sense. "Hey, you, step away from that guy. Unless you want trouble, seeeee. You don't want no trouble now, do you, sonny boy?"

"No. I don't want no trouble, mister. Granny always says to stay out of trouble. But I got to get my serve in. He owes Mr. Wang fourteen dollars and seventy-nine cents."

Minnow chortles. "Just step aside, and there'll be no trouble."

"I don't want no trouble. But I got to untie him, so I can get my serve in."

"Nobody's untying anybody, seeeee." Minnow begins to walk toward us, drawing a gun from his belt as he approaches. "Move away, sonny boy. And there'll be no trouble." He stops about ten feet from Robert.

I have a front-row seat. Major is still at the door. It's pretty clear that glimpsing the gun froze him in his tracks.

"Move it, seeeee."

"I can't do that. I got to do my job. I got to serve process. I like your gun. It's a Glock. I know all about guns from my magazines, but I can't have one Granny says."

"Move it, kid! That is, if you ever want to see your granny again."

"Nuh-uh."

Minnow begins to take a few cautious steps toward Robert, who's just standing there, innocently, process manual still in hand. He watches as Minnow approaches, moving his lips as if mumbling to himself. This is not going to be good. Then, all of the sudden, like an explosion, Robert charges, head down, rhino-style. A shot goes off as he helmet-rams Minnow square in the gut, bulldozing him backward. But Robert keeps going, lifting him off the floor until he finds himself slammed into the wall near where Major is standing. He falls to the ground, limp.

Robert takes a step back and looks down at him. Minnow's out cold.

Just like that.

"Sorry, mister," he says to the unconscious Minotero. "But I told you I got to get my serve in. I got to get my financial independence so Granny can stop her worrying."

"Robert!" I yell. "Quick! Pick up the gun!" He looks at the piece on the floor. It's resting next to Major's foot.

"I'm not allowed to play with no guns. Granny said." He looks at Major, several feet away, who has blood discoloring the left shoulder of his blue button-down oxford. He must've been grazed. There's a bullet hole in the wall slightly above his shoulder. He's looking downward.

"Mister," he says, "you got something dark staining up your shirt. I know a good dry cleaner. His name is Mr. Wang. He's a really nice man."

But Major's focused on the gun. Robert follows his line of sight, then looks back up.

"Mister, I got to hand these papers to my lawyer over there, so I have to untie him. That's the rules. But if you go for that gun, I think something bad is gonna happen to you. Real bad."

Process served.

21.

"Where are you?" Lily asks.

"On the street in front of the building. I just came up from the subway."

"Well, you've got a reception full of people. And your wife just dropped your daughter off. She's pissed you weren't here."

"Oh, crap, I forgot. Her GYN appointment." I'm supposed to take my daughter to her dance audition around the corner while Tyler gets her annual. Worse yet, she gave me a stern warning not to forget. In writing.

"Well, you better have a good excuse why you didn't pick up when she tried to contact you every which way a few minutes ago," Lily admonishes. I look at my watch: 9:32.

"I do. I was underground, having stopped off in the Bronx to get a plate of pastrami and eggs. You never know when the end is near—we could be living in the final days."

"Can I watch when you tell her that?"

I look at my phone. It shows that at nine-thirty there were ten missed calls, six voice messages, three e-mails, and three texts all ending with exclamation points. She's going to rain on my day of joy. No, not *that* day—today is Wednesday. The day I distribute client monies. I've got Robert and Cookie at my office to pick up their checks. I have to deal with Robert on an unrelated matter, as well.

Giving clients their compensation for the pain and suffering they've endured is the highlight of my professional existence. It doesn't return them to the physical condition they enjoyed prior to the traumatic event that landed them in my office, but it helps give them a sense of closure. And, in Cookie's case, the outcome also put her existence back on track. I enter my building, step into a waiting elevator, assess, and reflect.

Cookie, she was set free from her bondage. Enough said. Chris Charles, as it turned out, was clueless, simply a pawn for Major. He immediately turned the file back over to me, offering to waive his fee, but I insisted he take ten percent, over Henry's objection. In fact, it was really hush money. If First Medical Liability ever found out that Cookie's biggest element of damage—the repeated spinal taps—was unrelated to McElroy's malpractice, being chemically induced and reversible, they'd never have paid out two million. It would've been more like the two-fifty, based on McElroy's misplacement of that screw.

And Major—well, Cookie just wanted to forget the whole thing and move forward.

"Really?" I said in disbelief.

She countered, "Despite his despicable crime against me, the truth is I wouldn't be getting all this money if it weren't for him." I couldn't disagree, but still . . .

Both of us couldn't stop laughing when she said, "I once told Major that he didn't have an evil bone in his body. Boy, was I wrong about that bone." Yet it wasn't the last laugh.

I had that one with Major.

You see, I couldn't just let him walk away from this without consequence, despite Cookie's wishes. And she refused to let me report him to the District Attorney for his crimes against her, and also against me. So we resolved it civilly.

I said to him, "Hey, Major, 'time for tap' is over. Can you guess what it's time for now?" He didn't answer, so I told him. "Time for transfer." I had him sign over the title of his apartment to Cookie in exchange for his freedom.

Minnow, it turns out, had been Major's phlebotomist for a brief period when he had his private practice. He became a tough guy after doing a short stint in jail for second-degree sexual misconduct. He'd had a young girl disrobe for a blood draw he performed from her mammary vein. Why am I not surprised at such craziness?

When I walk into my office, Cookie's sitting on the couch. No halo. She looks splendid, positively glowing with health. And there on the floor, helmet on, playing jacks with my daughter, is Robert Killroy. He may not have killed no Roy or nobody, but he sure did head-ram Minnow into unconsciousness.

Born with fetal alcohol syndrome, Robert greets each day with an excess of determination and extraordinary acceptance. Granny said chances were slim that I'd ever get anything back from Robert for working his case for free, yet this iron-willed kid saved my life. I'd call that reciprocating karma. I'm happy to have made his and Granny's own lives easier, but there's no doubt in my mind Robert was already well on his way to achieving his own financial independence.

As for Ethel, her prognosis is looking good. I made a call to my mother's oncologist, who was able to switch her course of treatment to a different cocktail, and she seems to be headed in the direction of remission. She tells me her new group of doctors is "bona fide."

"Hi, everybody, I see you all met my daughter, Summer." They look at one another, confused.

"No, Dad," my special girl says, "it's Penelope." She returns her attention to the jacks on the floor in front of her. I look over at Robert, who finally looks up at me.

"You got Mr. Wang's fourteen dollars and seventy-nine cents?"

"Yes, Robert, I do. I hear he's a really nice man."

ACKNOWLEDGMENTS

A giant thank you to Michele Slung for embracing the wacky world of Tug Wyler. To be connected to someone in the literary industry with your background, expertise, and unparalleled insight is truly and honor. Another giant thank you to Otto Penzler. To be associated with a legend in the mystery, crime, and suspense genres is another great privilege. I also greatly appreciate your absolute professionalism when reverting back to me the rights of *Cookie's Case* from MysteriousPress.com and Open Road Media. Erin Mitchell, thank you for taking the reins and making Rockwell Press happen. Renata Di Biase, your artistic excellence in book design is unmatched, thank you. Fauzia Burke, thank you for your support and online publicity expertise.

Numerous individuals have influenced my writing in some way, shape, or form. Too many to mention out of fear of forgetting someone—but you know who you are. These people consist of my family and friends, trusted business associates, and those hardworking special people who make up my law firm. And . . . my brave clients.

On a personal note, I would like to I would like to thank my perfectly dysfunctional family for keeping me stimulated with its nutty antics. Your conduct has inspired me in immeasurable ways. Blake, Cooper and Phoebe—I love you with all that I have in me. And to my wife, Randi: Again, I knew it would piss you off to be the last person acknowledged. That's why I did it. Consider it foreplay. You inspire me, incite me, annoy me, put up with me, and everything else that provokes the intense energy that makes our marriage work. I love you dearly, and I always have. Well, most of the time.

BEHIND THE BOOK

When a guy's been practicing law in New York City for thirty years and has written several novels, you don't look at him and think, "Hey, in high school, they kept him in remedial reading through eleventh grade." But it's true. There I was, meeting three times a week with five other students in a room with a solid wooden door and a tiny window set up high to prevent kids from peeking. By junior year though, everybody was tall enough to look in.

From that classroom came my earliest identification with the underdog. Okay, I may have had more going on for me than the rest of the kids in there, but I'd been one of them. I knew what it felt like to be at a distinct disadvantage.

All things turn out to be connected. After I began practicing law, I quickly realized the little guys of this world—the ordinary joes unable to stand up for themselves—most needed my legal expertise and fighting spirit to take on large and powerful insurance companies.

Justice is something you shouldn't have to compete for, but it is.

It's common to diss personal injury lawyers—ambulance chasers they call us. But just remember: anyone, in an instant, can become a victim. Even you.

ABOUT THE AUTHOR

Andy Siegel maintains a special commitment to representing survivors of traumatic brain injury in his practice of law. He is on the Board of Directors of the New York State Trial Lawyers Association and of the Brain Injury Association of New York State. His many trial successes have regularly placed those outcomes among the "Top 100 Verdicts" reported in the state annually. A graduate of Tulane University and Brooklyn Law School, he now lives outside of the greater NYC area.

ABOUT THE SERIES

Tug Wyler will thrust readers headfirst into the emotionally charged high-stakes arena of medical malpractice law. At the center of each book lays the rush to cover up genuine wrongs. What keeps Tug digging deeper and deeper into the circumstances is his compulsion to make the system work for people at a disadvantage with their life situation stacked against them. Tug is unswerving in his dedication because justice is an outcome the big insurance companies—through their high paid lawyers—vigorously resist.

Suzy's Case

When Henry Benson, a high-profile criminal lawyer known for his unsavory clients, recruits Tug to take over a multimillion-dollar lawsuit representing a tragically brain-injured child, his instructions are clear: get us out of it; there is no case. Yet the moment Tug meets the disabled but gallant little Suzy and her beautiful, resourceful mother June, all bets are off. When his passionate commitment to Suzy's case thrusts him into a surreal, often violent sideshow, the ensuing danger only sharpens his obsession with learning what really happened to Suzy in a Brooklyn hospital. Did she suffer from an unpreventable complication from her sickle cell crisis that caused her devastating brain injury? Or, did something else happen . . .

Cookie's Case

Cookie, an angel in stiletto heels, is by far the most popular performer at Jingles Dance Bonanza. To her devoted audience, she's a friend, therapist, and shoulder to cry on, all rolled into one. While meeting an old pal at the club, Tug doesn't expect to pick up a new client but quickly realizes the gallant Cookie—dancing in a neck brace, each leg kick potentially her last—is in need of a committed champion. Believing that Cookie is the victim of a spine surgeon with a sloppy touch, Tug takes her case. But as he seeks both medical cure and a fair shake for Cookie, he realizes—a tad too late—that sinister sights are now trained on him.

Nelly's Case

Nelly Rivera, when Tug first sees her, lies helpless in a hospital bed. Once sassy, active and ambitious, she's now a young woman with an uncertain future and a present seemingly tied to dependency. Discovering exactly what happened to her in a dental office while under anesthesia and who was responsible, however, is just one of Tug's goals. For he soon enough learns Nelly has recently inherited a hefty sum from her late father's life insurance. Which definitely complicates matters. The closer Tug, committed as always to gaining justice, gets to the truth, the more elusive it becomes.

Elton's Case

Wrongfully locked up for a crime he didn't commit, the wheelchair-bound Elton Cribbs's immediate situation soon goes from bad to tragic. Could it have happened that, while in custody and being transported with less than suitable care in a police van, he suffered the injuries which rendered him a paraplegic? Certainly, ever since then—for the past decade—he's led the life of an aggrieved victim, seeking justice while rejecting pity. Retained now to litigate Elton's case even as the clock's ticking, Tug finds himself caught in the unlikeliest of conflicts. After all, what's he supposed to think when the defendant, otherwise known as the City of New York, begins offering him millions to settle while at the same time maintaining its allegation that Elton's case is a phony one?

Jenna's Case

A teen-aged girl can be among the most vulnerable of human beings. And the preyed-upon young woman at the dark center of Jenna's Case is certain to win the heart of readers. Believing Jenna Radcliff to be the victim of a Brooklyn doctor willing to put greed above his oath to do no harm, Tug takes on her case with deeply felt zeal. Yet what he quickly comes to understand is that his new client—once an obviously bright, outgoing girl (and ace neighborhood jump-roper)—is now a nearly mute shadow of her former self. As he proceeds to amass evidence against the conscienceless and defiant surgeon who'd willfully mutilated Jenna, Tug unfortunately soon discovers that the forces set against him are not only more numerous than he'd imagined but also more deadly.

Turn the page for an excerpt from the next book in the Tug Wyler Mystery Series, *Nelly's Case*.

Visit **andysiegel.com** for more.

nelly's case

A TUG WYLER MYSTERY

ANDY
SIEGEL

Two girls walk into a dentist's office . . . but only one walks out. Yet it's no joke, and there isn't a punch-line.

Instead, it's the start of another gripping one-of-a-kind case for the quick-thinking, frequently outrageous Tug Wyler, the New York City malpractice lawyer whose clients are as unpredictable as he is.

Nelly Rivera, when Tug first sees her, lies helpless in a hospital bed. Once sassy, active and ambitious, she's now a young woman with an uncertain future and a present seemingly tied to dependency. Discovering exactly what happened to her and who was responsible, however, is just one of Tug's goals. For he soon enough learns Nelly's recently inherited a hefty sum from her late father's life insurance. Which definitely complicates matters.

The fact that a witness was on hand—Jessie, her half-sister— looks a distinct advantage. But the closer Tug, committed as always to gaining justice, gets to the truth the more elusive it becomes. Both suspense—and menace—build as the stakes turn higher and Tug's determined path to the solution more uncharted. Not to mention, more hazardous to his own life and limb.

THE UNFORTUNATE EVENT

The door opens. In walks Dr. Grad. He's tall, lean, midsixties, with a thick head of salt-and-pepper hair, baby blues, and a strong chin. The knot of a dark-red tie, visible beneath his pristine dental smock, contrasts perfectly with his crisp white shirt.

"Hi, girls," he says, his manner engaging, yet professional.

"I'm Dr. Grad. And you," he says to the one reclining in the dental chair, "must be Nelly Rivera."

A timid nod reveals her as nervous. Shifting his attention, he speaks to the other girl. "And, young lady, you are?"

"I'm Nelly's sister, Jessie." He extends his hand.

They share a smile, but then it's back to business.

Looking down at Nelly—wearing a Yankees cap she bought just down the block at the stadium—Grad turns serious. "Let's have a brief talk, shall we?"

"Sure."

"Great. So I've reviewed Dr. Meyer's films," he says in a measured way. "And this is a routine procedure that can be done by numbing the area locally. Cavity work is quite simple and doesn't require anesthesia. So, before we begin, I'd like to suggest that you reconsider and allow Dr. Meyer to do the work. He's a good dentist, and I'm confident that, with your sister's support"—he acknowledges Jessie—"you can overcome this."

What he's talking about is Nelly's dental anxiety. Grad encourages these patients to address their fears before committing to going forward with anesthesia. Most of the time it's a losing battle and, therefore, why they've come to him in the first place.

"But he's not the Painless Dentist, is he now, Dr. Grad?" Jessie's teasing reference is to the ads Grad regularly runs in *Time Out New York*.

"No, I guess he's not," Grad answers. He's in a familiar scenario, one where he knows every move. It's his business, after all.

As he heads toward the IV pole, Nelly grabs the bottom of his smock, giving it a playful tug. He turns, looking down at her. There's no trace of a smile left on her face.

"Yes, dear?" he asks, his voice comforting.

"You *promise* it's not going to hurt?"

"Not even a pinch," he reassures. Nelly looks to Jessie, sitting at her right, who gives an "I told you so" nod of encouragement. The catch phrase of his ads is the line he's just used. That's why they're here.

He opens a cabinet and takes out two solution bags, hanging them on the pole. After accessing an arm vessel, he starts the flow of the larger one, dripping Ringer's Lactate hydrating solution. He then connects the much smaller bag to the drip line. He reaches up and slightly adjusts the mechanism that controls the flow of this anesthetic.

Nelly feels a chill where the fluid enters her arm, then warmth all over.

"Just relax and enjoy the peacefulness," he urges soothingly.

Her lids close as the drug takes its immediate effect. Grad observes her for several moments. He knows well what to expect. Her face wears that familiar tranquil expression he's induced so many times. He looks to Jessie, giving her a reassuring smile, then back to his patient, whose eyes are open just a slit.

"How are you feeling?"

"Drowsy," she's able to respond.

"Good. That's the place we want you to be. Drowsy but not out. That's how conscious sedation works. Now relax." He reaches up to the control mechanism and adjusts the flow of anesthesia. Then he maneuvers a curly plastic suction device under Nelly's tongue and rests the tubing on the protective blue bib covering her clothes. Glancing over at Jessie, he whispers, "Keep an eye on her, like a good big sister." After disposing of his sterile gloves, he slowly turns the knob, then leaves the room, carefully shutting the door.

Jessie smiles tenderly as she looks at Nelly lying there helpless. Here is the girl who once stood up, all alone, to a gang of boys who tried to steal her sneakers back in third grade. It hadn't been easy growing up in the Bronx, where the streets were a daily education all their own. Yet her sister—tough as Jessie knows her to be—still is scared to have a cavity filled.

A few moments later the door opens. Sensing someone's presence, Nelly manages to shift her head ever-so-slightly to the left. A woman enters. It's Rita, the dental assistant, who'd ushered them into the room. She walks to the pole and checks the flow dripping from the two bags at different rates. She looks over Nelly, who gathers the strength to flash an acknowledging smile. After smiling back, Rita disappears just as quickly as she entered.

Nelly, with great effort, slowly repositions herself. Her head tilting left. Deeper and deeper she falls into a restful, anesthetized state.

The door opens again. Or maybe not. Nelly can't be sure at this stage. But she believes she sees Debbie, the young receptionist Nelly saw being reprimanded earlier for wearing denims to work day two on the job. As Debbie moves toward the pole, a cardigan button comes into focus. Then this figure disappears too.

Now standing over her—for some reason—is Jessie.

Though Jessie, who's watching her, can't know it, Nelly is tumbling deeper and faster, deeper and faster, with every drop of the infusing anesthetic. What Jessie can see, however, is that her sister's chest is rising and falling in slow, rhythmic fashion. The infiltrating drugs, like all anesthetics, are respiratory depressants causing hypotension and rapid shallow breathing.

"Keep an eye on her," Dr. Grad had told Jessie when he'd left the room. So she's doing just that.

If we could ask Nelly, we'd learn that she's now at peace without a worry in the world, never having imagined a dental procedure could be so relaxing. Deeper and deeper she drops into that place where you go when anesthesia perfuses your bodily systems and centers of consciousness.

Her chest rises in a measured fashion. Just as slowly, it falls. Up and down, in rhythmic motion. Yet subtle changes occur as Nelly enters a more depressed physiologic state. Jessie, without quite realizing why, is feeling a sense of unease. What's happening?

Her sister's chest movements are difficult to register. Its expansions and contractions are hard to perceive.

Slower. And slower. Until—

"Help! Somebody! Help!" Jessie screams. "My sister stopped breathing! Help! Help!" she yells at the top of her lungs, bolting from the room. Two nearby exam doors pop open. Grad and Rita spring into the hall.

"Help! Please! My sister's not breathing!"

They jostle past her into the room. Nelly is ghost-white. Cadaver-white actually. Grad yanks out her IV. He lifts Nelly from the chair—exhibiting strength uncommon to men his age—now laying her flat on the floor.

"Move back! Move back!" he shouts to the crowd gathered at the door. He puts his ear to Nelly's chest. He cocks her head back, creating an airway. Sealing her mouth with his, he gives two quick breaths, raising her chest. Ear again on sternum. He looks up to Rita.

"Call 911! Call 911!"

"Debbie did!" she tells him. Her voice breaks.

He continues working on Nelly, alternating breaths with chest compressions. Nothing. Repeats for three more minutes. Nothing.

"Oh, my god! Help her! Help her!" Jessie cries out. "Don't let her die!" she yells. Grad continues his cardiopulmonary resuscitation, employing it with efficiency and skill.

But five minutes into arrest, there is still no response.

He checks her pupils. Fixed, ... doll's eyes, ... not good. He goes back to work, forcing air into her. He won't stop until she's officially pronounced dead by someone with the authority to do so. That's the protocol.

"Move! Move!" a firm voice commands from near the door. "Out of the way!" orders the emergency medical technician. "Move out of the way!"

Grad, Rita and Debbie, plus two curious patients, scramble out of the doorway, then jockey for position to watch the events. One EMT applies an oxygen mask and ambubags her. The other—with his fingers on her carotid—looks up at Grad.

"How long? How long!"

Grad checks his watch. He depresses the chronometer, angling its face toward him.

"Stop playing with your watch, goddamn it! How long?"

"Nine minutes, forty-three seconds."

"What did you give her?" Nodding toward the dangling lines.

"Midazolam."

"Reversals?"

"No," Grad replies.

"Move out of the way!" commands the EMT to the doorway spectators. His partner, now at Nelly's feet, counts, "One, ... two, ... three," and they lift, whisking her in one fluid motion from the room and onto a waiting stretcher.

"Oh, my god!" Jessie repeats. Then says, "Please don't let her die!"

They wheel Nelly down the hall and exit as fast as they can. The entourage of onlookers follows suit. All watch somberly as the stricken young woman is loaded into the ambulance. A throng of city sidewalk bystanders stops to spectate too.

"Let's go!" Grad orders, pulling Jessie's arm. Moments later they enter his car parked at the curb and pull out right behind the siren-blaring ambulance.

It's a race against time. Fighting city traffic.

Jessie turns to Grad, now drenched in sweat.

"Do you think she's going to live?" She can't help but ask.

He answers, keeping his sight fixed on the road. "She'll make it. She's young. She's strong."

But Jessie's not convinced. His tone lacked the certainty she had hoped to hear.

"Dr. Grad?" she asks, in a tone seeking answers.

"Yes, dear?" His concentration doesn't waver.

"After you started the anesthesia . . . "

"Yes, dear, go on," he encourages. "After I started the anesthesia, what?" He glances over the way drivers do. For just an instant, they lock eyes.

"Why did you leave the room?"

Made in the USA
Middletown, DE
12 August 2018